Alexandre Dumas

Lady of the Camillias

Volume 6

Alexandre Dumas

Lady of the Camillias
Volume 6

ISBN/EAN: 9783337118792

Printed in Europe, USA, Canada, Australia, Japan

Cover: Foto ©Andreas Hilbeck / pixelio.de

More available books at **www.hansebooks.com**

Chapter VIII

"*We left our places to go up to the box of Madame Duvernoy.*

"*Scarcely had we opened the door of the orchestra seats when we were compelled to stop in order to allow to pass Marguerite and the duke, who were going.*

"*I would have given ten years of my life to have been in the place of that old gentleman.*"

BIBLIOTHÈQUE DES CHEFS-D'ŒUVRE DU ROMAN CONTEMPORAIN

THE LADY OF THE CAMELLIAS

ALEXANDRE DUMAS *FILS*
OF THE ACADÉMIE FRANÇAISE

PRINTED FOR SUBSCRIBERS ONLY BY
GEORGE BARRIE & SONS, Philadelphia

THIS EDITION OF

THE LADY OF THE CAMELLIAS

WITH A PREFACE BY

JULES JANIN

AND A HITHERTO UNPUBLISHED PREFACE BY THE AUTHOR
HAVE BEEN COMPLETELY TRANSLATED

BY

WILLIAM WALTON

THE ETCHINGS ARE BY

EUGENE-ANDRE CHAMPOLLION
PIERRE-AUGUSTIN MASSE

AND DRAWINGS BY

ALBERT LYNCH

MONSIEUR CALMANN LEVY

MY DEAR CALMANN:

You ask of me a preface for a new edition, illustrated, of the *Dame aux Camélias*. You prefer this request to precisely the only man in the world who can say neither good nor evil of this book. Janin has related concerning Marie Duplessis everything that there is to relate; he has even embroidered a little, here and there. I have recalled, for my part, either in the preface to the play, or in the notes to the *Edition des comédiens*, everything that my memory has preserved of this charming young woman who has had so great an influence on my literary life, since it is to her I owe my first success as a novelist and my first success as a playwright. Monsieur de Contades has, quite recently, published in the review *Le Livre* a series of studies and of details concerning her, most exact and most interesting; I have nothing further to say. How it was that I wrote this book, in three weeks, on the corner of a table, at Saint-Germain-en-Laye, in a chamber for which I paid a franc a day, in the inn of the *Cheval blanc*, the only one that I found open one evening when I had missed the last train? Have I not already related it? Moreover, is it interesting? Would it be better to make philosophical reflections upon prostitution, and the fatal influence of courtesans? Evidently not. Well, then, here goes for the history of the origin of this book!

I had then missed the railway train, and I slept at the *Cheval blanc*, in the high street; that was thirty-seven or thirty-eight years ago. I was accompanied by a friend who had come to dine with me, at my father's, at Monte-Christo. We each of us took a room in this inn, the regular customers of which were the carriers and the diligence conductors who maintained the service of the neighboring villages. The next morning, when we arose, the weather was fine. Instead of returning immediately to Paris, we conclude to hire some horses from Ravelet and take a ride in the forest. You did not know Ravelet. I regret it for your sake. Ravelet kept a riding-school, or, rather, a stable, at the first Rond-point of the terrace of Saint-Germain. He was celebrated in our generation. He bought up all the rejected horses, kicking, rearing, running away, of the garrison of Saint-Germain, and riders came expressly from Paris, by companies, to break them in. At thirty sous the hour, all summer from seven o'clock in the morning to nine o'clock in the evening, they were soon rid of the vices that had caused them to be excluded

from the regiment. They were provided indifferently
with men's saddles or women's. When they were once
duly mounted by a client they were pushed out of the
stables by a plentiful use of the lash, and for good luck
or bad! But it served, youth and laughter aiding.
Everybody did not fall off; in any case, they got up
again. Happy times!

This Ravelet establishment was, as you may well
imagine, a fine rendezvous. Between 1840 and 1860,
the date at which, I believe, the improvements carried
out in the terrace caused his place to disappear, Ravelet
saw his noble steeds mounted by all the pretty women
of the gay life of Paris, including Marie Duplessis,
who was one of the frequenters of the place and
whose feverish nature took delight in these reckless
excursions.

I recall a sufficiently droll incident concerning a
cherry-tree that was the finest ornament of the court-
yard of this stable. One day I went there to get a horse
to ride. While waiting I asked Ravelet if I could eat
some of the cherries on his tree. He was as phlegmatic
as was necessary : "You can," he said to me, "there is
some one there already." I saw, in fact, a ladder leaning against a tree; I ascended it, and I perceived, as my
friend had said, a young woman, pretty, although a
brunette, seated at her ease in the fork of two branches
tranquilly eating cherries. "You will permit me,
madame?" I said to her. "Certainly, monsieur, with

the greatest pleasure." And there we sat, eating cherries and talking of that of which would naturally
talk, on a fine June morning, a youth of twenty and a
pretty girl who met in a cherry-tree. Four or five years
ago I went into a curiosity shop to price a Louis XVI.
mirror. There I found a saleswoman, very pleasant,
whose hair was turning gray, was even quite gray, but
whose black eyes were still lively and whose fine teeth
were still white. I said to myself: "I have seen that
face somewhere." She looked at me and smiled. I
examined her so attentively that she perceived I was
searching some souvenir. "Yes," she said, "the cherry-
tree of Saint-Germain!"

My friend, seeing this fine weather, was of the opinion
that we might remain two or three days more at Saint-
Germain. He proposed to me to go to Paris to get
whatever we might need of linen and outside garments
for this improvised village life. During this time I
would go to see my father in whose house I offered to
establish him with myself rather than to remain at the
Cheval blanc; but he feared that we would disturb the
author of the "Musketeers," and the proximity of
Ravelet, of the horses, of the cherry-tree and of all the
consequences that might flow from these different things,
offered him superior attractions. Scarcely had he
departed, scarcely had I found myself alone on this
terrace where I had walked so often with Marie Duplessis, when I began to think of her, and when the idea

of writing her story, or, rather, a story concerning her,
came into my mind, and so imperiously that I bought
three or four quires of large paper, pens and ink, and
returned to my twenty-sou chamber where I commenced
this book while waiting for my friend. When he returned to dinner, he found me hard at work and in such
an enthusiasm that I did not wish to leave Saint-Germain
until I had written the last word. This was an affair of
three or four weeks. My friend ended by becoming so
interested in my work that he made a fair copy of it as
fast as I wrote it, on the conditions that I should give
him my original manuscript, which I did give him in
fact and which he carried with him on a voyage which
he made to India, long before the opening of the Suez
Canal. He rounded the Cape of Good Hope, where the
ship was assailed by such a tempest that they threw
overboard everything they could to lighten her. The
manuscript of the " Lady of the Camellias " was in one
of the trunks sacrificed. What an appropriate ending !

When the story was finished, I carried it to Cadot,
the publisher, who received me as he was in the habit of
receiving the writers who worked for him, and by whom
he would say he was ruined when he had given them
four or five hundred francs for an unpublished volume.
He consented, after making many difficulties, to give
me a thousand francs for my book, for an edition of two
volumes in octavo of twelve hundred copies, which he
sold to the very last one. He wished afterwards, for

the sum of two hundred francs, to publish a second edition in duodecimo of fifteen hundred copies which he sold also ; but when I asked him to publish a third, he sent me about my business. I followed his advice and, passing through the Rue Vivienne, I entered your brother's, where he finally welcomed my heroine whom the house of Quantin is about to present again to the public, but adorned, this time, with the finest ornaments that she has ever had. Thanks for her. Good luck and plenty to you.

A. DUMAS FILS.

MLLE. MARIE DUPLESSIS

There was, in the year of grace 1845, in those years of peace and abundance when all the favors of wit, of talent, of beauty and of fortune enveloped this France of a day, a young and beautiful woman with a most charming face, who attracted to herself, by her mere presence, a certain admiration mingled with deference from whoever, seeing her for the first time, knew neither her name nor her profession. She had, in fact, and most naturally, the candid look, the action that revealed nothing, the bearing at once courageous and modest, of the most accomplished woman of the world. Her expression was serious, her smile was imposing, and from simply seeing her walk, it might have been said of her as Ellevíou said one day of a lady of the Court: "She is evidently either a courtesan or a duchess."

Alas! this one was not a duchess, she had been born at the foot of the difficult ladder, and she had needed to be in reality beautiful and charming to have ascended with so light a foot the first steps, at the age of eighteen, which she may have attained at this period. I remember having met her one day, for the first time, in the abominable foyer of a theatre of the boulevards, badly lit and crowded with that buzzing multitude usually attracted by spectacular melodramas. There were there more blouses than coats, more round caps than bonnets with feathers, and more worn paletots than new costumes; the conversation was on all subjects, the dramatic art and fried potatoes; the plays at the Gymnaise and the galette[1] of the Gymnaise; well, when this woman appeared on this alien threshold, you would have said that she illuminated all these rough or absurd things with the glance of her beautiful eyes. Her foot touched this muddy floor as if she were crossing the boulevard on a rainy day. She lifted her dress instinctively, that it might not sweep this dried filth, and without any thought of showing—why should she?—her carefully shod foot terminating a rounded limb covered with a silk stocking with fine open-work. Her entire toilet was in harmony with this supple and youthful figure; this countenance, of a fine oval, and a little pale, corresponded with the grace which she diffused like an undefinable perfume around her.

She entered then; she traversed this astonished mob with her head high, and we were very much surprised, Liszt and I, when she came and seated herself familiarly on the sofa where we were, for neither he nor I had ever spoken to her; she was a woman of intelligence, of taste, and of good sense, and she immediately addressed the great artist; she related to him that she had but lately

*heard him, and that he had made her reflect. He,
meanwhile, like those sonorous instruments which respond
to the first breath of the breeze of May, he listened with
a sustained attention to this beautiful speech, full of ideas,
this speech melodious, eloquent, and reflective all at once.
With that marvellous instinct which he possesses, and that
long familiarity with the highest official world, and the
highest artistic world, he asked himself who this woman
could be, so familiar and so noble, who accosted him
the first, and who, after the exchange of the first words,
treated him with a certain reserve, as though it were
he who had been presented to her, at London, in the
Queen's drawing-room, or in that of the Duchess of
Sutherland.*

*However, the three solemn strokes which announced
the raising of the curtain resounded through the room,
and the foyer was promptly emptied of all this crowd of
spectators and critics. The unknown lady, her female
companion, and ourselves alone were left—she even drew
near to the fire and placed her two shivering feet before
those niggardly brands, so that we could readily contemplate her, quite at our ease, from the embroidered folds of
her petticoat to the little locks of her black hair on her
temples; her hand gloved as though it were in a picture,
her handkerchief wonderfully ornamented with a royal
lace; in her ears, two Oriental pearls that would have
rendered a queen envious. She carried all these beautiful things as though she had been born in silk and in*

*velvet, under some gilded ceiling of the grand faubourgs,
a crown on her head, a world of flatterers at her feet.
Thus her bearing corresponded with her language, her
thoughts with her smile, her toilet with her person, and
one would have sought vainly, in the highest places in the
world, for a being who was in more beautiful and more
complete harmony with her ornaments, her dress, and her
conversation.*

*Liszt, meanwhile, very much astonished at this marvel
in such a place, at this gay entr'acte in so terrible a
melodrama, gave free vent to his imagination. He is
not only a great artist, but also an eloquent man. He
knows how to talk with women, passing, as they do, from
one idea to the other, and selecting the most opposite.
He adores paradoxes, he touches on the serious, on the
burlesque, and I cannot describe to you with what art,
what tact, what infinite taste, he ranged, with this
woman whose name he did not know, through all the
commonplace gamuts and all the elegant flourishes of
daily conversation.*

*They conversed thus during the whole of the third act
of the aforesaid melodrama, for, as far as I was concerned, a question was put to me once or twice through
politeness ; but as I was precisely in one of those moments
of ill-humor in which every species of enthusiasm is forbidden to the human soul, I took it for granted that the
lady considered me perfectly surly, perfectly absurd, and
that she was quite right.*

*That winter passed, then the summer, and in the fol-
lowing autumn once again; but this time in all the
splendor of a benefit performance, in full opera, we saw
suddenly open, with a certain flourish, one of the great
proscenium boxes, and in the front of this box advance, a
bouquet in her hand, this same beauty whom I had seen
at the boulevard. It was she! but this time in the full
dress of a woman of the world, and brilliant with all the
splendors of conquest. Her coiffure was ravishing, in
her beautiful hair were diamonds and flowers, and her
tresses were drawn up with that studied grace which
gives them movement and life, her arms were bare, and
her bust, and she had collars, and bracelets, and emer-
alds. She held in her hand a bouquet—of what color?
I would not be able to tell you; it would be necessary to
have the eyes of a young man and the imagination of a
child to distinguish well the color of a flower over
which bends a beautiful face. At our time of life, we
see only the cheek and the light of the glance, we care
but little for the accessories, and if we amuse ourselves
by drawing consequences, we draw them from the persons themselves, and find ourselves sufficiently occupied,
verily.*

*On that evening, Duprez was in the first stages of his
conflict with that rebellious voice the definite revolt of
which he already foresaw; but he alone had this presentiment, and the public as yet had no suspicions.
Only, among the most attentive hearers, a few amateurs*

divined the fatigue under the skill, and the exhaustion of the artist under the immense efforts which he made to deceive himself. The beautiful creature of whom I speak was evidently an accomplished judge, and, after the first few minutes of attention, it could be seen that she was not under the influence of the usual spell, for she threw herself suddenly back in her box, and, no longer listening, she betook herself to examining through her opera-glass the countenances of the audience.

It was very evident that she was acquainted with many of the most select among the spectators. One might have known, merely by the movement of her lorgnette, that the fair spectatress could have related more than one history concerning certain young men with the highest names; she looked sometimes at one, sometimes at another, without making any choice, according this one no more attention than that one, indifferent to all, and each one acknowledged, with a smile or with a very brief little gesture, or with a quick and rapid glance, the attention she had given him. From the depths of dark boxes and from the midst of the orchestra, other glances, burning like volcanoes, were thrown at this charming person; but these she did not see. If by chance her lorgnette was turned upon the ladies of the real Parisian world, she revealed suddenly in her attitude an undefinable resigned and humiliated air which was painful to see. On the contrary, she looked bitterly aside, if unfortunately her look chanced to fall on one of those doubtful celebrities and those charming heads which usurp the finest stalls in the theatre on the great occasions.

Her companion—for this time she had a cavalier—was a handsome young man, half-Parisian, and still retaining some opulent remnants of the paternal estate which he had been devouring, acre by acre, in this city of perdition. The young man, still in the morning of his youth, was evidently very proud of this beauty in full splendor, and he was not at all displeased to do himself honor by demonstrating that it was indeed his by offering her continuously those thousand little attentions so precious to a young woman when they come from the beloved lover, so displeasing when they are addressed to a soul occupied elsewhere —— There is listening without hearing, there is looking without seeing —— What was he saying? The lady did not know, but she endeavored to reply, and these words, devoid of meaning, became fatiguing to her.

Thus, all unknown to them, they were not alone in this box, the price of which represented the bread of a family for six months. Between them had established himself the assiduous companion of sick souls, of wounded hearts, of exhausted minds,—ennui, that immense Mephistopheles of the wandering Marguerites, of the lost Clarissas, of all those divinities, daughters of chance, who go astray in life to ruin.

She wearied herself then, this sinning one, surrounded by the adoration and the homage of youth, and this weariness even should serve her for pardon and excuse,

since it was the chastisement of her transient prosperity.
Ennui had been the great evil of her life. Through
having seen all her affections crushed, through yielding to
the necessity of her ephemeral liaisons and passing from
one love to another love, without knowing! alas, why it
was that she strangled so promptly this inclination which
commenced to reveal itself and these tendernesses in their
birth, she had ended by becoming indifferent to all things,
forgetting the love of yesterday, and scarcely thinking
more of the love of to-day than of to-morrow's passion.

The unfortunate one! she had such need of soli-
tude ——, she saw herself ceaselessly importuned. She
had need of silence ——, she heard ceaselessly and with-
out end the same words in her wearied ear! she wished
to have quiet! —— she was forever drawn into festi-
vals and distractions. She would have wished to be
loved! —— she was told that she was beautiful! Thus
she abandoned herself, unresistingly, to the whirlpool
which swept her away! What a youth! —— and how
we are enabled to comprehend that speech of Mademoi-
selle de Lenclos, when, at the height of her prosperity, as
in the fairy-stories, the friend of the Prince de Condé
and of Madame de Maintenon, she said, with a profound
sigh of regret: " Had any one foretold me such a life,
I should have died of fright and of sorrow."

When the opera was ended, this charming creature
departed, although the performance was scarcely half
over. There were still to come Bouffé, Mademoiselle

Déjazet, and the comedians from the Palais-Royal, without counting the ballet in which La Carlotta was to dance, light and charming in the first days of her poetical intoxication ——— She would not wait for the vaudeville; she wished to depart immediately to return home, whilst there were still for so many three hours of pleasure to come, to the sound of the music and under these brilliant lights!

I saw her leave her box and envelope herself with her own hands in her cloak lined with the fur of young ermine. The young man who had brought her seemed vexed, and as he could no longer make use of her to flatter his vanity, he did not trouble himself as to whether she were cold or not. I even remember to have assisted her to lift the cloak on her shoulder, which was very white, and she looked at me without recognizing me and with a little painful smile which she turned on the tall young man, who was occupied at that moment in paying the box-opener and in making her change a five-franc piece. "Keep it all, madame," she said to the woman, making her a pretty gesture. I saw her descend the grand stairway to the right, her white dress contrasting with her red cloak, and her handkerchief around her head, fastened under her chin; the jealous lace falling a little over her eyes; but what did it matter! the lady had played her part, her day was over, and she no longer cared whether she were beautiful ——— She must have left the young man at her door that night.

*There was one thing worthy of remark and altogether
to her praise, and that is that this young woman, who in
her youthful hours expended silver and gold by handfuls—
for she united benevolence to caprice, and she valued but
slightly this fatal money which cost her so dearly—was
the heroine of none of those histories of ruin and of
scandal, of gambling, of debts and of duels, which so
many other women, in her place, would have scattered in
their passage. On the contrary, around her there was
talk only of her beauty, of her triumphs, of her taste for
beautiful furnishings, of the fashions which she knew
how to discover and of those which she set for others.
There were never related concerning her stories of lost
fortunes, imprisonments for debts, and treacheries, which
form the usual accompaniment of these doubtful loves.
There was certainly around this creature, so early carried
away by death, a certain restraint, a certain decency that
was resistless. She lived apart, even in the world apart
in which she dwelt, and in a region more calm and more
serene, although, alas! in truth, she lived in the regions
in which everything is lost.*

*I saw her again, for the third time, at the inauguration
of the railway du Nord, in those fêtes which Brussels
gave to France, now become her neighbor and her com-
mensal. In that depot, the immense rendezvous of all
the railways of the North, Belgium had brought together
all her splendors,—the plants of her conservatories, the
flowers of her gardens, the diamonds of her crowns. An*

incredible crowd of uniforms, of orders, of diamonds, and of dresses of gauze thronged this locality of a festival which will not be seen again. The French peerage and the German nobility, and the Spanish Belgium and Flanders and Holland, adorned with their antique jewels, contemporaries of the king Louis XIV. and his court, all the heavy and massive acquisitions of industry, and more than one elegant Parisienne, resembling so many butterflies in a hive of bees, had assembled for this festival of industry and of travel, and of iron conquered and of flame obeying vanquished time. A strange medley, in which all the forces and all the graces of creation were represented, from the oak to the flower, and from pit-coal to the amethyst. In the midst of all this movement of peoples, of kings, of princes, of artists, of iron-smiths, and of the great coquettes of Europe, there was to be seen, or rather I alone saw, paler still and whiter than usual, this charming creature already touched by the invisible malady that was to bring her to the tomb.

She had entered this ball, notwithstanding her name, and protected by her dazzling beauty! She attracted all eyes, she was followed by the homage of all. A flattering murmur saluted her passage, and even those who knew her inclined before her; she, meanwhile, always calm and intrenched in her habitual disdain—she accepted these homages, as if these homages were justly due her. She was not in the least surprised—far from it—to tread the carpet which the queen herself had trod!

More than one prince arrested his steps to see her, and his eyes told her that which women comprehend so readily: "I think you beautiful, and I go away regretfully!" She gave her arm, that evening, to another stranger, a newcomer, blond as a German, impassible as an Englishman, over-dressed, very much buttoned up in his coat, very stiff, and who believed himself to be committing, it could be seen from his manner, one of those nameless audacities with which men reproach themselves to their last day.

This man's attitude was certainly displeasing to the sensitive creature who took his arm; she perceived it with that sixth sense which was in her, and she redoubled her haughtiness, for her marvellous instinct told her that the more this man was astonished at his own action, the more she herself should be insolent, and tread under with a scornful foot the remorse of this frightened fellow. Few can comprehend that which she must have suffered at this moment,—a woman without a name, on the arm of a man without a name, this man seeming to give, himself, the signal of disapprobation, and his threatening attitude indicating, with sufficient clearness, an unquiet soul, an undecided heart, a spirit ill at ease. But this Anglo-German was cruelly punished for his inward remorse when, at a turn of the great alley of light and of verdure, our Parisienne met a friend of hers, a friend without pretensions, who asked her, from time to time, a touch of her hand and a smile of her lips; an artist of our world,

*a painter who knew better than any one who had seen
her but little how perfect a model she was of all that is
elegant and of all that is attractive in youth.*

*"Ah! you here!" she said to him, "give me your
arm and let us dance!" And, quitting the official arm
of her cavalier, she launched into the* valse à deux temps,
*which is seduction itself when it obeys the inspiration of
Strauss, and when it comes all enamored of the banks of
the German Rhine, its true country! she danced marvellously well, not too quickly, nor too languidly, obedient to
the inward cadence as well as to the outward measure,
touching with a light foot the elastic floor, and swaying
and reposing, and her eyes in the eyes of her partner.*

*They made a circle around one and the other, and it
was who could be touched by this beautiful hair which
followed the movement of the rapid waltz, and it was
who could graze this light dress diffusing light perfumes,
and, little by little the circle contracting, and the other
dancers stopping to see them, it came to pass that the tall
young man—he who had brought her to this ball—lost
her in the crowd, and that he wished in vain to find
again that charming arm, to which he had lent his own
with so much repugnance —— The arm and the person
and the artist, they could no longer be found.*

*Two days after this festival she came from Brussels to
Spa, on a beautiful day, at the hour when these mountains
covered with verdure allow the sun to penetrate, a charming hour! There were to be seen then hastening thither*

all kinds of happy invalids, who came to repose from the
festivities of the past winter, in order to be better prepared for the joys of the winter to come. At Spa, no
other fever is known than the fever of the ball, and
no other languors than those of absence, and no other
remedies than conversation and dancing and music, and
the emotion of play, in the evenings, when La Redoute is
illumined with all its lights, when the echoes of the mountains send back in a thousand fragments the intoxicating
strains of the orchestra.   At Spa, the Parisienne was
received with a fervor sufficiently rare in this somewhat
timid village, which abandons willingly enough to Baden,
its rival, the beautiful creatures without names, without
husbands, and without any official position.   At Spa,
also, there was a general surprise when it was learned
that so young a woman was seriously ill, and the sorrowful physicians declared that, in fact, they had rarely met
with so much resignation united with so much courage.

Her health was investigated with great care, with
great zeal, and after a serious consultation she was recommended quiet, repose, sleep, silence, those beautiful
dreams of her life ! At these counsels she began to smile,
shaking her head with a little air of incredulity, for she
knew that everything was possible for her except the
securing of those chosen hours, which are the portion of
certain women, and which belong to them alone.   She
promised, however, to obey for a few days and to restrict
herself to this regimen of isolation ; but they were vain

efforts, and she was seen a short time afterwards, wild and intoxicated with a factitious joy, traversing on horse- back the most difficult defiles, astonishing by her gayety that passage of Sept-Heures which had seen her thought- ful and reading with a low voice under the trees.

Presently she became the celebrity of these beautiful localities. She presided at all the fêtes ; she gave the initiative to every ball ; she imposed her favorite airs on the orchestra, and when the night came, at the hour in which a little sleep would have been so beneficial to her, she terrified the most intrepid players by the heaps of gold which collected before her, and which she lost all at a stroke, indifferent to the gain, indifferent to the loss. She had taken to play as a sort of appendix to her profession, as a means of killing the hours which killed her. Such as she was, however, she had still this happy fortune—in the cruel game of her life she had preserved some friends, a rare thing ! and it is one of the signs of these fatal liaisons that they leave but cinders and dust, vanity and nothingness, after the adorations !—And how many times has the lover passed by his mistress without recognizing her, and how many times has the unhappy one called him, but in vain, to her aid !—— How many times has that hand consecrated to flowers vainly been extended for alms and for a crust of bread !

It was not thus for our heroine : she fell without com- plaint, and, when fallen, she found again aid, support, and protection among the passionate adorers of her days of

*prosperity.   Those who had been rivals, or perhaps ene-
mies, came to an understanding among themselves to
watch at the bedside of the invalid, to expiate nights of
folly by nights of devotion, when death approaches, and
when the vail is rent, and when the victim lying there
and her accomplice comprehend finally the truth of that
solemn word :* Væ ridentibus ! *Woe to those who laugh !
Woe ! that is to say, woe to the profane joys, woe to the
volatile loves, woe to the changing passions, woe to youth
that goes astray in the paths of evil, for, at certain turnings
of the path, it is obliged, inevitably, to retrace the steps, and
to fall into the abysses which await the youth of twenty.*

*Thus she died, softly cradled and consoled by a thousand
soothing words, a thousand fraternal cares; she had no
longer any lovers —— never had she had so many friends,
and yet she did not regret life.   She knew what it was
that awaited her if she returned to health, and that she
would be obliged to lift again to her pale lips that cup of
pleasure of which she had drained the dregs prematurely;
she died, then, in silence, concealed in her death even more
than she had been revealed in her life, and, after so much
luxury and so many scandals, she had the supreme good
taste to wish to be interred at the break of day, in some
concealed and solitary spot, without ostentation, without
celebrity, quite like an honest mother of a family who goes
to rejoin her husband, her father, her mother and her
children, and all that she has loved, in the quiet cemetery
over yonder.*

It happened, however, despite her, that her death was a species of important event; it was a three days' wonder; and that is a great deal in this city of knowing passions and of festivities incessantly renewed which never pall. At the end of three days the closed door of her house was opened.—The long windows which looked out on the boulevard, facing the church of the Madeleine, her patron saint, permitted the air and the sun to enter again these rooms in which she had passed away. It seemed as though this young woman would appear again in this habitation. Not one of the odors of death still clung to the folds of these silken curtains, to these long hangings with their agreeable reflections, to this Gobelin carpet in which the flowers had seemed to spring to life, scarcely touched by this youthful foot.

Each piece of furniture of this sumptuous apartment was still in its place; the bed on which she had died was scarcely disarranged. At the bedside an ottoman preserved still the print of the knees of the man who had closed her eyes. This clock of former times, which had struck the hour for Madame de Pompadour and for Madame du Barry, struck the hour still, as then; the silver candelabra were furnished with candles prepared for the last social converse of the evening; in the vases the damask roses and the hardy heather resisted death in their turn. They were dying for want of a little water —— their mistress had died for want of a little happiness and hope.

Alas! on the walls were hung the paintings by Diaz, whom she had been one of the first to adopt as the veritable painter of the springtime of the year, and her portrait which Vidal had executed aux trois crayons. *Vidal had made of this beautiful head a chaste and ravishing study, of a finished elegance, and since the death of this divinity he has ever refused to depict any but chaste women, having made for this one an exception which served so well for the rising renown of the painter and of the sitter!*

Everything spoke of her still! The birds were singing in their gilded cage; in the Boule cabinets, through the transparent glass, there could be seen a collection, of an admirable choice and one worthy of a wealthy and critical antiquary, the rarest masterpieces of the manufacture of Sèvres, the most exquisite paintings of Saxony, the enamels of Petitot, the nudities of Klinstadt, the Pampines of Boucher. She loved this little coquettish, graceful, elegant style, in which vice itself has its wit, in which innocence has its nudities; she loved the shepherds and the shepherdesses in biscuit, *the Florentine bronzes, the terra-cottas, the enamels, all the refinements of taste and of luxury of exhausted societies. She saw in them so many emblems of her beauty and of her life. Alas! she was, she also, a useless ornament, a fancy, a frivolous toy which breaks at the first blow, a brilliant product of an expiring society, a bird of passage, a momentary aurora.*

She had carried so far the science of personal comfort and the worship of self that nothing could compare with her garments, her linen, with the smallest details of her daily service, for the adornment of her beauty had been, everything considered, the most cherished and the most charming occupation of her youth.

I have heard the ladies of the highest society and the most accomplished coquettes of Paris express their astonishment over the art and the studied elegance of her most insignificant toilet articles. Her comb was bid in at a fantastic price; her hair-brush was paid for at its weight in gold. Gloves that she had worn were sold, so beautiful were her hands. Shoes that she had used were sold, and virtuous women disputed among themselves as to who should assume those Cinderella slippers. Everything was sold, even her oldest shawl which had had three years of use; even her Aras parrakeet of brilliant plumage, which repeated a little melody sufficiently sorrowful that his mistress had taught him; her portraits were sold, her love-letters were sold, her ringlets were sold, everything was disposed of, and her family, who had turned their heads away when she had driven by in her carriage with armorial panels, at the full speed of her English horses, glutted themselves triumphantly with all the gold that these spoils had produced. They kept nothing which had belonged to her, for themselves. Chaste souls!

Such was this woman set apart, even in the midst of the Parisian passions, and you may judge of my surprise

*when this book appeared, of an interest so keen and above
all of a truthfulness quite fresh and quite young, and
which was entitled* La Dame aux Camélias. *It became
immediately a theme for discussion, as are discussed those
works stamped with the sincere emotion of youth, and
every one was glad to aver that the son of Alexandre
Dumas, barely out of college, already followed with a
sure step in the brilliant career of his father. He had
his vivacity and his inward emotion; he had his style,
lively, rapid, and with something of that dialogue, so
natural, so easy, and so varied, which gives to the
romances of this great inventor the charm, the taste, and
the accent of Comedy.*

*Thus the book obtained a great success; but presently
the readers, in reviewing their fugitive impressions, were
led to this observation, that the* Dame aux Camélias *was
not merely a romance in the air; that this woman must
have lived, and that she had lived recently; that this
drama was not one invented at pleasure, but on the
contrary an intimate tragedy, the representation of which
was quite true and quite warm from the heart. Then
there was much inquiry as to the name of the heroine,
as to her position in the world, as to her fortune, her
adornments, and the reports concerning her amours. The
public which wishes to know everything, and which
learns everything in the end, was informed, one after the
other, of all these details, and, the book once read, it was
desired to read it again, and it happened, very naturally*

*that the truth, once known, gave fresh interest to the
recital.*

*Therefore, this is how it happened, by an extraordinary
fortune, that this book, struck off with the ease of a futile
romance, scarcely destined to live a day, is republished
to-day with all the honors of a book universally accepted.
Read it, and you will recognize in its least details the
affecting history of which this young man so happily
endowed has written the elegy and the drama with so
many tears, with such success and good fortune.*

JULES JANIN.

---

[1] The galette of the Gymnaise.—A celebrated cake-shop adjoining the theatre of the same name and sharing its reputation, said to
be European in extent. This same M. Jules Janin pronounced in
1865 the funeral oration of the galette, but, as events proved, a
premature one.—NOTE BY TRANSLATOR.

THE

LADY OF THE CAMELLIAS

I

It is my opinion that no one can create characters unless he has greatly studied men, as it is impossible to speak a language excepting under the conditions of having learned it.

Not having yet reached the age at which one invents, I have contented myself with relating.

I therefore require the reader to be convinced of the reality of this history, all the personages of which, with the exception of the heroine, are still living.

Moreover, there are in Paris persons cognizant of the greater number of the facts which I have gathered here, and who could confirm them, if my testimony be not sufficient. A peculiar circumstance has enabled me alone to write them out, for I alone have been the confidant of the last details without which it would be impossible to give a complete and interesting recital.

Now, this is how these details came to my knowledge. On the 12th of the month of March, 1847, I read, in the Rue Laffitte, a great yellow poster which announced a sale of furniture and of valuable articles of curiosity. This sale was one after the decease of the owner. The

3

poster did not give the name of the deceased person,
but the sale was to take place in the Rue d'Antin, No. 9,
on the 16th, from noon to five o'clock.

The poster furthermore declared that the apartment
and the furniture could be inspected on the 13th and
the 14th.

I have always been an amateur of curiosities. I
promised myself that I would not miss this occasion, if
not of purchasing, at least of seeing them.

The next day I went to the Rue d'Antin, No. 9.

It was early, and yet there were in the apartment
already a number of visitors, and even lady visitors,
who, although clothed in velvet, arrayed in cashmeres
and with their elegant coupés waiting at the door,
looked with astonishment, even with admiration, at the
luxury which was displayed before their eyes.

I was able to comprehend this admiration and this
astonishment later, for, beginning to examine the articles myself, I readily recognized that I was in the
apartment of a kept mistress. Now, if there is one
thing that the women of the world desire to see, and
there were present here women of the world, it is the
household interiors of these women, whose equipages
spatter mud on their own, who have, as well as they,
and by the side of theirs, their boxes at the Opera and
at the Italiens, and who display openly in Paris the
insolent opulence of their beauty, of their jewels, and
of their scandals.

She in whose house I found myself was dead; the most virtuous wives could therefore penetrate even into her bed-chamber. Death had purified the air of this splendid cloaca, and, moreover, they had for an excuse, if necessary, that they had come to a public sale without knowing in whose house it was. They had read the posters, they wished to inspect that which the posters promised and make their selections in advance; nothing was more simple; all of which did not prevent them from seeking, in the midst of all these marvels, traces of that life of the courtesan of which, doubtless, they had heard such strange stories.

Unfortunately, the mysteries had all died with the goddess, and, notwithstanding their good-will, these ladies succeeded in discovering only that which was for sale since the decease, and nothing of that which was sold during the life-time of the inmate.

For the rest, there was abundant opportunity for purchases. The furnishing was superb. Pieces in rosewood and of Boule, vases of Sèvres and of China, Dresden statuettes, satin, velvet and laces, nothing was lacking.

I walked about in the apartment, and I followed the distinguished curious ones who preceded me. They entered a chamber hung with a Persian stuff, and I was about to enter also when they came out again almost immediately and smiling as if they were somewhat ashamed of this new curiosity. I only desired all the

more keenly to penetrate into this chamber. It was the
dressing-room, furnished with its most minute details,
in which the prodigality of the dead woman appeared
developed to its highest degree.

On a large table, placed against the wall, a table
three feet wide by six long, glittered all the treasures of
Aucoc and of Odiot. This was a magnificent collection, and not one of these thousand objects, so necessary
to the toilet of a woman such as the one in whose house
we were, but was in gold or silver. And this collection
could only have been made piece by piece, and it was
not the same love that had furnished the whole of it.

I, who am not terrified at the sight of the dressing-
room of a kept mistress—I amused myself by examining
the various articles such as they were, and I perceived
that all these utensils magnificently chiseled bore various
initials and different coronets.

I contemplated all these things, each one of which
represented to me a prostitution of the poor girl, and I
said to myself that God had been lenient to her, since
He had not permitted her to be brought to the usual
punishment, and since He had allowed her to die in
her luxury and her beauty, before old age, that first
death of the courtesans.

In fact, what is more sorrowful to see than the old
age of vice, above all in a woman? Then, it is attended
with no dignity and inspires no interest. This lasting
repentance, not for the evil courses followed, but for

miscalculations and misspent money, is one of the most saddening things that can be witnessed. I have known a former woman of pleasure to whom there remained of her past nothing but a daughter almost as beautiful as, according to the testimony of her contemporaries, the mother had been. This poor child, to whom her mother had never said: "Thou art my daughter," except when she laid her commands on her to take care of her in her old age as she herself had taken care of her infancy, this poor creature was named Louise, and, in obedience to her mother, she yielded herself without willingness, without passion, without pleasure, as she would have taken up a trade or profession if any one had thought to instruct her in one.

The constant familiarity with a life of debauchery, a precocious debauchery, aided by the continual state of ill health of this young girl, had extinguished in her the knowledge of good and evil which God had given her perhaps, but which it had occurred to no one to develop in her.

I still remember this young girl, who passed on the Boulevards every day at almost the same hour. Her mother always accompanied her, quite as assiduously as a real mother would have accompanied her real daughter. I was very young at that time, and quite ready to accept the easy morality of my century. I remember, however, that the sight of this scandalous surveillance filled me with contempt and disgust.

And to this it may be added that never did the face
of a virgin express such a sentiment of innocence, wear
such an expression of melancholy suffering.

It might have been accepted as the countenance of
Resignation.

One day, the face of this young girl lighted up.   In
the midst of the debauchery which her mother super-
vised, it seemed to the sinning one that God had granted
her a happiness.   And, after all, why should God, who
had made her without strength, have left her entirely
without consolation, under the sorrowful burden of her
life?   One day, then, she discovered that she was
enceinte, and all that was left in her of chastity trembled with joy.   The soul has strange asylums.   Louise
hastened to announce to her mother this news, which
rendered her so joyous.   It is a shameful thing to
relate — but we are not concerned here with the
pleasure of immorality, we are relating a true fact,
which we would perhaps do better to conceal if we
did not believe that, from time to time, it was necessary to reveal the martyrdom of these beings, who are
condemned without being heard, who are despised
without being judged; it is shameful, as we say,
but the mother replied to her daughter that they
already had none too much for two, and that they
certainly would not have enough for three; that such
children were unnecessary and that a lying-in was
time lost.

The next day, a midwife, whom we shall indicate only as a friend of the mother, came to see Louise, who remained for some days confined to her bed and who rose from it paler and more feeble than ever.

Three months later, a man took pity upon her and undertook her cure, moral and physical; but the last shock had been too violent, and Louise died from the effects of this miscarriage.

The mother is still living: how? God knows.

This story had come into my mind while I was contemplating the toilet articles in silver, and, as it appeared, a certain length of time had been passed in these reflections, for there was no longer in the room any one but myself and a guardian who, from the doorway, was watching attentively that I did not make away with anything.

I approached this honest man in whom I inspired such grave disquietude.

"Monsieur," I said to him, "could you give me the name of the person who lived here?"

"Mademoiselle Marguerite Gautier."

I had known this young woman by name and by sight.

"What!" I said to the guardian, "Marguerite Gautier is dead?"

"Yes, monsieur."

"And how long ago?"

"About three weeks, I think."

"And why is the apartment thrown open to the public?"

"The creditors thought that it could not but aid the sale. People would be enabled to see in advance the effect made by the draperies and the furniture; you understand, that encourages them to bid."

"She had debts, then?"

"Oh, monsieur, plenty of them."

"But the sale will doubtless cover them?"

"And over."

"To whom will the surplus go?"

"To her family."

"She has, then, a family?"

"So it seems."

"Thank you, monsieur."

The guardian, reassured concerning my intentions, saluted me, and I passed out.

"Poor girl!" I said to myself as I returned homewards, "her death must have been a sad one, for, in her world, no one has any friends excepting in health and prosperity." And, despite myself, I felt pity for the fate of Marguerite Gautier.

This will perhaps appear ridiculous to many, but I have an inexhaustible indulgence for the courtesans, and I do not even give myself the trouble to discuss this indulgence.

One day, going to procure a passport at the prefecture, I saw in one of the adjacent streets a woman of the town whom two gendarmes were leading away. I do not know what this woman had done; all that I can say is that she was weeping bitterly while embracing an infant of a few months from whom she would be separated by her arrest. Since that day, I have no longer been able to despise a woman at first sight.

II

The sale was for the 16th.

An interval of a day had been left between the inspection and the sale in order to give the furnishers time to take down the hangings, curtains, etc.

At this period I had just returned from a journey. It was natural enough that no one had informed me of the death of Marguerite as one of those great pieces of news which one's friends always communicate to one returning to the capital of all news. Marguerite was pretty, but just in proportion as the notorious life of these women makes a noise, just so little does their death make. They are suns which set as they rose, without disturbance. Their death, when they die young, is known to all their lovers at the same time, for, in Paris, nearly all the lovers of a known woman live on terms of intimacy. Some souvenirs are exchanged concerning her, and the lives of all continue without being troubled by this incident, even to the extent of a tear.

Nowadays, when one has reached the age of twenty-five, tears become something so very rare that they cannot be given to the first comer. It is the utmost that

13

can be expected if the parents, who pay for being wept, receive the worth of their money.

As for myself, though my monogram was not to be found on any of Marguerite's articles, this instinctive indulgence, this natural pity, which I have just avowed, made me think of her death longer perhaps than it merited I should think of it.

I remembered having met Marguerite very frequently in the Champs-Élysées, where she came assiduously, every day, in a little blue coupé drawn by two magnificent bay horses, and to have then remarked in her a distinction very uncommon among her kind, a distinction which was made all the more noticeable by a truly exceptional beauty.

These unfortunate creatures are always, when they go out, accompanied by no one knows whom.

As no man will consent to proclaim publicly the nocturnal love which he bears for them, as they have a horror of solitude, they take with them either those, less fortunate, who have no carriage of their own, or one of those elegantly arrayed old ladies whose elegance can in no wise be accounted for, and to whom you can address yourself without any misgivings when you wish to have any information whatever concerning the woman they are accompanying.

It was not thus with Marguerite. She arrived on the Champs-Élysées always alone in her carriage, in which she made as little display as possible, in winter enveloped in a great cashmere wrap and in summer dressed very simply; and although there were on her favorite promenade many men whom she knew, when by chance she smiled at them, the smile was visible for them alone, and a duchess might have smiled in the same manner.

She did not drive merely from the Rond-point to the entrance of the Champs-Élysées, as did, and do still, all her colleagues. Her two horses carried her rapidly to the Bois. There, she descended from her carriage, walked about for an hour, got into her coupé again and returned home at a rapid trot.

All these circumstances, of which I had formerly been the witness, passed before me again, and I regretted the death of this woman as the total destruction of a beautiful work is regretted.

It must be said, there was no more charming beauty than Marguerite's to be seen.

Tall and slight, even to exaggeration, she possessed to a supreme degree the art of causing this slight neglect on the part of nature to disappear by the simple arrangements of the articles that she wore. Her cashmere, the point of which touched the ground, allowed to escape on each side the large flounces of a silk dress, and the thick sleeve which concealed her hands and which she carried against her breast was surrounded by folds so skillfully managed that the eye had nothing to complain of, however exacting it may have been, in the contour of her forms.

Her head, a marvel, was the object of a peculiar
coquetry.   It was very small, and her mother, as
De Musset would have said, seemed to have made it
thus in order to make it carefully.

In an oval of indescribable grace, place black eyes
under brows of so pure an arch that they seemed to
have been painted; veil these eyes with long lashes
which, when lowered, cast a shadow upon the pink
tint of the cheeks; design a nose, fine, straight, spirit-
ual, with nostrils slightly dilated by an ardent aspira-
tion towards the sensual life; trace a regular mouth,
the lips of which opened graciously over teeth as
white as milk; color the skin with that velvet softness
which covers the peaches that no hand has touched,
and you will have a general idea of this charming
head.

Her hair, black as jet, whether waved naturally or
not, parted over the forehead in two large bandeaux
and disappeared behind the head, allowing the tips
of the ears to be seen, in each of which glittered a
diamond of the value of four or five thousand francs.

How was it that her ardent life left on Marguerite's
face the virginal, even infantile, expression which
characterized it?   This is something that we are
obliged to admit without comprehending it.

Marguerite had had a marvellous portrait of herself
executed by Vidal, the only man whose crayon could
have reproduced her.   Since her death, I have had

this portrait at my disposition for a few days, and it was so astonishing a resemblance that it has aided me to give some indications for which my memory alone perhaps might not have sufficed.

Among the details of this chapter, there are some that did not come to me till later; but I write them all down here so as not to have to return to them when we shall have begun the anecdotal history of this woman.

Marguerite was present at all the first nights of the theatres, and devoted all her evenings either to the drama or the ball. Whenever a new piece was given she was always to be seen with three articles which never left her and which constantly occupied the front of her stage-box,—her opera-glasses, a paper of bon-bons, and a bouquet of camellias.

During twenty-five days of the month her camellias were white, and for five days they were red; no one ever knew the reason for this variety of colors, which I notice without being able to explain it, and which her friends and the habitués of the theatres where she went most frequently had remarked, like myself.

She was never seen with any other flowers than camellias. Thus, in the establishment of Madame Barjon, her florist, she came to be known finally as the Lady of the Camellias, and this appellation clung to her.

I knew, in addition, like all those who live in a certain world in Paris, that Marguerite had been the

mistress of some of the most elegant young men, that
she admitted it openly, and that they, themselves,
boasted of it, which proved that the lovers and the
mistress were well satisfied with each other.

However, for about the last three years, ever since a
trip to Bagnères, she lived, it was said, only with an old
duke, a foreigner, enormously rich, and who had endeavored to detach her, as much as possible, from all her
past life, which, moreover, she had seemed sufficiently
willing to do.

This is what was related to me on this subject :

In the spring of 1842, Marguerite was so delicate,
her health was so impaired, that the physicians ordered
her to take the waters, and she departed for Bagnères.

At this place, among the invalids, was the daughter of
this duke, who had not only the same malady, but even
the same countenance, as Marguerite, to such a degree
that they would have been taken for two sisters. Unfortunately, however, the young duchess was in the last
stages of consumption, and died a few days after
Marguerite's arrival.

One morning the duke, who had remained at Bagnères
as one remains on the soil in which a portion of his
heart has been interred, perceived Marguerite at the
angle of an alley.

It seemed to him that he saw the shade of his child
passing by, and, going up to her, he took her hands,
embraced her weeping, and, without asking her who

she was, implored her permission to visit her and to love in her the living image of his dead daughter.

Marguerite, who was alone at Bagnères with her *femme de chambre*, and who, moreover, had no fear of compromising herself, granted the duke all that he asked.

There happened to be at Bagnères some who knew her, and they officially notified the duke of the true position of Mademoiselle Gautier. This was a heavy blow for the old man, for all resemblance to his daughter ceased here; but it was too late. The young woman had become indispensable to his heart, and his sole pretext, his sole excuse for still living.

He offered her no reproaches, he had the right to make none, but he asked her if she felt herself capable of changing her mode of life, offering her in exchange for this sacrifice all the compensations which she could desire. She promised.

It must be observed that at this period Marguerite, an enthusiastic temperament, was ill. Her past appeared to her as one of the principal causes of this illness, and a species of superstition led her to hope that God would still leave to her her beauty and health in recompense for her repentance and conversion.

In fact, the waters, the walks, the natural fatigue and sleep, had almost restored her to health by the end of the summer.

The duke accompanied Marguerite to Paris, where he continued to visit her as at Bagnères.

This liaison, of which no one knew either the true origin nor the true motive, caused a great sensation here, for the duke, known already by his great fortune, now made himself further known by his prodigality.

This connection between the old duke and the young woman was generally attributed to that libertinism so frequent among rich old men. Everything was supposed, excepting that which really was.

Nevertheless the sentiments of this father towards Marguerite had a cause so chaste that any other relations than those of the heart with her would have seemed to him incestuous, and he had never addressed to her a word that his daughter might not have heard.

Far be it from us to think of making of our heroine anything other than that she really was. We will say, then, that so long as she remained at Bagnères the promise given to the duke had not been difficult to keep, and that she had kept it; but, once returned to Paris, it had seemed to this young woman, accustomed to a life of dissipation, to balls, to orgies even, that her solitude, broken only by the periodic visits of the duke, would cause her to die of ennui, and the burning breath of her former life passed at once over her head and her heart.

Add to this that she had returned from this journey more beautiful than she had ever been, that she was twenty years of age, and that her malady, lulled but not vanquished, continued to inspire in her those feverish desires which are almost always excited by pulmonary affections.

The duke experienced then a great sorrow on the day when his friends, ceaselessly on the watch to discover some scandal concerning the young woman with whom he was compromising himself, as they said, came to apprise him and to prove to him that at the hour in which she was sure that he would not come, she received other visits, and that these were frequently prolonged even to the next day.

When interrogated, Marguerite avowed everything to the duke, advising him, quite honestly, to take no further interest in her, as she did not feel herself strong enough to fulfill the engagements she had made and did not wish to receive longer the benefactions of a man whom she deceived.

For the space of a week the duke did not appear; this was all that he could do, and, on the eighth day, he came to entreat her to receive him still, promising to accept her such as she was, provided that he could see her, and swearing to her that, were he to die for it, he would never reproach her.

This was the state of affairs three months after Marguerite's return, that is to say, in November or December, 1842.

III

At one o'clock on the 16th of the month I returned to the Rue d'Antin.

The voices of the auctioneers could be heard even from the porte-cochère.

The apartment was filled with a curious crowd.

In it there were to be seen all the celebrities of this life of elegant vice, stealthily watched by great ladies who had availed themselves once more of this pretext of the sale in order to inspect more nearly these women whom they would never have. an opportunity to meet again, and whose facile pleasures they perhaps envied secretly.

Madame la duchesse de F—— was elbowing Mademoiselle A——, one of the saddest examples of our modern courtesans; Madame la marquise de T—— hesitated to purchase an article of furniture which was being priced by Madame D——, the most elegant and the best-known adulterous wife of our epoch; the duc de Y——, who is accounted in Madrid to be ruining himself in Paris, and in Paris to be ruining himself in Madrid, and who, in all, does not even spend his

23

revenue, while conversing with Madame M——, one of our most spirituelle romancers, who is quite willing from time to time to write what she says and to sign what she writes, exchanged confidential glances with Madame de N——, that beautiful promenader of the Champs-Élysées, dressed almost always in pink or in blue and whose carriage is drawn by two great black horses which Tony sold to her for ten thousand francs and —— for which she paid him; finally Mademoiselle R——, who with her single talent realizes the double of that which the women of the world do with their dot, and the triple of that which the others do with their amours, had come, notwithstanding the cold, to make some purchases, and she was not the least looked at.

We could cite the initials of many more who had met together in this salon and who were greatly surprised to find themselves together; but we should fear to weary the reader.

Let us say only that everybody was in a very gay mood, and that among all those there assembled there were many who had known the dead woman and who did not appear in the least to remember her.

The laughter was loud; the auctioneers cried at the top of their lungs; the dealers, who had taken possession of the benches before the sales tables, endeavored in vain to impose silence, in order to carry on their negotiations tranquilly. Never had a reunion been more varied, more noisy.

I slipped humbly through the midst of this tumult, which was saddening when I reflected that it took place adjoining the chamber in which had expired the poor creature whose furniture was being sold in order to pay her debts.   I had come to examine rather than to purchase, and I looked at the faces of the furnishers who had caused the sale, and whose features expanded with joy each time that an object attained a price which they had not hoped for.

Honest souls who had speculated upon the prostitution of this woman, who had made a hundred per cent. out of her, who had pursued her with legal papers during the last moments of her life, and who came after her death to gather the fruits of their honorable calculations at the same time with the interests of their shameful credits.

How very right were the ancients who had but one god for the merchants and the thieves !

Dresses, cashmeres, jewels, were disposed of with an incredible rapidity.   Nothing of all these appealed to me, and I waited for something further.

Suddenly I heard the cry :

"One volume, in perfect binding, gilt edges, *entitled :* Manon Lescaut.   *There is something written on the first page :* Ten francs."

"Twelve," said a voice after a sufficiently long silence.

"Fifteen," said I.

Why? I did not know in the least. Doubtless because of that *something written*.

" Fifteen," repeated the auctioneer.

"Thirty," said the first bidder, in a tone which seemed to defy any one to go higher.

This had become a real contest.

"Thirty-five!" I then cried in the same tone.

"Forty."

" Fifty."

" Sixty."

" A hundred."

I must confess that if I had wished to make an effect, I had completely succeeded, for at this bid there fell a great silence, and every one looked at me to see who was this monsieur who seemed so determined to possess this volume.

It appeared that the accent given to my last word had convinced my antagonist; he therefore preferred to abandon a combat which would have only served to make me pay for this volume ten times its price, and, bowing, he said to me very graciously, although a little late :

" I yield, monsieur."

No one having anything further to say, the book was knocked down to me.

As I feared a new obstinacy which my self-respect would perhaps have sustained but which my purse would certainly have taken very ill, I gave my name, had the volume put to one side, and I departed. I must have excited much curiosity among those, witnesses of this scene, who doubtless asked themselves with what object I had come to pay a hundred francs for a book which I could get anywhere for ten or fifteen francs at the most.

An hour later I sent for my purchase.

On the first page was written with a pen, and in a handsome handwriting, the dedication of the donor of this book. This dedication consisted in these words only:

MANON TO MARGUERITE,
HUMILITY.

It was signed: Armand Duval.

What was the meaning of this word: humility?

Did Manon recognize in Marguerite, in the opinion of this Monsieur Armand Duval, a superiority of debauchery or of the heart?

The second interpretation was the more probable, for the first would have been only a frank impertinence which would not have been accepted by Marguerite, whatever might have been her opinion of herself.

I left the house a second time, and I did not concern myself with this book again until that night when I retired.

Certainly *Manon Lescaut* is a touching story, every detail of which is known to me, and yet whenever I find this volume under my hand, my sympathy for it always attracts me; I open it, and for the hundredth time I am living again with the heroine of the Abbé Prévost. This heroine is indeed so very life-like that it seems to me that I have known her. Under these novel circumstances, the species of comparison established between her and Marguerite gave this reading an unexpected attraction for me, and my indulgence was augmented by pity, almost by love for the poor girl to whose estate I owed this volume. Manon had died in a desert, it is true, but in the arms of a man who loved her with all the energy of his soul, who, when she was dead, had dug her grave, watered it with his tears, and buried in it his heart; whilst Marguerite, a sinner like Manon and perhaps converted like her, had died in the midst of sumptuous luxury, if what I had seen could be believed, in the very bed of her past life, but also in the midst of that desert of the heart, much more arid, much more vast, much more pitiless than that in which Manon had been interred.

Marguerite, in fact, as I had learned from some friends informed of the last circumstances of her life, had not seen any real consolation seated at her bedside, during the two months of her last slow and painful illness.

Then from Manon and Marguerite my thoughts travelled to those whom I knew and whom I saw on the road, singing gayly, to an almost invariable death.

Poor creatures! If it be a wrong to love them, it is the least we can do to pity them. You pity the blind man who has never seen the daylight, the deaf who has never heard Nature's accords, the mute who can never express the voice of his soul, and, under a false pretext of modesty, you are not willing to pity that blindness of the heart, that deafness of the soul, that dumbness of the conscience, which deprives the unfortunate afflicted one of her judgment and which makes her, despite herself, incapable of seeing the good, of hearing the voice of the Lord and of uttering the pure language of love and of faith.

Hugo has created *Marion Delorme*, Musset has created *Bernerette*, Alexandre Dumas has created *Fernande*, the thinkers and the poets of all times have brought to the courtesan the offering of their compassion, and sometimes a great man has rehabilitated them with his love and even with his name. If I thus dwell upon this point, it is because, among those who are about to become my readers, many perhaps are already prepared to throw down this book in which they fear to find only an apology for prostitution and vice,—and the age of the author doubtless contributes not a little to this fear. Let those who are of this way of thinking undeceive themselves, and let them continue reading if it is this fear alone which deters them.

I am quite sincerely convinced of one principle, which is this:—For that woman whom education has not instructed in good, God opens almost always two pathways which may bring her back to it; these pathways are sorrow and love. They are very difficult; those who enter them traverse them with bleeding feet, with torn hands, but at the same time they leave on all the brambles of the wayside the tinseled trappings of vice, and they arrive at their destination in that nudity for which no one blushes before the Lord.

Those who encounter these courageous pilgrims should give them aid and comfort and relate to all that they have met them, for, in making it public, they show the way to all.

It is not a question of setting up quite frankly at the entry of life two posts, bearing, one of them, this inscription: *The Path of Virtue*, and the other, this warning: *The Path of Vice*, and of saying to all who present themselves: "Choose;" it is necessary, like Christ, to show the paths which conduct from the second road to the first those who have allowed themselves to be tempted by the easiness of access; and it is above all necessary that the commencement of these roads should not be too painful nor appear to be too impenetrable.

We have the support of Christianity, with its wonderful parable of the prodigal son, to counsel us to indulgence and pardon. Jesus was filled with love for these

souls wounded by men's passions, and of which he loved
to heal the wounds, drawing from them the balm which
should cure them of the wounds themselves. Thus he
said to the Magdalen: "Much shall be forgiven thee,
because thou hast loved much," a sublime speech which
should awaken a sublime faith.

Why should we make ourselves more severe than
Christ himself? Why, in clinging obstinately to the
opinions of that world which makes itself hard in order
that it may be thought strong, should we reject with it
souls bleeding often with wounds from which, like the
corrupted blood of an invalid, issues the evil of their
past life, and waiting only for a friendly hand which
shall bind them up and restore them to the convalescence of the heart?

It is to my own generation that I address myself, to
those for whom the theories of Monsieur de Voltaire
fortunately do not exist, to those who, like myself, comprehend that humanity has been for the last fifteen years
in one of its most courageous transports. The knowledge of good and of evil is forever acquired; faith is
restored, respect for sacred things is given us again, and,
if the world is not making itself all at once virtuous, it
is at least making itself better. The efforts of all intelli-
gent men tend to the same end, and all the great wills
attach themselves to the same principle: be honest, be
youthful. be true! Evil is only a vain thing; have the
pride of virtue, and, above all, do not despair. Do not

despise the woman who is neither mother, nor sister, nor daughter, nor wife. Do not restrict respect to the family only, indulgence to egotism. Since there is more joy in heaven over one sinner who repenteth than over a hundred just ones who have never sinned, let us endeavor to make heaven rejoice. It may return it to us with usury. Let us leave upon our road the alms of our forgiveness for those who have been lost through earthly desires, but whom a divine hope will, perhaps, save, and, as the old women say when they advise a prescription of their simples, if that does no good, at least it will do no harm.

Certainly, it must appear very hardy in me to wish to develop these great results from the slight subject which I am treating; but I am of those who believe that every-thing is in the little. The child is small, he encloses the man; the brain is narrow, it shelters the thought; the eye is but a point, and it covers leagues.

IV

Two days later the sale was entirely completed. It had produced a hundred and fifty thousand francs.

The creditors had divided two-thirds among themselves, and the family, consisting of a sister and a grand-nephew, had inherited the remainder.

This sister had opened her eyes in astonishment when the business man wrote her that she had inherited fifty thousand francs.

It had been six or seven years since this young girl had seen her sister, who had disappeared one day, and of whose life since the moment of her disappearance no one had ever had the slightest knowledge, either through herself or through others.

She therefore came to Paris in hot haste, and great was the astonishment of those who had known Marguerite when they saw that her only heir was a plump and handsome country wench who had never before left her natal village.

Her fortune was made at one stroke, without her knowing even from what source there came to her this unhoped-for fortune.

33

She returned, as I have been told since, to her country
home, carrying with her because of the death of her
sister a great sadness, which was consoled nevertheless
by the investment at four and a half per cent. which she
had made.

All these circumstances, which had been repeated in
Paris, the mother city of scandals, were beginning to be
forgotten, and I had almost forgotten myself the part I
had taken in these events, when a new incident made
me acquainted with the whole life of Marguerite and
informed me of details so touching that I resolved to
write this history, and that I wrote it.

For the last three or four days the apartment, emptied of all its furniture sold at the auction, had been
offered for rent, when there was a ring at my door one
morning.

My servant, or, rather, my porter, who took the place
of a servant, opened the door and brought me a card,
saying that the person who had given it to him desired
to speak to me.

I glanced at this card and I there read these two words:
Armand Duval.

I endeavored to remember where I had seen this
name before, and I recalled the first leaf of the volume
of *Manon Lescaut.*

What could he want with me, the person who had
given this book to Marguerite? I directed that he
should be immediately admitted.

I saw then a blond young man, tall, pale, wearing a travelling costume which he apparently had not taken off for several days and had not even taken the trouble to brush since entering Paris, for he was covered with dust.

This Monsieur Duval, who was strongly agitated, made no effort to conceal his emotion, and it was with tears in his eyes and a trembling in his voice that he said to me:

"Monsieur, you will excuse, I entreat you, my visit and my costume; but, outside of the fact that among young people we do not observe the formalities very strictly, I wished so much to see you that I did not even take time to stop at the hotel to which I have sent my trunks, and I hastened here, fearing even then not to find you, although it is so early."

I asked Monsieur Duval to take a seat near the fire, which he did, drawing at the same time from his pocket a handkerchief with which he concealed his face a moment.

"You cannot comprehend," he went on, sighing mournfully, "what this unknown visitor can want with you, at such an hour, in such a costume, and weeping as he does.

"I come quite frankly, monsieur, to ask of you a great service."

"Speak, monsieur; I am entirely at your disposition."

"You were present at the Marguerite Gautier sale?"

At this word the young man's emotion, which he had overcome for a moment, was stronger than he, and he was compelled to carry his hands to his eyes.

"I must appear very ridiculous to you," he added; "excuse me again for this, and believe that I shall never forget the patience with which you listen to me."

"Monsieur," I replied, "if the service which it seems I can render you should be able to calm your grief a little, tell me quickly in what I may be of use to you, and you will find in me a man happy to oblige you."

There was something in Monsieur Duval's sorrow that was sympathetic, and, despite myself, I would have wished to have pleased him.

He then said to me :

"You bought something at Marguerite's sale?"

"Yes, monsieur, a book."

"*Manon Lescaut?*"

"That is it."

"Have you this book still?"

"It is in my bedroom."

At this intelligence Armand Duval seemed relieved of a great weight and thanked me as if I had already commenced to do him a service by keeping the volume.

I rose, I went into my chamber to get the book and handed it to him.

"That is it, indeed," he said, looking at the dedication on the first page and turning over the leaves; "that is it, indeed."

And two big tears fell on the pages.

"Well, monsieur," said he, lifting his face toward me, and not even endeavoring to conceal from me that he had wept, and that he was near to weeping again, "do you value this book greatly?"

"Why, monsieur?"

"Because I have come to ask you to yield it to me."

"Forgive my curiosity," I said; "but it was then you who gave it to Marguerite Gautier?"

"It was I, myself."

"The book is yours, monsieur, take it, I am happy to be able to return it to you."

"But," replied Monsieur Duval in embarrassment, "it is the least I can do to give you the price which you paid for it."

"Permit me to offer it to you. The price of a single volume in such a sale as that is a trifle, and I no longer remember what I did pay for this one."

"You paid for it a hundred francs."

"That is true," said I, embarrassed in my turn. "How do you know it?"

"It is very simple. I hoped to arrive in Paris in time for Marguerite's sale, and I arrived only this morning. I was strongly desirous of having some object that had belonged to her, and I hastened to the auctioneer's establishment to ask of him permission to see the list of objects sold and the names of the purchasers. I saw that this volume had been bought by you, I resolved to

ask you to give it up to me, although the price which you
had paid for it made me fear that you yourself connected
the possession of this volume with some souvenir."

In speaking thus it was evident that Armand feared
that I had known Marguerite as he had known her.

I hastened to reassure him.

"I knew Mademoiselle Gautier only by sight," I
said to him; "her death made upon me the impression
which the death of a pretty woman whom he has had
pleasure in meeting always makes on a young man. I
wished to buy something at her sale, and I was obstinate
in bidding on this volume, I know not why, for the
pleasure of aggravating a monsieur who was furiously
interested and seemed to defy me to get it. I therefore
repeat to you, monsieur, this book is at your disposition,
and I entreat you again to accept it so that you shall
not have obtained it from me as I obtained it from the
auctioneer, and that it shall be between us a pledge of a
longer acquaintance and of more intimate relations."

"It is well, monsieur," said Armand, offering me his
hand and grasping mine; "I accept, and I shall be
grateful to you all my life."

I had a great desire to question Armand about Marguerite, for the dedication of the book, the young man's
journey, his desire to possess this volume, excited my
curiosity; but I feared, in questioning my visitor, to
appear to have refused his money only for the purpose of
having the right to interfere in his affairs.

It would seem that he was aware of my desire, for he said to me :

"You have read this volume?"

"All through."

"What did you think of the two lines which I wrote?"

"I understood at once that in your eyes the poor girl to whom you had given this volume was not to be included in the usual category, for I could not see in these lines only a commonplace compliment."

"And you were right, monsieur. This girl was an angel. See," he said to me, "read this letter."

And he extended to me a paper which seemed to have been read a great many times.

I opened it ; this is what it contained :

"My Dear Armand : I have received your letter; you are still kind, and I thank God for it. Yes, my friend, I am ill, and with one of those maladies which never forgive; but the interest which you are still willing to take in me serves to greatly lessen my sufferings. I doubtless shall not live long enough to have the happiness of clasping the hand which has written the kind letter which I have just received, and the words of which would cure me, if anything could cure me. I shall not see you, for I am very near to death, and hundreds of leagues separate you from me. Poor friend! your Marguerite of other days is indeed changed, and it

is perhaps better that you should not see her again than
to see her as she is. You ask me if I forgive you? Oh!
with all my heart, friend, for the pain which you gave
me was only a proof of the love which you had for me.
I have been confined to my bed for a month, and I
cling so much to your esteem that each day I write up
the journal of my life, from the moment when we separated up to the moment when I shall no longer have the
strength to write.

"If the interest which you take in me is real, Armand,
on your return go to see Julie Duprat. She will give to
you this journal. You will find in it the reason and the
excuse for that which has passed between us. Julie is
very kind to me; we often talk together of you. She was
present when your letter came, we wept in reading it.

"In case you should not have sent me any news of
yourself, she is charged to transmit these papers to you
on your arrival in France. Do not be grateful to me.
This daily return to the only happy moments of my life
is of immense benefit to me, and, if you should find in
this reading the excuse for the past, I, for my part, find
in it a continual solace.

"I would wish to leave you something which would
recall me always to your mind, but everything has been
seized in my apartment, and nothing belongs to me.

"Do you understand, my friend? I am dying, and
from my bed-chamber I can hear walking in the salon
the guardian whom my creditors have placed there to

see that nothing is carried away and that nothing shall be left me in case I do not die. It is to be hoped that they will wait for the end before selling.

"Oh! men are pitiless! or, rather, I deceive myself, it is God who is just and inflexible.

"Well, dearly beloved, you will come to my sale and you will purchase something, for, if I should put aside the least object for you and it should be detected, they would be capable of attaching you for unlawful conveyance of articles levied upon.

"What a sorrowful life is that which I leave!

"How good God would be if he should permit me to see you again before dying! In all probability, it is farewell, my friend; forgive me if I do not write to you more at length, but those who say they will cure me are exhausting me with blood-lettings, and my hand refuses to write more.   "MARGUERITE GAUTIER."

In fact, the last words were scarcely legible.

I returned this letter to Armand, who had doubtless re-read it in his memory as I had read it on the paper, for he said to me as he took it:

"Who would ever believe that it was a kept mistress who had written that?" And, carried away by his memories, he looked for some time at the writing of this letter, which he finally carried to his lips.

"And when I think," he went on, "that she is dead without my having been able to see her again and that I shall never see her again; when I think that she has done for me that which a sister would not have done, I cannot forgive myself for having allowed her to die thus.

"Dead! dead! while thinking of me, while writing and uttering my name, poor dear Marguerite!"

And Armand, giving a free course to his thoughts and his tears, extended his hand to me and continued:

"I would be considered very childish if I should be seen lamenting thus over a death like this; it would be because it was not known how I had made this woman suffer, how cruel I had been, how good and resigned she had been. I thought that it was my place to pardon her, and to-day I find myself unworthy of the pardon which she grants me. Oh! I would give ten years of my life to weep one hour at her feet."

It is always difficult to find consolation for a sorrow which you do not share, and yet I was filled with so keen a sympathy for this young man, he made me so frankly the confidant of his grief, that I thought that my words might not be indifferent to him, and I said to him:

"Have you not relatives, friends? Have hopes, go to see them, and they will console you, for I can only pity you."

"That is true," said he, rising and walking hastily about in my chamber, "I annoy you. Forgive me, I did not reflect that my sorrow must be of little matter to you, and that I am importuning you with a thing which cannot and should not interest you in the least.''

"You are mistaken in the meaning of my words, I am entirely at your service ; only, I regret my inability to calm your grief. If my society and that of my friends can give you any distraction; if, in short, you have need of me in anything whatever, I desire that you should be well assured of all the pleasure which it would give me to be of service to you.''

" Pardon, pardon,'' he said, " sorrow intensifies all the sensations. Allow me to remain a few moments longer, time enough to dry my eyes, so that the ninnies in the street shall not look, as though he were a curiosity, at the big boy who is crying. You have made me very happy by giving me this book ; I shall never know how to acknowledge that which I owe you.''

" By giving me a little of your friendship,'' I said to Armand, "and in telling me the cause of your grief. Consolation is found in relating our own sufferings.''

"You are right ; but to-day I have too much need of tears, and I would say to you only disconnected words. Some day I will inform you of this history, and you will see if I have cause for regretting the poor girl. And now,'' he added, rubbing his eyes for the last time and looking at himself in the mirror, "tell me that you do not think me too silly, and permit me to come again to see you."

This young man's look was good and gentle; I was on the point of embracing him.

As for him, his eyes began again to be veiled in tears, he saw that I perceived them and he turned away his glance.

"Come," I said to him, "have courage."

"Adieu," he replied.

And, making an incredible effort not to weep, he fled out of my apartment rather than went out of it.

I lifted the curtain of my window, and I saw him get into the cabriolet which was waiting for him at the door; but scarcely had he taken his seat when he broke into tears and hid his face in his handkerchief.

V

A considerable length of time elapsed without my hearing anything of Armand, but, as if in compensation, there was much discussion of Marguerite.

I do not know whether you have observed it, but if the name of a person who apparently should have remained unknown to you, or at the least entirely indifferent, be pronounced once before you, a multitude of details come, little by little, to group themselves around this name, and you hear all your friends speaking to you of something which they never mentioned to you before. You then discover that this person was very near to you, you perceive that he has passed through your life many times without being noticed; you find in the events which are related to you a coincidence, a real affinity with certain events of your own existence. It was not precisely thus with me concerning Marguerite, since I had seen her, met her, and since I knew her face and her habits; however, since this sale, her name had come so frequently to my ears, and, under the circumstances which I have related in the last chapter, this name

45

had been accompanied by so sincere a grief, that my astonishment had been increased, augmenting my curiosity.

It thus happened that I no longer accosted my friends, to whom I had never before spoken of Marguerite, without saying to them :

"Did you know a girl named Marguerite Gautier?"

"The Lady of the Camellias?"

"The same."

"Very well!" These "very wells!" were sometimes accompanied by smiles that left no possible doubt as to their significance.

"Well, what was she, that girl?" I continued.

"A nice girl."

"Was that all?"

"Good Lord! yes, more wit and perhaps a little more heart than the others."

"And you know nothing particular about her?"

"She ruined the Baron de G——."

"He only?"

"She was the mistress of the old Duc de ——."

"Was she indeed his mistress?"

"So it was said; in any case, he gave her a great deal of money."

Always the same general details.

However, I would have been interested to learn something concerning the liaison of Marguerite and of Armand.

One day I met one of those who live in intimate acquaintance with known women. I questioned him.

" Did you know Marguerite Gautier?"

The same *very well* was my answer.

" What kind of a girl was she?"

"A pretty, nice girl. I was very sorry to hear of her death."

" Did she not have a lover named Armand Duval?"

" A tall blond?"

" Yes."

" That is true."

" Who was this Armand?"

" A youth who devoured with her the little that he had, I believe, and who was compelled to leave her. It is said that he was crazy over her."

"And she?"

"She loved him a good deal, too, it is said, but as such women love. They should not be asked for more than they can give."

" What has become of Armand?"

" I don't know. We knew him very slightly. He stayed with Marguerite five or six months, but in the country. When she came back, he had departed."

" And you have never seen him since?"

" Never."

Neither had I seen Armand since. I had come to the point of asking myself whether, when he had presented himself in my rooms, the recent intelligence of

Marguerite's death had not served to exaggerate his former love and consequently his grief, and I said to myself that perhaps he had already forgotten with the dead one the promise made to come and see me again.

This supposition would have been probable enough with regard to any other, but there had been sincere accents in Armand's despair, and, passing from one extreme to the other, I imagined to myself that his grief had led to an illness, and that, if I had no news of him, it was because he was ill, and perhaps indeed dead.

I was interested, despite myself, in this young man. Perhaps in this interest there was some selfishness; perhaps I had had in this grief an intimation of an affecting story of the heart; perhaps, in short, my desire to hear it counted for a good deal in the anxiety which I felt over Armand's silence.

As Monsieur Duval did not come back to see me, I resolved to go and see him. A pretext was not difficult to find; unfortunately, I did not know his address, and among all those whom I had questioned, no one had been able to give it to me.

I went to the Rue d'Antin. The porter of Marguerite's house would perhaps know where Armand lived. There was a new porter. He was as ignorant as I was. I then inquired concerning the cemetery in which Mademoiselle Gautier had been interred. It was the Montmartre cemétery.

April had come again, the weather was fine, the tombs should no longer have that dolorous and desolate aspect which the winter gives them ; in short, it was already sufficiently warm for the living to remember the dead and to go to visit them. I went to the cemetery, saying to myself: "At the first sight of Marguerite's tomb I shall see whether Armand's grief still survives, and I shall learn perhaps what has become of him."

I entered the keeper's lodge, and I asked him if, on the 22d of the month of February, a woman named Marguerite Gautier had not been buried in the cemétery Montmartre.

This man turned over the pages of a great book in which are inscribed and numbered all those who enter this last asylum, and replied that in fact, on the 22d of February, at noon, a woman of that name had been buried.

I asked him to conduct me to the tomb, for there is no method of finding your way without a guide in this city of the dead, which has its streets like a city of the living. The guardian called a gardener to whom he gave the necessary directions, and who interrupted him by saying: "I know, I know —— Oh! that tomb is very easy to find," he continued, turning towards me.

"Why?" I asked him.

" Because it has flowers very different from the others."

" It is you who take care of it ?"

"Yes, monsieur, and I wish that all the relatives would take care of their deceased as does the young man who recommended that one to me."

After making a few turns in the alleys, the gardener stopped and said to me:

"Here we are."

In fact, I had before my eyes a square of flowers which would never have been taken for a tomb were it not for a white marble bearing a name.

This marble was upright, an iron railing defined the purchased plot of ground, and this space was covered with white camellias.

"What do you say to that?" asked the gardener.

"It is very beautiful."

"And every time that a camellia fades, I have orders to renew it."

"And who gave you that order?"

"A young man who wept a great deal, the first time that he came; an old lover of the dead woman, doubtless, for it seems that she was a gay one. They say that she was very pretty. Did monsieur know her?"

"Yes."

"Like the other?" said the gardener, with a malicious grin.

"No, I never spoke to her."

"And you come to see her here; that is very considerate in you, for those who come to see the poor girl do not crowd the cemetery."

"No one comes, then?"

"No one, except that young gentleman who came once."

"Once only?"

"Yes, monsieur."

"And he has not returned?"

"No, but he will return when he comes back again."

"He is then on a journey?"

"Yes."

"And do you know where he is?"

"He has, I believe, gone to see the sister of Mademoiselle Gautier."

"And what is he doing there?"

"He has gone to ask of her an authorization to have the body exhumed so that it may be buried elsewhere."

"Why should he not leave her here?"

"You know, monsieur, that people have notions about the dead. We see that every day, we here. This lot has only been bought for five years, and this young man wants a perpetual lease and a larger lot; in the new quarter it would be better."

"What do you call the new quarter?"

"The new ground now for sale, at the left. If the cemetery had always been kept as it is now, there would not be one like it in the world; but there is still a great deal to do before it will be altogether what it should be. And then people are so queer."

"What do you mean?"

"I mean to say that there are people who are proud even in here. Thus, this demoiselle Gautier, it appears that she led a gay life, excuse the expression. Now, the poor demoiselle, she is dead; and there is left of her just as much as of those of whom there is nothing to say and whom we sprinkle every day; well, when the relatives of the persons who are buried beside her learned who she was, did they not take it into their heads to say that they objected to having her here, and that there should be separate grounds for this sort of women, as there are for the poor! Did any one ever hear of such a thing? I have said fine words about them, I have; great fat proprietors who do not come four times a year to visit their dead friends, who bring their flowers themselves, and such flowers! who consider every expense for those whom they say they mourn, who engrave on their tombs tears which they have never shed, and who come to make things disagreeable for their neighbors. You may believe me if you like, monsieur, I was not acquainted with this demoiselle, I do not know what she did; well, I love her, this poor thing, and I take care of her, I give her the camellias at the lowest price. She is my favorite dead one. We here, monsieur, we are indeed obliged to love the dead, for we are so busy that we have scarcely time to love anything else."

I looked at this man, and some of my readers will understand, without any necessity of explanation on my part, the emotion which I experienced in hearing him.

Doubtless he perceived it, for he continued:

" They say that there were those who ruined themselves for this girl, and that she had lovers who adored her; well, when I think that there is not one of them who comes to buy her a flower even, it is that which is curious and sad. And yet, she has no cause to complain, for she has her grave, and if there is only one who thinks of her, he does the thing for all the others. But we have here the poor girls of the same style and the same age who are thrown into the common trench, and that breaks my heart when I hear their poor bodies fall in the earth. And no one at all takes any interest in them, once they are dead! It is not always cheerful, the trade which we follow, above all when we have a little heart left. What would you have? it is stronger than I. I have a fine tall daughter of twenty years, and, when they bring here a dead girl of her age, I think of her, and, whether it be a great lady or a street-walker, I cannot help being affected.

" But I weary you, doubtless, with my stories, and it was not to hear them that you came here. I was told to bring you to the tomb of Mademoiselle Gautier, here you are; can I be of service to you in anything further?"

" Do you know the address of Monsieur Armand Duval?" I asked him.

" Yes, he lives Rue de ——, it was there, at least, that I went to get the price of all the flowers which you see here."

" Thank you, my good man."

I threw a last look upon this flowery tomb, of which, despite myself, I would have wished to have sounded the depths to see what the earth had made of the beautiful creature who had been thrown into it, and I withdrew very mournfully.

" Does monsieur wish to see Monsieur Duval?" resumed the gardener, who was walking beside me.

" Yes."

" It is because I am very sure that he has not returned, otherwise I should have seen him here before this."

" You are then convinced that he has not forgotten Marguerite ?"

" Not only am I convinced of it, but I would be willing to bet that his desire to change the tomb is only the desire to see her again."

" How is that ?"

" The very first thing that he said to me when he came to the cemetery was : ' How could I see her again ?' This could not be done without changing the grave ; and I gave him information on all the formalities to be fulfilled in order to obtain this change, for you know that to transfer a body from one grave to another it is necessary to identify it, and the family only can authorize this operation, at which must be present a police commissioner. It is to obtain this authorization that Monsieur Duval went to see the sister of

Mademoiselle Gautier, and his first visit on his return will evidently be here."

We had arrived at the gate of the cemetery; I thanked the gardener again, putting into his hand several pieces of money, and I took my way to the address which he had given me.

Armand had not returned.

I left a word for him, asking him to come and see me on his arrival, or to let me know where I could find him.

Early next morning I received a letter from Duval in which he informed me of his return and entreated me to come to see him, adding that, as he was exhausted by fatigue, it was impossible for him to go out.

VI

I found Armand in bed.

When he saw me, he extended to me his burning hand.

"You have a fever," I said to him.

"That will not amount to anything,—the fatigue of a rapid voyage, that is all."

"You come from Marguerite's sister."

"Yes, who told you?"

"I know it, and you have obtained that which you wished?"

"Yes, again; but who informed you of the journey and of the object which I had in making it?"

"The gardener of the cemetery."

"You have seen the grave?"

I scarcely dared to reply, for the tone in which this phrase was pronounced proved to me that he who uttered it was still a prey to the emotion of which I had been a witness, and every time that his thoughts or the speech of another brought him back to this sorrowful subject, for a long time yet to come this emotion would be stronger than his will.

I therefore contented myself by replying with a sign of the head.

" He has taken good care of it?" continued Armand.

Two great tears rolled down the cheeks of the sick man, who turned his head to conceal them from me. I appeared not to have perceived them, and I endeavored to change the conversation.

" It is now three weeks since you departed?" I said to him.

Armand passed his hand over his eyes, and replied :

"Three weeks exactly."

" Your journey was long?"

" Oh, I was not traveling all the time, I was sick for two weeks, otherwise I would have returned long ago; but, scarcely had I arrived there than I was taken down with the fever, and I was obliged to keep my room."

" And you came away without being entirely cured?"

" If I had remained a week longer in that country, I would have died."

" But, now that you have returned, it will be necessary for you to be taken care of: your friends will come to see you. I, the first of all, if you will permit me."

" In two hours I shall get up."

" What imprudence ! "

" It is necessary."

" What have you then to do that is so pressing?"

" It is necessary that I should go to the commissioner of police."

"Why do you not entrust to some one this mission which may make you still more ill?"

"It is the only thing that can cure me. It is necessary that I should see her. Ever since I heard of her death, and above all since I have seen her tomb, I can no longer sleep. I cannot convince myself that this woman whom I left so young and so beautiful is dead. I must assure myself by my own testimony. I must see what God has made of that being which I have so much loved, and perhaps the disgust of the spectacle will replace the despair of the remembrance; you will accompany me, will you not? —— if that does not annoy you too much?"

"What did her sister say to you?"

"Nothing. She seemed to be very much astonished that a stranger should wish to buy a plot of ground and make a tomb for Marguerite, and she signed for me immediately the authorization which I asked of her."

"Listen to me, wait for this transferral until you are more nearly cured."

"Oh! I shall be well, be assured. Moreover, I should go mad if I did not carry out as quickly as possible this resolution, the accomplishment of which has become an absolute requirement of my grief. I swear to you that I cannot be calm until I shall have seen Marguerite. It is perhaps a thirst of the fever which burns me, a dream of my insomnias, a result of my deliriums; but, should I make myself a Trappist

monk like Monsieur de Rancé, after having seen, I will
see."

"I understand that," said I to Armand, "and I am
entirely at your service; have you seen Julie Duprat?"

"Yes. Oh! I saw her the very day of my first
return."

"Did she give you the papers which Marguerite had
left with her for you?"

"Here they are."

Armand drew a roll from under his pillow and immediately replaced it there.

"I know by heart what these papers contain," he
said to me. "For the last three weeks I have read
them ten times a day. You shall read them also,
but later, when I shall be more calm and when I
shall be able to make you comprehend all that this
confession reveals of heart and of love.

"For the moment, I have a service to ask of you."

"What is it?"

"You have a carriage below?"

"Yes."

"Well, will you take my passport and go to ask
at the *poste restante* if there are any letters for me?
My father and my sister must have written to me at
Paris, and I went off so precipitately that I did not take
the time to get news of them before I left. When you
come back, we will go together to notify the police
commissioner of the ceremony for to-morrow."

Armand handed me his passport, and I went off to the Rue Jean-Jacques-Rousseau.

There were two letters addressed to the name of Duval, I took them and returned.

When I reappeared, Armand was up and dressed and ready to go out.

"Thanks," he said to me, taking his letters. "Yes," he added, after looking at the addresses—"yes, they are from my father and my sister. They must have been entirely unable to understand my silence."

He opened the letters, divined them rather than read them, for they were four pages long, each one, and at the end of a moment he had folded them up again.

"Let us go," he said to me, "I will reply to-morrow."

We went to the police commissioner, to whom Armand handed the power of attorney of Marguerite's sister.

The commissioner gave him in exchange a notification for the keeper of the cemetery; it was arranged that the transferral should take place the next day, at ten o'clock in the morning, that I should come for him an hour earlier, and that we should go together to the cemetery.

I was curious, also, to be present at this spectacle, and I admit that I did not sleep at all that night.

To judge by the thoughts that assailed me, this must have been a long night for Armand.

When I entered his room at nine o'clock the next morning, he was horribly pale, but he seemed to be calm.

He smiled at me and offered me his hand.

His candles were burned down to the end, and, before going out, he took a very thick letter addressed to his father, and containing doubtless his confidences concerning his impressions of the night.

Half an hour later we arrived at Montmartre.

The commissioner was already waiting for us.

We took our way slowly in the direction of Marguerite's tomb. The commissioner walked first, Armand and I followed a few steps behind.

From time to time I felt the arm of my companion shudder convulsively, as if he suddenly shivered in all his body. Then I would look at him; he understood my glance and smiled at me, but since we left his house we had not exchanged a single word.

Shortly before we reached the tomb Armand halted to wipe his face, which was covered with great drops of sweat.

I profited by this halt to get my breath, for I myself felt my heart compressed as in a vice.

Whence comes the painful pleasure which we take in these spectacles! When we arrived at the grave, the gardener had taken away all the pots of flowers, the iron railing had been removed, and two men were excavating the earth.

Armand leaned against a tree and looked on.

All his life seemed to have passed into his eyes.

Suddenly one of the two pickaxes grated against a stone.

At this noise Armand recoiled as if he had received an electric shock, and grasped my hand with such force that he gave me pain.

One of the grave-diggers took a large shovel and emptied the grave little by little; then, when there was nothing left but the stones with which the coffin was covered, he threw them out, one by one.

I was watching Armand, for I feared at each moment that his sensations, which he was visibly concentrating, would overcome him; but he was looking steadily, his eyes fixed and open as in madness, and only a slight trembling of the cheeks and of the lips showing that he was a prey to a violent nervous crisis.

As for myself, I can only say one thing, that is, that I regretted having come.

When the coffin was entirely uncovered, the commissioner said to the grave-diggers :

"Open it."

These men obeyed, as if it were the most simple thing in the world.

The coffin was in oak, and they began to unscrew the upper portion which formed the cover. The dampness of the earth had rusted the screws, and it was not without an effort that the coffin was opened. A tainted odor exhaled from it, notwithstanding the aromatic herbs with which it was spread.

"Oh, my God ! my God !" murmured Armand, and he turned still paler.

The grave-diggers themselves recoiled.

A great white shroud covered the body, some of the forms of which it revealed. This shroud was almost completely eaten away at one of the ends and allowed one of the feet of the dead woman to appear.

I was on the point of being ill, and, at the hour at which I write these lines, the memory of this scene appears before me again in all its imposing reality.

"Be quick," said the commissioner.

Then one of the two men extended his hand, began to rip up the shroud, and, taking it by the end, suddenly uncovered the face of Marguerite.

It was terrible to see, it is horrible to relate.

The eyes were no longer anything but two holes, the lips had disappeared, and the white teeth were clenched against each other. The long hair, black and dry, was glued against the temples and veiled somewhat the greenish cavities of the cheeks, and yet I recognized in this visage the white, pink, and joyous visage which I had so often seen.

Armand, without the power to turn his eyes from this face, had carried his handkerchief to his mouth and was biting it.

Chapter VI

"Be quick," said the commissioner.

Then one of the two men extended his hand, began to rip up the shroud, and, taking it by the end, suddenly uncovered the face of Marguerite.

It was terrible to see, it is horrible to relate.

For myself, it seemed to me that a circle of iron was compressing my head, a veil covered my eyes, a buzzing and humming filled my ears, and the utmost that I could do was to open a flask which I had brought at a venture and inspire strongly the salts it contained.

In the midst of this stupefaction I heard the commissioner say to Monsieur Duval :

" Do you recognize her ? "

" Yes," answered the young man dully.

" Then close it up and take it away," said the commissioner.

The grave-diggers threw the shroud again over the face of the dead, closed the coffin, took each of them an end of it, and directed their steps towards the locality which had been designated to them.

Armand did not stir. His eyes were riveted on this empty grave ; he was as pale as the corpse which he had just seen —— It seemed as though he were petrified.

I foresaw that which would happen when his distress should be diminished by the absence of the spectacle, and consequently would no longer sustain him.

I approached the commissioner.

" Will the presence of this gentleman be necessary any longer ? " said I to him, indicating Armand.

" No," he replied, " and I should even advise you to take him away, for he seems to be ill."

" Come," I said to Armand, taking him by the arm.

"What?" he replied, looking at me as though he had not recognized me.

"It is over," I added, "you must go away, my friend, you are pale, you are cold, you will kill yourself with all these emotions."

"You are right, let us go away," he replied mechanically, but without taking a step.

Then I seized him by the arm and I dragged him away.

He allowed himself to be conducted like a child, murmuring only from time to time:

"Did you see the eyes?"

And he turned back, as if this vision had recalled him.

However, his steps became irregular; he seemed to advance only by jerks; his teeth chattered, his hands were cold, a violent nervous agitation took possession of his whole person.

I spoke to him, he did not reply to me.

All that he could do was to allow himself to be conducted.

At the gate we found our carriage. It was high time.

Scarcely had he taken his seat when his shivering increased and he experienced a true nervous attack, in the midst of which the fear of terrifying me caused him to murmur while pressing my hand:

"It is nothing, it is nothing, I wish I could weep."

And I could hear his chest inflate, and the blood came into his eyes, but no tears.

I caused him to smell the flask which I had brought, and by the time we arrived at his house the shiverings alone manifested themselves.

With the aid of the servant I put him to bed, I caused a great fire to be lit in his room, and I hastened away in search of my physician, to whom I related all that had passed.

He came promptly.

Armand was purple; he was in delirium and stammering disconnected words, in the midst of which only the name of Marguerite could be distinctly heard.

"Well?" said I to the doctor when he had examined the patient.

"Well, he has a brain fever, neither more nor less, and it is very fortunate, for I think, God forgive me, that he was going mad. Luckily, the physical malady will kill the mental malady, and in a month he will be cured of the one, and perhaps of the other."

VII

Maladies such as that with which Armand had been attacked have this of fortunate about them, that they kill on the spot or they allow themselves to be very quickly overcome.

Two weeks after the events which I have just recited Armand was in full convalescence, and we were united by a firm friendship. I had scarcely left his chamber during the entire time that he had been ill.

The spring had scattered in profusion her flowers, her leaves, her birds, her songs, and my friend's window opened cheerfully on his garden the wholesome exhalations of which ascended to him.

The physician had permitted him to leave his bed, and we often remained talking, seated near the open window at the hours in which the sun is the warmest, between noon and two o'clock.

I was very careful about conversing of Marguerite, fearing always that this name would awaken a sorrowful remembrance concealed under the apparent calmness of the invalid; but Armand, on the contrary, seemed to take pleasure in speaking of her, not as formerly with tears in his eyes, but with a soft smile which reassured me as to the state of his mind.

I had remarked that, since his last visit to the ceme-tery, since the spectacle which had brought about in him this violent crisis, the measure of his mental malady seemed to have been completed by his illness, and that the death of Marguerite no longer appeared to him under its former aspect. A species of consolation had resulted from the certainty acquired, and, in order to drive away the sombre image which often presented itself before him, he took refuge in the happy memories of his liaison with Marguerite and seemed no longer willing to accept anything but them.

His body was too exhausted by the attack and even by the cure of the fever to permit in his mind a violent emotion, and the springtime and universal joy with which he was surrounded carried his thoughts, despite himself, to smiling images.

He had always obstinately refused to inform his family of the danger he had been in, and when he was safe his father was still ignorant of his illness.

One evening we had remained at the window later than usual ; the day had been magnificent and the sun was sinking in a splendid twilight of azure and gold. Although we were in Paris, the verdure which surrounded us seemed to isolate us from the world, and there was scarcely, from time to time, the sound of a distant carriage to trouble our conversation.

"It was very nearly at this time of the year, and on the evening of a day like this, that I first knew Marguerite," said Armand to me, following his own thoughts, and not that which I had been saying to him.

I made no reply. Then he turned toward me and said :

"It is, however, necessary that I should relate to you this story ; you will make of it a book which no one will believe, but which, perhaps, will be interesting to make."

"You can tell that to me later, my friend," I said to him ; "you are not yet strong enough."

"The evening is warm, I have eaten the white meat of my chicken," he said smiling ; "I have no fever, we have nothing to do, I am going to tell you all."

"Since you will have it so, I will listen."

"It is a very simple history," he added, "and one which I will relate to you following the order of the incidents. If you make something of it later, you are free to tell it otherwise."

This is what he related to me, and I have scarcely changed any words in this touching recital.

"Yes," resumed Armand, letting his head fall on the back of his easy-chair—"yes, it was on an evening like this ! I had passed my day in the country with one of my friends, Gaston R——. We came back to Paris in the evening, and, not knowing what to do, we went into the theatre of the Variétés.

" Between the acts we went out, and in the corridor we saw passing a tall woman to whom my friend bowed.

" ' To whom are you speaking ?' I asked him.

" ' Marguerite Gautier,' he replied.

" ' It seems to me that she is very much changed, for I did not recognize her,' I said with an emotion which you will comprehend presently.

" ' She has been ill ; the poor girl will not live long.'

" I recall these words as if they had been said to me yesterday.

" It is necessary that you should know, my friend, that for the last two years the sight of this girl, whenever I encountered her, had had a strange effect upon me.

" Without knowing why, I became pale and my heart beat violently. I have a friend who occupies himself with the occult sciences, and who would call that which I experienced the affinity of fluids; for my part, I believe quite simply that I was destined to fall in love with Marguerite and that I had a presentiment of it.

" However this may be, it is very certain that she produced a real impression upon me, that several of my friends had been witnesses thereof, and that they had laughed a great deal when they recognized the source of this impression.

" The very first time that I saw her it was on the Place de la Bourse, at the door of Susse. An open calash was stationed there, and a woman dressed in white had descended from it. Her entrance in the store was greeted by a murmur of admiration. As for myself, I remained nailed to my place, from the moment when she entered to the moment when she came out. Through the windows I saw her in the shop selecting her purchases. I could have entered, but I did not dare. I did not know who this woman was, and I feared that she would divine the cause of my entrance and take offence at it. However, I did not feel that I should see her again.

"She was elegantly dressed ; she wore a muslin dress covered with flounces, an India shawl with the corners embroidered with gold and with flowers in silk, a hat of Leghorn straw and a single bracelet—a heavy chain of gold of a kind that was just coming into fashion.

"She took her seat in her calash again and departed.

"One of the attendants of the store remained at the door, following with his eyes the carriage of this elegant customer. I approached him and asked him for the name of this lady.

"'It is Mademoiselle Marguerite Gautier,' he replied.

"I did not dare to ask him her address, and went away.

"The memory of this vision, for it was a veritable one, did not leave me, like very many visions which I had already seen, and I sought everywhere for this lady in white so royally beautiful.

"A few days later, there was a grand representation at the Opéra-Comique. I was present. The first person whom I saw in a proscenium box of the gallery was Marguerite Gautier.

"The young man in whose company I was recognized her also, for he said to me, naming her: ' Look at that pretty girl.'

".At this moment Marguerite was looking in our direction through her glasses; she perceived my friend, smiled at him, and made a sign to come and make her a visit.

" ' I am going to say good-evening to her,' he said to me, ' and I will be back in a moment.'

"I could not prevent myself from saying: ' You are very fortunate ! '

" ' In what ? '

" ' In going to see that girl.'

" ' Are you in love with her ? '

" ' No,' said I, reddening, ' for I do not really know anything about her; but I should very well like to make her acquaintance.'

" ' Come along with me, I will present you.'

" ' Ask her permission first.'

" ' Ah ! *pardieu*, you need not stand on ceremony with her; come.'

" What he said troubled me. I trembled for fear of acquiring the certainty that Marguerite was not worthy of that which I felt for her.

"There is in a book by Alphonse Karr, entitled *Am Rauchen*, a man who follows one evening a woman very elegant in appearance and with whom, at the first sight, he has fallen in love, so beautiful is she. Merely to kiss this woman's hand he feels in himself the strength to undertake anything, the will to conquer anything, the courage to accomplish anything. Scarcely does he venture to look at the coquettish ankle which she reveals by lifting her dress so as not to soil it by contact with the pavement. While he is dreaming of all that he would do to possess this woman, she stops at the corner of the street and asks him if he will go home with her.

"He turns his head away, crosses the street, and returns to his lodgings very sorrowful.

"I recalled this study, and for myself, who would have wished to suffer for this woman, I feared that she would accept me too quickly and give me too promptly a love for which I would have wished to pay by a long waiting or by a great sacrifice. We are thus constituted, we men; and it is very fortunate that the imagination yields this poetry to the senses, and that the desires of the body make this concession to the dreams of the soul.

"In short, if it had been said to me: 'You shall have this woman to-night, and you shall be killed to-morrow,' I would have accepted. If it had been said to me: 'Give ten louis and you shall be her lover,' I would have refused and wept like an infant who sees vanish at his waking the fairy castle dreamed of in the night.

"However, I wished to know her; it was a means, and even the only one, of establishing my relations with her.

"I accordingly said to my friend that I still wished that he would obtain permission from her to present me, and I wandered about in the corridors, imagining to myself that from that moment our acquaintance would begin, and that I should not know how to appear before her.

"I endeavored to put together the words which I was going to say to her.

"What a sublime childishness is love!

"A moment later my friend descended again.

"'She is waiting for us,' he said to me.

"'Is she alone?' I asked.

"'With another woman.'

"'There are no men?'

"'No.'

"'Let us go.'

"My friend directed his steps toward the entrance of the theatre.

"'Well, that is not the way,' I said to him.

"'We are going to get some bonbons. She asked me for some.'

"We entered a confectioner's in the Passage de l'Opéra.

"I would have wished to have bought out the whole shop, and I was even looking about to see what this sacking would produce when my friend said:

"'A pound of grapes _glacés_.'

"'Do you know whether she likes them?'

"'She never eats any other kind of bonbons, that is well known.'

"'Now!' he continued when we had gone out, 'do you know to what kind of a woman I am going to present you? Do not imagine to yourself that it is a duchess, it is quite simply a kept woman, everything that there is of kept, my dear fellow; do not make yourself uncomfortable, then, and say anything that comes into your head.'

"'Very well!' I stammered, following him, and saying to myself that I was going to be cured of my passion.

"When we entered the box, Marguerite was laughing aloud.

"I would have wished that she were sad.

"My friend presented me. Marguerite made me a slight inclination of the head and said:

"'And my bonbons?'

"'Here they are.'

"As she took them, she looked at me. I lowered my eyes, I blushed.

"She leaned over to her neighbor's ear, whispered something to her, and both of them broke out laughing.

"Very certainly I was the cause of this hilarity; my embarrassment was redoubled by it. At this period I had for mistress a little bourgeoise, very tender and very sentimental, whose sentiments and whose melancholy letters made me laugh. I comprehended now the

pain which I must have given her by that which I experienced myself, and, for the space of five minutes, I
loved her as never was woman loved.

"Marguerite ate her grapes without paying any further
attention to me.

"My introducer was not willing to leave me in this
ridiculous position.

"'Marguerite,' said he, 'you must not be surprised
if Monsieur Duval has nothing to say to you, you so
upset him that he cannot find a word.'

"'I thought rather that monsieur accompanied you
hither because it bored you to come alone.'

"'If that were true,' said I in my turn, 'I would not
have asked Ernest to request your permission to present
me.'

"'That was perhaps only a means of delaying the
fatal moment.'

"However little you may have lived with women of
Marguerite's class, you become acquainted with the
pleasure they take in malicious wit and in teasing those
whom they see for the first time. It is doubtless a
revenge for the humiliations to which they are forced to
submit from those whom they see daily.

"Thus, to reply to them, it is necessary to have a certain familiarity with their world, a familiarity which I
had not; moreover, the idea which I had formed of
Marguerite exaggerated her mocking in my eyes.
Nothing concerning this woman was indifferent to me.

So I rose, saying with an alteration of voice which it was impossible for me to conceal completely :

" 'If that is what you think of me, madame, it only remains for me to ask your pardon for my indiscretion and to take my leave of you, assuring you that it shall not happen again.'

"Whereupon I bowed and went out.

"Scarcely had I closed the door when I heard a third burst of laughter. I should have been very willing to be jostled by some one at that moment.

"I returned to my seat.

"The three knocks for the raising of the curtain were heard.

"Ernest returned to his place beside me.

" 'How you go on!' he said as he seated himself; 'they think you are crazy.'

" 'What did Marguerite say after I left?'

" 'She laughed, and assured me that she had never seen anything as absurd as you. But it is not necessary to consider yourself beaten; only, do not do those women the honor to take them seriously. They do not know what elegance and politeness are; they are like dogs to whom you give perfumes, they think they are offensive and go and roll in the gutter.'

" 'After all, what does it matter to me?' said I, endeavoring to assume an indifferent air, 'I shall never see that woman again, and, if I were attracted by her before I knew her, it is very different now that I have met her.'

"'Bah! I do not despair of one day seeing you in the back of her box and of hearing it said that you are ruining yourself for her. For the rest you are right, she has no education; but she is a charming mistress to have.'

"Fortunately the curtain rose, and my friend was silent. It would be impossible for me to say what the play was. All that I remember is that, from time to time, I lifted my eyes to the box which I had so brusquely quitted, and that the faces of new visitors constantly succeeded each other in it.

"However, I was far from no longer thinking of Marguerite. Another sentiment had taken possession of me. It seemed to me that I had her insult and my own ridicule to cause to be forgotten; I said to myself that, should I expend in it all that I possessed, I would have this woman and would take as a right the place which I had so quickly abandoned.

"Before the play was ended, Marguerite and her friend left their box.

"In spite of myself, I quitted my seat.

"'You are going?' said Ernest to me.

"'Yes.'

"'Why?'

"At that moment he perceived that the box was empty.

"'Go ahead, go ahead,' he said, 'and good luck to you, or, rather, better luck.'

" I went out.

" I heard in the stairway the rustle of dresses and the sound of voices. I placed myself at one side and I saw pass by, without being seen, the two women and the two young men who accompanied them.

" Under the peristyle of the theatre a small servant presented himself to them.

" 'Go tell the coachman to wait at the door of the Café Anglais,' said Marguerite, 'we are going to walk that far.'

" Some minutes later, while strolling on the boulevard, I saw, at a window of one of the large cabinets of the restaurant, Marguerite, leaning on the balcony, stripping one by one the petals from the camellias of her bouquet.

" One of the two young men was leaning over her shoulder and speaking to her in a low voice.

" I went and installed myself in the Maison d'Or, in the salons of the first floor, and I did not lose sight of the window in question.

" At one o'clock in the morning Marguerite took her carriage again with her three friends.

" I engaged a cabriolet, and I followed her.

" The carriage stopped in the Rue d'Antin, No. 9.

" Marguerite descended from it and entered her house alone.

" It was doubtless a chance, but this chance rendered me very happy.

"After that day I often met Marguerite at the theatre, in the Champs-Élysées. Always the same gayety on her part, always the same emotion on mine.

"Two weeks passed, however, without my seeing her again anywhere. I met Gaston, of whom I asked news of her.

"'The poor girl is very sick,' he replied.

"'What is the matter with her?'

"'The matter with her is, that she is consumptive, and, as she leads a life that is not calculated to cure her, she is in her bed, and that she is dying.'

"The heart is a strange thing; I was almost satisfied because of this illness.

"I went every day to hear news of the patient, without, however, inscribing my name or leaving my card. I thus learned of her convalescence and of her departure for Bagnères.

"Then, as time passed on, the impression, if not the memory, seemed to disappear little by little from my mind. I travelled; liaisons, daily habits, work, took the place of this idea, and, when I thought of this first adventure, I was willing to see in it only one of those passions which you have when you are very young, and at which you laugh a little while later.

"For that matter, there would not have been much merit in triumphing over this memory, for I had lost sight of Marguerite since her departure, and, as I have

told you, when she passed me in the corridors of the
Variétés, I did not recognize her.

" She was veiled, it is true ; but however deeply she
might have been veiled two years before, I should not
have needed to have seen to have recognized her,—I
would have divined her.

" This did not prevent my heart from beating when I
knew that it was she ; and the two years passed without
seeing her and the results which this separation should
have brought about vanished in the same smoke at the
mere touch of her dress.

VIII

"However," continued Armand after a pause, "while comprehending that I was still in love, I felt myself stronger than formerly, and, in my desire to find myself again with Marguerite, there was also the determination to make her see that I had become her superior.

"How many methods the heart takes and how many reasons it gives itself in order to arrive at that which it desires! But I could not remain long in the corridors, and I returned to take my place in the orchestra, throwing a rapid glance through the house to see which box she occupied.

"She was in the proscenium box on the stage, and all alone. She was changed, as I said; I did not find around her mouth any longer her indifferent smile. She had suffered, she was still suffering.

"Although the season was as far advanced as April, she was still dressed as in winter and quite enveloped in velvets.

"I looked at her so obstinately that my eyes attracted hers.

" She considered me some moments, took her lorgnette to see me better ; and doubtless thought she recognized me, without being able to positively identify me, for, when she laid down her glasses, a smile, that charming salutation of women, strayed over her lips, to respond to a salutation which she seemed to expect from me ; but I did not respond in the least, as though to obtain the advantage over her and to seem to have forgotten when she had remembered.

" She thought she was mistaken, and turned her head away.

" The curtain rose.

" I have seen Marguerite at the theatre many times, I have never seen her pay the slightest attention to what was going on on the stage.

" For my part, the play also interested me very little, and I occupied myself only with her, but in taking the greatest possible care that she should not perceive it.

" I thus saw her exchanging glances with the occupant of the box facing hers ; I turned my eyes on this box and I recognized in it a woman with whom I was sufficiently well acquainted.

" This woman was a former kept mistress, who had endeavored to go on the stage, who had not succeeded, and who, counting upon her relation with the fashionables of Paris, had gone into business and had opened a dress-making establishment.

"I saw in her a means of meeting Marguerite, and I profited by a moment when her eyes were turned in my direction to recognize her with my hand and my looks.

"That which I had foreseen arrived, she summoned me to her box.

"Prudence Duvernoy, such was the fortunate name of the modiste, was one of those plump women of forty with whom there is no need of much diplomacy to make them say that which you wish to know, above all when that which you wish to know is as simple as that which I had to ask of her.

"I took advantage of a moment when she was recommencing her signals to Marguerite to say to her:

"'Who is that looking at you so?'

"'Marguerite Gautier.'

"'You know her?'

"'Yes; I am her dress-maker, she is my neighbor.'

"'You live, then, in the Rue d'Antin?'

"'No. 7. The window of her dressing-room faces mine.'

"'They say that she is a charming girl.'

"'You do not know her?'

"'No, but I should well like to know her.'

"'Would you like me to tell her to come to our box?'

"'No, I should like better that you would present me to her.'

"'In her own house?'

"'Yes.'

"'That is more difficult.'

"'Why?'

"'Because she is protected by an old duke, very jealous.'

"'*Protected* is charming.'

"'Yes, protected,' replied Prudence. 'The poor old fellow, he would be very much embarrassed to be her lover.'

"Prudence then related to me the circumstances of Marguerite's having made the acquaintance of the duke at Bagnères.

"'That is the reason, then, that she is alone here?' I asked.

"'Exactly.'

"'But who will take her home?'

"'He.'

"'He will then come for her?'

"'In a moment.'

"'And you, who will take you home?'

"'No one.'

"'I offer my services.'

"'But you are with a friend, I believe.'

"'We will offer ourselves then.'

"'Who is he, your friend?'

"'He is a charming fellow, very clever, and who will be enchanted to make your acquaintance.'

" ' Very well, it is agreed, we will go, all four of us, after this piece, for I know the last one.'

" ' Willingly, I will go and notify my friend.'

" ' Go.'

" ' Ah!' said Prudence to me as I was about to leave, ' there is the duke coming into Marguerite's box.'

" I looked.

" A man of seventy, in fact, had just seated himself behind the young woman, handing to her at the same time a bag of bonbons, into which she immediately plunged, smiling, then she put it forward on the front of her box, making to Prudence a sign which could be translated :

" ' Will you have some ? '

" ' No,' signed Prudence.

" Marguerite took the bag again, and, turning round, began to talk with the duke.

" The recital of all these details seems childish, but everything which related to this girl is so fresh in my memory that I cannot refrain from recalling it to-day.

" I descended to notify Gaston of that which I had just arranged for him and for me.

" He accepted.

" We left our places to go up to the box of Madame Duvernoy.

" Scarcely had we opened the door of the orchestra seats when we were compelled to stop in order to allow to pass Marguerite and the duke, who were going.

"I would have given ten years of my life to have been in the place of that old gentleman.

"When they reached the boulevard. he seated her in a phaeton which he drove himself, and they disappeared, carried away by two superb horses at a trot.

"We entered Prudence's box.

"When the piece was ended, we went down and took a simple hackney coach which conducted us to No. 7, Rue d'Antin. At the door of her house Prudence invited us to ascend to see her establishment, which we did not know, and of which she seemed very proud. You may judge of the alacrity with which I accepted.

"It seemed to me that I was drawing nearer and nearer to Marguerite. I soon had the conversation turned again upon her.

"'Is the old duke in your neighbor's house?' I said to Prudence.

"'Not at all ; she must be alone.'

"'But she must bore herself horribly,' said Gaston.

"'We pass nearly all our evenings together, or, when she comes in, she calls me. She never goes to bed before two o'clock in the morning. She cannot sleep sooner.'

"'Why?'

"'Because she has a lung trouble and nearly always a fever.'

"'She has no lovers?' I asked.

" ' I have never seen any one stay when I left ; but I cannot say that no one comes after I have gone ; I have often met in her apartments in the evening a certain Comte de N——, who thinks to advance his interests by making his visits at eleven o'clock, by sending her all the jewels that she wants ; but she will really have nothing to do with him. She is in the wrong ; he is a very rich fellow. I have often said to her from time to time : " My dear child, there is the man for you ! " She who listens to me well enough ordinarily, she turns her back on me and replies that he is too stupid. That he is stupid, I admit ; but that would be a position for her, whereas the old duke may die any day. The old men are selfish ; his family are constantly reproaching him with his affection for Marguerite,—there are two reasons why he will leave her nothing. I preach to her, but she always replies that it will be time enough to take the count when the duke is dead.

" ' It is not always amusing,' continued Prudence, ' to live as she does. I know very well, for my part, that it would not suit me, and that I would very soon send the goodman about his business. He is insipid, that old fellow ; he calls her his daughter, he takes care of her as though she were a child, he is forever on her back. I am certain that at this hour one of his servants is watching in the street, to see who comes out, and, above all, who enters.'

"'Ah! the poor Marguerite!' said Gaston, seating himself at the piano and playing a waltz, 'I did not know that, for my part.   However, I thought she seemed less gay for some time back.'

"'Hush!' said Prudence, listening.

"Gaston stopped.

"'She is calling me, I think.'

"We listened.

"In fact, a voice was calling Prudence.

"'Come, messieurs, be off with you,' said Madame Duvernoy to us.

"'Ah! is that what you call hospitality?' said Gaston laughing; 'we will go away when we see fit.'

"'Why should we go away?'

"'I am going to see Marguerite.'

"'We will wait here.'

"'That cannot be.

"'Then we will go with you.'

"'Still less.'

"'I know Marguerite, I do,' said Gaston; 'I can very well go and pay her a visit.'

"'But Armand does not know her.'

"'I will present him.'

"'It is impossible.'

"We heard again the voice of Marguerite still calling Prudence.   The latter hastened into her dressing-room. I followed her there with Gaston.   She opened the window.

" We concealed ourselves in such a manner as not to be seen from the outside.

" ' I have been calling you for the past ten minutes,' said Marguerite from her window in a tone of voice that was almost imperious.

" ' What do you want with me?'

" ' I want you to come in immediately.'

" ' Why?'

" ' Because the Comte de N—— is still here and he is boring me to death.'

" ' I cannot now.'

" ' What prevents you?'

" ' I have in the house two young men who will not go away.'

" ' Tell them that it is necessary that you should go out.'

" ' I have told them so.'

" ' Well, leave them in your house; when they see you go out, they will leave.'

" ' After having turned everything topsy-turvy!'

" ' But what is it they want?'

" ' They wish to see you.'

" ' What are their names?'

" ' You know one of them, Monsieur Gaston R——.'

" ' Ah! yes, I know him; and the other?'

" ' Monsieur Armand Duval. You do not know him?'

" ' No; but bring them in all the same, I like anything better than the count. I am waiting for you, come quickly.'

"Marguerite closed her window again, and Prudence, hers.

"Marguerite, who for a moment had recalled my face, had not remembered my name. I would have preferred some souvenir to my disadvantage to this forgetfulness.

"'I knew very well,' said Gaston, 'that she would be enchanted to see us.'

"'Enchanted is not the word,' replied Prudence, putting on her shawl and her bonnet, 'she receives you in order to make the count go away. Try to be more agreeable than he, or, I know Marguerite, she will quarrel with me.'

"We followed Prudence, who went down-stairs.

"I was trembling; it seemed to me that this visit was going to have a great influence upon my life.

"I was still more affected than on the evening of my presentation in the box of the Opéra-Comique.

"When we arrived at the door of the apartment which you know, my heart was beating so strongly that my thoughts were confused.

"Some strains of a piano came to our ears.

"Prudence rang.

"The piano was silenced.

"A woman who had rather the appearance of a lady's companion than that of a femme de chambre came to open to us.

"We passed into the salon, from the salon into the boudoir, which was at that period such as you saw it later.

"A young man was leaning against the chimney-piece.

"Marguerite, seated before the piano, was allowing her fingers to stray over the keys and commencing bits that she did not complete.

"The character of this scene was ennui, resulting, for the man, from the embarrassment caused by his nullity; for the woman, from the visit of this dreary personage.

"At the sound of Prudence's voice Marguerite rose, and, coming towards us, after having exchanged a glance of thanks with Madame Duvernoy, she said to us:

"'Come in, messieurs, and be welcome.'

IX

"'Good-evening, my dear Gaston,' said Marguerite to my companion, 'I am very glad to see you. Why did you not come to my box at the Variétés?'

"'I feared to be indiscreet.'

"'Friends,' and Marguerite emphasized the word, as though she wished those who were present to understand that, notwithstanding the familiar fashion in which she welcomed him, Gaston was not and had never been anything but a friend, 'friends are never indiscreet.'

"'Then you will permit me to present to you Monsieur Armand Duval?'

"'I have already authorized Prudence to do so.'

"'For that matter, madame,' I said, bowing and succeeding in making sounds almost intelligible, 'I have already had the honor of being presented to you.'

"The charming eye of Marguerite seemed to search among her souvenirs, but she did not remember, or appeared to not remember.

"'Madame,' I then continued, 'I am grateful to you for having forgotten that first presentation, for I was then very ridiculous and must have appeared to you

97

very wearisome. This was two years ago, at the Opéra-Comique; I was with Ernest de ——'

"'Ah! I remember!' said Marguerite, with a smile. 'It was not that you were ridiculous, it was that I was teasing, as I am still a little, but less so, however. You have forgiven me, monsieur?'

"And she extended to me her hand, which I kissed.

"'That is true,' she resumed. 'Imagine, if you can, that I have the bad habit of wishing to embarrass people whom I see for the first time. It is very stupid. My doctor says that it is because I am nervous and always suffering,—do believe my doctor.'

"'But you look to me to be very well.'

"'Oh! I have been very sick.'

"'I know it.'

"'Who told it to you?'

"'Everybody knew it; I came often to inquire after you, and I heard of your convalescence with pleasure.'

"They never sent me your card."

"'I never left it.'

"'Could it have been you, that young man who came every day to inquire after me during my illness, and who would never leave his name?'

"'It was I.'

"'Then you are more than indulgent, you are generous. You would not have done that, count," she added, turning toward Monsieur de N——, and after having given me one of those glances in which the women sum up their opinion of a man.

"'I have only known you for two months,' replied the count.

"'And monsieur who has know me only five minutes! You always answer stupidities.'

"The women are pitiless for those whom they do not love.

"The count reddened and bit his lips.

"I had compassion on him, for he seemed to be genuinely in love, like myself, and the curt frankness of Marguerite must have rendered him very unhappy, especially in the presence of two strangers.

"'You were having some music when we entered,' I said, to change the conversation; 'will you not give me the pleasure of treating me like an old acquaintance, and will you not continue?'

"'Oh!' she said, throwing herself on the sofa and making us a sign to be seated, 'Gaston knows very well the kind of music I make. It will do when I am alone with the count, but I should not wish to make you endure such torture.'

"'You have this preference for me?' said Monsieur de N——, with a smile which he endeavored to render fine and ironical.

"'You do wrong to reproach me with it; it is the only one.'

"It was decided that this poor fellow should not say a word. He threw upon the young woman a look that was truly supplicating.

"'Tell me, Prudence,' she continued, 'have you done that which I asked you to do?'

"'Yes.'

"'That is well, you shall tell me about it later. We shall have to have a talk, you will not go away until I have spoken to you.'

"'We are doubtless indiscreet,' I said, 'and, now that we have, or rather that I have, obtained a second presentation to make the first forgotten, we will retire, Gaston and I.'

"'Not the least in the world; it is not for you that I say that. I wish, on the contrary, that you should remain.'

"The count drew out a very elegant watch, which he consulted.

"'It is time that I should go to the club,' he said.

"Marguerite made no reply.

"The count accordingly left the chimney-piece, and, coming toward her:

"'Adieu, madame.'

"Marguerite rose.

"'Adieu, my dear count, you are going away already?'

"'Yes, I fear to weary you.'

"'You do not weary me any more to-day than at other times. When shall we see you?'

" ' Whenever you permit me.'

" ' Adieu, then ! '

" It was cruel, you must admit.

" The count had, fortunately, a very good education and an excellent character. He contented himself with kissing the hand which Marguerite extended to him very nonchalantly, and with departing, after having bowed to us.

" As he crossed the threshold, he looked at Prudence.

" She shrugged her shoulders with an air which signified :

" ' What would you have? I have done all that I could.'

" ' Nanine ! ' cried Marguerite, 'light Monsieur le Comte.'

" We heard the door open and shut.

" ' At last,' exclaimed Marguerite, reappearing, ' he has gone ; that fellow wears horribly on my nerves.'

" ' My dear child,' said Prudence, ' you are really too hard with him, he who is so good and so thoughtful for you.   See, here on your mantel-piece is another watch which he has given you, and which cost him at least a thousand écus, I am sure of it.'

" And Madam Duvernoy, who had approached the chimney-piece, toyed with the jewel of which she spoke and threw upon it covetous looks.

" ' My dear,' said Marguerite, seating herself at her piano,'when I weigh on one hand that which he gives

me, and on the other that which he says to me, I find
that I give him his visits very cheaply.'

" 'That poor fellow is in love with you.'

" 'If I were obliged to listen to all those who are in
love with me, I should not have time enough to dine.'

"And she let her fingers run over the piano, after
which, turning to us, she said :

" 'Would you take something? for my part, I should
very well like a little punch.'

" 'And I, I should like to eat a bit of chicken,' said
Prudence ; 'suppose we have supper?'

" 'That is it, let us go to supper,' said Gaston.

" 'No, we are going to have supper here.'

"She rang.   Nanine appeared.

" 'Send and get something for supper.'

" 'What would you like?'

" 'Anything you please, but quickly, quickly.'

"Nanine went out.

" 'That is it,' said Marguerite, jumping like a child,
'we are going to have supper.   How tedious is that
imbecile of a count !'

"The more I saw of this woman, the more she enchanted me.   She was ravishingly beautiful.   Her thin-
ness even was a grace.

"I was wrapped in contemplation.

"That which was passing within me, I should have
difficulty in explaining it.   I was full of indulgence for
her life, full of admiration for her beauty.   This proof

of disinterestedness which she gave in refusing to accept a young man, rich and elegant, quite ready to ruin himself for her, condoned in my eyes all her past faults.

"There was in this woman something like candor.

"It could be seen that she was still in the virginity of vice. Her assured walk, her supple figure, her nostrils pink and dilated, her large eyes with their faint circles of blue, denoted one of those ardent natures which diffuse around them a perfume of voluptuousness, like those flasks from the Orient, which, no matter how firmly they are closed, allow to escape the perfume of the liquid which they contain.

"Finally, whether it were constitutional or a result of her state of illness, there shone from time to time in the eyes of this woman lightings of desire the expansion of which would have been a heavenly revelation to one she loved. But those who had loved Marguerite were no longer to be considered, and those whom she had loved were no more to be considered than they.

"In fine, there was to be recognized in this young woman the virgin whom a nothing had made a courtesan, and the courtesan whom a nothing would have made the most loving and purest of virgins. There were still in Marguerite pride and independence,—two sentiments which, when offended, are capable of replacing modesty. I said nothing, my soul seemed to have passed entirely into my heart, and my heart into my eyes.

" ' Then,' she suddenly resumed, ' it was you who came to inquire after me when I was ill ? '

" ' Yes.'

" ' Do you know that was very nice, that was! And what can I do to thank you ? '

" ' Permit me to come from time to time to see you.'

" ' As often as you like, from five o'clock to six, from eleven to midnight. I say, Gaston, play for me the *Invitation à la valse.*'

" ' Why ? '

" ' To please me, in the first place, and secondly because I cannot succeed in playing it myself.'

" ' What is it that troubles you in it ? '

" ' The third part, the passage in sharps.'

" Gaston rose, placed himself at the piano, and began that marvellous melody of Weber, the music of which was open on the stand.

" Marguerite, one hand resting on the piano, watched the score, following with her eyes each note which she accompanied very softly with her voice, and, when Gaston arrived at the passage which she had mentioned to him, she sang, aloud, beating time with her fingers on the top of the piano.

" ' *Re, mi, re, do, re, fa, mi, re,* that is what I cannot do. Commence it again.'

" Gaston recommenced, after which Marguerite said to him :

" ' Now let me try.'

"She took his place and played in her turn, but her rebellious fingers constantly went astray over one of the notes just indicated.

" 'Is it not incredible,' she said, with a truly childish intonation, 'that I cannot learn to play that passage ! Would you believe it that I stay sometimes even to two o'clock in the morning over it.   And when I think that that imbecile of a count plays it without music and admirably, it is that which renders me furious against him, I believe.'

"And she began again, always with the same results.

" 'May the devil fly away with Weber, the music, and the pianos ! ' she exclaimed, throwing the music-book to the other end of the chamber; 'could any one believe that I could not play eight sharps in succession ? '

"And she crossed her arms, looking at us and tapping with her foot.

"The blood came into her cheeks, and a slight cough parted her lips.

" 'Come, come,' said Prudence, who had taken off her bonnet and who was smoothing her hair before the glass, 'you are going to put yourself in a passion again and do yourself harm; let us go to supper, that will be better; for my part, I am dying with hunger.'

"Marguerite rang again; then she resumed her place at the piano and commenced in a minor key a libertine song, the accompaniment of which she played without impediment.

"Gaston knew this song, and they made of it a sort of duet.

"'Do not sing those dirty things,' said I familiarly to Marguerite and in a tone of entreaty.

"'Oh! how chaste you are?' she said to me, smiling and offering her hand.

"'It is not for myself, it is for you.'

"She made a gesture which seemed to say: 'Oh! it is a long time since I finished with chastity.'

"At this moment Nanine appeared.

"'Is supper ready?' asked Marguerite.

"'Yes, madame, in a moment.'

"'Apropos,' said Prudence to me, 'you have not seen the apartment, come and I will show it to you.'

"As you know, the salon was a marvel.

"Marguerite accompanied us a short distance, then she called Gaston and passed with him into the dining-room to see if the supper were ready.

"'Ah!' said Prudence aloud, looking at an étagère and taking from it a little figure in Dresden china, 'I had not seen this little man here!'

"'Which one?'

"'A little shepherd who holds a cage with a bird in it.'

"'Take it, if it pleases you.'

"'Ah! but I should fear to deprive you of it.'

"'I was going to give it to my femme de chambre, I think it hideous; but since it pleases you, take it.'

"Prudence saw only the gift, and not the manner in which it was made. She put her little figure to one side and led me into the dressing-room, where, showing me two miniatures which hung opposite to each other, she said to me:

"'This is the Comte de G——, who was very much in love with Marguerite; it was he who launched her. Do you know him?'

"'No. And this one?' I asked, indicating the other miniature.

"'That is the little Vicomte de L——. He was obliged to depart.'

"'Why?'

"'Because he was nearly ruined. Ah! there was one who loved Marguerite!'

"'And she doubtless loved him greatly?'

"'She is a queer sort of a girl, you never know where to find her. The evening of the day on which he went away she was at the theatre, as usual, and yet she wept at the moment of his departure.'

"At that moment Nanine appeared, announcing to us that the supper was served.

"When we entered the dining-room, Marguerite was leaning against the wall, and Gaston, holding her hands, was speaking to her in a low tone of voice.

"'You are crazy,' replied Marguerite to him, 'you know very well that I do not want you. It is not after knowing a woman like me for two years that one asks to become her lover. We women, we give ourselves at once or never. Come, messieurs, to table.'

"And, escaping from Gaston's hands, Marguerite seated him at her right, me at her left, then she said to Nanine:

"'Before you sit down, notify the cook not to open if any one rings.'

"This notification was given at one o'clock in the morning.

"There was much laughing, drinking, and eating at this supper. At the expiration of a few moments the gayety had descended to the lowest limits, and those words which a certain class finds amusing and which always soil the mouth which utters them, broke out from time to time, loudly acclaimed by Nanine, Prudence, and Marguerite. Gaston was amusing himself frankly; he was a fellow with a good heart, but whose mind had been somewhat perverted by his early habits. For a moment I had wished to stupefy myself, to make my heart and my thoughts indifferent to the spectacle which I had before my eyes and take part in this gayety which seemed one of the dishes of the repast; but, little by little, I had become isolated in this tumult, my glass remained empty, and I was almost mournful in seeing this beautiful creature of twenty drink, talk like a fish-wife, and laugh all the more loudly as that which was said was the more scandalous.

"However, this gayety, this manner of speaking and of drinking, which seemed to me in the other guests to be the results of the debauch, of habits or of active energy, appeared to me to be in Marguerite a need of forgetfulness, a feverishness, a nervous irritability. At each glass of champagne her cheeks were flushed with a feverish red, and a cough, slight at the commencement of the supper, had become in the end so violent as to compel her to throw her head back on the top of her chair and compress her chest with her hands every time she coughed.

"I suffered in thinking of the injury which must be inflicted on this frail organization by these daily excesses.

"Finally, something occurred which I had foreseen and which I feared. Near the end of the supper, Marguerite was seized with an attack of coughing more violent than any of those which I had seen. It seemed to me that her chest was rending itself internally. The poor girl became purple, closed her eyes with the pain, and carried to her lips her napkin which was reddened by a drop of blood. Then she rose suddenly and ran into her dressing-room.

"'What is the matter with Marguerite?' asked Gaston.

"'The matter is that she has laughed too much and that she is spitting blood,' said Prudence. 'Oh! it will be nothing, that happens to her every day.

She will come back. Leave her alone, she prefers that.'

"As for me, I could no longer contain myself, and, to the great stupefaction of Prudence and Nanine, who called me back, I went to rejoin Marguerite.

X

"The chamber in which she had taken refuge was lit only by a single candle placed on a table. Reclining upon a large sofa, her dress opened, she held one hand upon her heart and allowed the other to hang idly. On the table there was a silver hand-basin half full of water; this water was marbled with threads of blood.

"Marguerite, very pale and with her mouth partly opened, was endeavoring to get her breath. At moments her bosom heaved with a long sigh which, when exhaled, seemed to soothe her a little, and left her for a few seconds with a feeling of relief.

"I approached her, she remained motionless, I seated myself and took that one of her hands which was lying on the sofa.

"'Ah! it is you?' she said to me with a smile.

"It seems that my countenance showed distress, for she added:

"'Are you, too, ill?'

"'No; but you, are you still suffering?'

"'Very little;' and she wiped away with her handkerchief the tears which the coughing had brought into her eyes; 'I am used to that now.'

"'You are killing yourself, madame,' I said to her in a voice of emotion; 'I would I were your friend, your relative, to prevent you from injuring yourself thus.'

"'Ah! it is not worth while that you should alarm yourself,' she replied in a somewhat bitter tone; 'you see that the others do not concern themselves about me in the least; they know very well that there is nothing to be done for this trouble.'

"After which she rose, and, taking the candle, she placed it on the mantel-piece and looked at herself in the glass.

"'How pale I am!' she said, refastening her dress and passing her fingers over her roughened hair. 'Ah! bah! let us go and take our places again at the table. Will you come?'

"But I was seated and I did not move.

"She comprehended the emotion which this scene had caused me, for she approached me and, extending to me her hand, she said:

"'Come, let us go.'

"I took her hand, I carried it to my lips, wetting it, despite myself, by two tears which I had long retained.

"'Well, what a child you are!' she said, seating herself again at my side; 'here it is you who are crying! What troubles you?'

"'I must seem to you very silly, but that which I have just seen has distressed me greatly.'

Chapter IX

"*Finally, something occurred which I had foreseen and which I feared. Near the end of the supper, Marguerite was seized with an attack of coughing more violent than any of those which I had seen. It seemed to me that her chest was rending itself internally. The poor girl became purple, closed her eyes with the pain, and carried to her lips her napkin which was reddened by a drop of blood.*"

"'You are very good! What would you have! I cannot sleep, I must amuse myself a little. And then, of
women like me, one more or less, what does that matter?
The doctors say to me that the blood which I spit up
cor es from the bronchial tubes; I appear to believe
them, it is all that I can do for them.'

"'Listen to me, Marguerite,' I exclaimed with a
sudden expansion which I could not restrain, 'I do not
know what influence you should exercise on my life; but
that which I do know is, that at this hour, there is no
one, not even my sister, in whom I am interested as I
am in you. It has been thus ever since I first saw you.
Well, in the name of Heaven, do take care of yourself
and do not continue to lead this life any longer.'

"'If I should take care of myself, I should die. That
which sustains me is the feverish life which I lead.
Then, to take care of yourself, that is very well for
women of society who have a family and friends; but
we, just as soon as we can no longer serve either for the
vanity or the pleasure of our friends, they abandon us,
and the long evenings follow the long days. I know all
about it, come now, I was two months in my bed; at
the end of three weeks no one any longer came to see
me.'

"'It is true that I am nothing to you,' I replied;
'but, if you were willing, I would take care of you like
a brother, I would not leave you, and I would cure you.
Then, when you are strong enough, you may take up

again the life which you lead, if it seem good to you;
but, I am certain of it, you will like better a tranquil
existence which would make you happier and which
would keep you pretty.'

"'You think so this evening, because your wine has
made you see things mournfully, but you would not have
the patience of which you boast.'

"'Permit me to say to you, Marguerite, that you were
sick for two months, and that, during those two months,
I came every day to inquire after you.'

"'That is true, but why did you not come up to see
me?'

"'Because I did not know you then.'

"'Is any one considerate with a woman such as I?'

"'One is always considerate with a woman; at least,
that is my opinion.'

"'Thus, you would take care of me?'

"'Yes.'

"'You would remain with me all day?'

"'Yes.'

"'And even all night?'

"'Just as long as I did not weary you.'

"'What is it that you call that?'

"'Devotion.'

"'And whence comes this devotion?'

"'From an irresistible sympathy which I have for you.'

"'Therefore you are in love with me? say it at once,
it is much more simple.'

"'It is possible; but if I should say it to you some day, it is not to-day.'

"'You would do better to never say it to me.'

"'Why?'

"'Because there could result from this avowal only two things.'

"'Which?'

"'Either that I would not accept you, then you would quarrel with me, or that I would accept you, then you would have a sad mistress; a woman, nervous, ill, melancholy, or gay with a gayety sadder than grief, a woman who spits blood and who spends a hundred thousand francs a year, that is all very well for a rich old man like the duke; but it is very tiresome for a young man like you, and the proof of it is, that all the young lovers I have had have very quickly left me.'

"I made no reply, I listened. This frankness which verged on confession, this mournful life of which I caught glimpses under the gilded veil which covered it, and the reality of which the poor girl took refuge from in debauchery, drunkenness, and insomnia, all this made such an impression upon me that I could not find a single word.

"'Come,' continued Marguerite, 'we are talking childishness. Give me your hand and let us go back to the dining-room. It were better not to know what our absence may mean.'

"'Go back, if it seem best to you; but I ask your permission to remain here.'

"'Why?'

"'Because your gayety distresses me.'

"'Very well, I will be sad.'

"'Listen, Marguerite, let me say to you something which you have doubtless heard very often, and which the habit of hearing perhaps prevents you from believing, but which is none the less real, and which I will never say to you again.'

"'That is?——' she said, with the smile of the young mothers listening to some childish foolishness.

"'That is, that ever since I saw you, I do not know how or why, you have taken a place in my life; that is, that however I might drive your image from my thoughts it always returned; that is, that to-day when I met you, after having been two years without seeing you, you assumed over my heart and my mind an ascendancy still greater; that is, finally, that now that you have received me, that I know you, that I know of all that there is strange in you, you have become indispensable to me, and that I shall go mad, not only if you do not love me, but if you do not allow me to love you.'

"'But, unfortunate that you are. I would say to you that which Madame D—— said: "You are then very rich!" But you do not know, then, that I spend six or seven thousand francs a month, and that this expenditure has become necessary to my life? but you do not know, then, my poor friend, that I should ruin you in no time, and that your family would have the management of your own affairs taken from you to teach you to live with a creature like me? Love me as you like, like a good friend, but in no other way. Come to see me, we will laugh together, we will talk together, but do not exaggerate to yourself my worth, for I am not worth very much. You have a good heart, you need to be loved, you are too young and too sensitive to live in our world. Take some married woman. You see that I am an honest girl and that I speak to you frankly.'

" 'Ah there! what the devil are you doing?' cried Prudence, whom we had not heard coming, and who suddenly appeared in the doorway with her hair half unloosened and her dress opened. I recognized in this disorder the hand of Gaston.

" 'We are talking sensibly,' said Marguerite, 'leave us alone a little; we will rejoin you presently.'

" 'Good, good, talk away, my children,' said Prudence, going away and closing the door behind her as if to emphasize the tone in which she pronounced these last words.

" 'Thus, it is arranged,' resumed Marguerite when we were alone, 'you will love me no more?'

" 'I will go away.'

" 'It is as bad as that?'

"I had gone too far to draw back, and, moreover, this girl confounded me. This mingling of gayety, of

sadness, of candor, of prostitution, this very malady
which should develop in her the sensitiveness of impressions as the irritability of the nerves, everything made
me comprehend that if, from the very beginning, I
did not assume the empire over this light and forgetful
nature, she would be lost to me.

"'Come, now, that is then serious, what you are
saying?' she asked.

"'Very serious.'

"'But why did you not say that to me sooner?'

"'When should I have said it to you?'

"'The next day after you were presented to me at
the Opéra-Comique.'

"'I believed that you would have received me very
badly if I had come to see you.'

"'Why?'

"'Because I had been stupid the evening before.'

"'Yes, that is true.   But, however, you loved me
already at that period?'

"'Yes.'

"'Which did not prevent you from going to bed and
sleeping very peacefully after the theatre.   We know all
about those great loves.'

"'Well, that is where you are mistaken.   Do you
know what I did on the evening of the Opéra-Comique?'

"'No.'

"'I accompanied you to the door of the Café Anglais.
I followed the carriage which took you away, you and

your three friends, and when I saw you descend alone and enter your house alone, I was very happy.'

"Marguerite began to laugh.

"'Why do you laugh?'

"'At nothing.'

"'Tell it to me, I entreat you, or I shall believe that you are still mocking me.'

"'You will not be offended?'

"'By what right should I be offended?'

"'Well, there was a good reason why I should return alone.'

"'What one?'

"'I was waited for here.'

"She could have given me a stab with a knife that would have wounded me less. I rose, offering her my hand.

"'Adieu,' I said to her.

"'I knew very well that you would be offended,' she said. 'The men have an insatiable desire to hear that which will give them pain.'

"'But I assure you,' I added coldly, as if I wished to prove to her that I was forever cured of my passion, 'I assure you that I am not offended. It was very natural that some one should be waiting for you, just as it is quite natural that I should go away at three o'clock in the morning.'

"'Have you also some one waiting for you at your house?'

" ' No, but I must go.'

" ' Adieu, then.'

" ' You send me away ? '

" ' Not the least in the world.'

" ' Why do you give me pain ? '

" ' What pain have I given you ? '

" ' You tell me that some one was waiting for you.'

" ' I could not keep from laughing at the idea that you had been so happy at seeing me return alone, when there had been such a good reason for my doing so.'

" ' One often gives one's self a childish joy, and it is wicked to destroy that joy when, by allowing it to remain. you can render still more happy he who has found it.'

" ' But with whom do you think you have to do? I am neither a virgin nor a duchess. I have only known you from to-day, and I am not responsible to you for my actions. Admitting that I should become some day your mistress, it is necessary that you should know that I have had other lovers. If you make scenes of jealousy with me before, what will it be, then, afterwards, if ever the afterwards comes to pass! I have never seen a man like you.'

" ' That is because no one has ever loved you as I love you.'

" ' Come now, frankly, you love me then very much ? '

" ' As much as it is possible to love, I think.'

" ' And that has lasted since —— ? '

" ' Since one day I saw you get out of a calash and enter Susse's, three years ago.'

" ' Do you know that is very fine? Well, what must I do to acknowledge this great love?'

" ' You must love me a little,' said I, with a beating of the heart which almost prevented my speaking ; for, notwithstanding the half-mocking smiles with which she had accompanied all this conversation, it seemed to me that Marguerite was beginning to share my trouble, and that I was approaching the hour so long waited for.

" ' Well, and the duke?'

" ' What duke?'

" ' My old jealous.'

" ' He will know nothing about it.'

" 'And if he should know it?'

" ' He will forgive you.'

" '*He*, no, he will abandon me, and what then will become of me?'

" ' You risk that abandonment very freely for another.'

" ' How do you know?'

" ' By the order which you gave to allow no one to enter to-night.'

" ' That is true ; but that one is a serious friend.'

" ' To whom you are not very much attached, since you close your door to him at such an hour.'

" ' It is not for you to reproach me with it, since it was to receive you, you and your friend.'

"Little by little I had approached Marguerite, I had passed my hands around her waist and I felt her supple body lean lightly against my joined hands.

"'If you knew how I love you!' I said to her in a low voice.

"'Truly?'

"'I swear it to you.'

"'Well, if you promise me to do everything I wish without saying a word, without making any observations to me, without questioning me, I will love you perhaps.'

"'Everything that you wish!'

"'But, I warn you, I wish to be free to do whatever seems good to me, without giving you the slightest details of my life. It is a long time that I have been looking for a young lover, without any will of his own, loving without suspicion, loved without having any rights. I have never been able to find one. The men, instead of being satisfied with being given for a long time that which they scarcely hoped to obtain once, demand of their mistress an account of the present, of the past, and even of the future. In proportion as they become accustomed to her, they wish to rule her, and they become all the more exacting as they are given all that they desire. If I decide now to take a new lover, I wish that he shall have three very rare qualities, that he shall be confiding, submissive, and discreet.'

"'Very well, I will be everything that you require.'

" ' We shall see.'

" ' And when shall we see ? '

" ' Later.'

" ' Why ? '

" ' Because,' said Marguerite, disengaging herself from my arms and taking from a great bouquet of red camellias which had been brought in that morning, a camellia which she placed in my buttonhole, ' because treaties cannot always be executed on the day on which they are signed.'

" ' That is easy to understand.'

" ' And when shall I see you again ? ' I asked, clasping her in my arms.

" ' When this camellia changes its color.'

" ' And when will it change its color ? '

" ' To-morrow, from eleven o'clock to midnight. Are you satisfied ? '

" ' You ask me that ? '

" ' Not a word of all this, neither to your friend, nor to Prudence, nor to any one whatever.'

" ' I promise you.'

" ' Now, then, kiss me, and let us go back into the dining-room.'

" She offered me her lips, smoothed her hair again, and we issued from this chamber, she singing and I, half beside myself.

" In the salon she said to me in a low tone, stopping a moment:

"'This must seem strange to you that I should have the air of being ready to accept you thus off-hand; do you know why that is?

"'That is,' she continued, taking my hand and pressing it against her heart, of which I could feel the violent and constant beating, 'that is because, having less time to live in than other people, I have promised myself to live more rapidly.'

"'Do not speak to me in such a manner, I entreat you.'

"'Oh! console yourself,' she continued, laughing. 'However little time I may have to live, I shall live longer than you will love me.'

"And she entered singing into the dining-room.

"'Where is Nanine?' she asked, seeing Gaston and Prudence alone.

"'She is asleep in your chamber, waiting till you should go to bed,' replied Prudence.

"'The poor thing! I am killing her! Come, messieurs, retire; it is time.'

"Ten minutes later Gaston and I left. Marguerite grasped my hand when saying good-night, and remained with Prudence.

"'Well,' asked Gaston when we were in the street, 'what do you say of Marguerite?'

"'She is an angel, and I am crazy over her.'

"'I thought so; did you tell her so?'

"'Yes.'

" ' And did she promise to believe you ? '

" ' No.'

" ' She is not like Prudence.'

" ' She has promised you ? '

" ' She has done better, my dear fellow ! It would not be believed, but she is still very nice, that fat Duvernoy ! "

XI

At this point in his recital Armand stopped.

"Will you close the window?" he said to me, "I begin to be cold. Meanwhile, I will go to bed."

I closed the window. Armand, who was still very weak, took off his dressing-gown and lay down in bed, resting his head for some moments on his pillow, like a man fatigued with a long course, or agitated by painful thoughts.

"You have perhaps talked too much," I said to him; "would you like me to go away and let you sleep? You can relate to me some other day the end of this story."

"Does it tire you?"

"Quite the contrary."

"I will continue, then; if you should leave me alone, I would not sleep.

"When I returned home," he resumed, without having had to stop to collect his thoughts, so vividly were all these details still present in his memory, "I did not go to bed; I set myself to reflecting on the day's adventure. The meeting, the presentation, the engagement with Marguerite, everything had been so rapid,

127

so unhoped for, that there were moments in which I thought I had dreamed.   However, this was not the first time that a girl like Marguerite had promised herself to a man for the day after that on which he had asked her.

"I had much need of this reflection, the first impression produced upon me by my future mistress having been so strong that it still asserted itself.   I was still obstinate in refusing to see in her a girl like the others, and, with the vanity so common to all men, I was ready to believe that she inevitably felt for me the same attraction that I had for her.

"However, I had very contradictory examples before my eyes, and I had often heard it said that Marguerite's love had passed into the state of a commodity more or less costly, according to the season.

"But also how, on the other hand, was this reputation to be reconciled with the continual refusals of the young count whom we had found in her house?

"You will say to me that he was displeasing to her, and that, as she was splendidly maintained by the duke, when it came to taking another lover, she preferred having a man who pleased her.   Well, then, why did she not take Gaston, charming, clever, rich, and why did she seem to wish for me, whom she had found so ridiculous the first time that she had seen me?

"It is true that there are incidents of the moment which count for more than a year's courting.

"Of all those who were at the supper, I was the only one who had been anxious in seeing her leave the table. I had followed her, I had been so affected as not to be able to conceal it, I had wept in kissing her hand. This circumstance, taken in connection with my daily visits during the two months in which she had been ill, might have led her to see in me another man than those she had known up to this time, and perhaps she had said to herself that she might very well do for a love expressed in this manner what she had done so many times before, that which had had no serious consequences for her before.

"All these suppositions, as you see, were sufficiently probable; but, whatever might have been the reason for her consenting, there was one thing certain, that she had consented.

"Now, I was in love with Marguerite, I was about to have possession of her, I could ask of her nothing more. However, I repeat it to you, although she was a kept woman, I had so much—perhaps to poetize it—made of this love a hopeless one, that the nearer the moment approached in which I would no longer have even need to hope, the more I doubted.

"I did not close my eyes that night.

"I did not recognize myself. I was half-beside myself. At times I considered myself neither sufficiently handsome, nor sufficiently rich, nor sufficiently elegant to possess such a woman, at times I felt myself filled with

vanity at the thought of this possession; then I began
to fear that Marguerite would have for me only a caprice
of a few days' duration, and foreseeing a misfortune in
a prompt rupture, I would perhaps do better, I said to
myself, not to go to her house that evening and to
depart after communicating to her my fears in writing.
From this, I passed to limitless hopes, to a boundless
confidence. I had a dream of an incredible future; I
said to myself that this girl would owe to me her cure,
physical and moral, that I would pass all my life with
her, and that her love would render me more happy
than the most virginal loves.

"In short, I could not repeat to you the thousand
thoughts which ascended from my heart to my head and
which were extinguished, little by little, in the slumber
which overcame me at daybreak.

"When I arose, it was two o'clock. The weather was
magnificent. I do not remember that life had ever appeared to me to be so beautiful and so full. The memories
of the evening before presented themselves to my mind,
without shadows, without obstacles, and gayly escorted by
the hopes of the evening to come. I dressed myself hastily.
I was well satisfied, and capable of the finest actions.
There were moments when my heart bounded with joy
and with love in my chest. A soft fever agitated me. I no
longer troubled myself with the reasons which had occupied me before I slept. I saw only the result, I thought
only of the hour in which I should see Marguerite again.

"It was impossible for me to remain in my rooms. My chamber seemed to me too small to contain my happiness; I felt the need of nature herself in which to expand myself.

"I went out.

"I went through the Rue d'Antin. Marguerite's coupé was waiting for her at her door; I directed my steps toward the Champs-Élysées. I loved, without even knowing them, every one whom I met.

"How love softens us!

"At the end of an hour, during which I promenaded from the horses of Marly to the Rond-point, and from the Rond-point to the horses of Marly, I saw in the distance Marguerite's carriage; I did not recognize it, I divined it.

"As she turned the angle of the Champs-Élysées she caused her coachman to stop, and a tall young man left a group in which he had been conversing and went to speak to her.

"They talked together for a few minutes; the young man rejoined his friends, the horses set off again, and I, who had approached the group, I recognized in him who had spoken to Marguerite that Comte de G—— whose portrait I had seen and whom Prudence had indicated to me as the one to whom Marguerite owed her position.

"It was to him that she had closed her door the evening before; I supposed that she had stopped her carriage to give him the reason for this closing, and I hoped that at the same time she had found some new pretext for not receiving him the following night.

"How the rest of the day passed, I do not know ; I walked about, I smoked, I talked ; but of what I said, whom I met, up to ten o'clock in the evening, I have no remembrance.

"All that I can recollect is, that I returned to my apartment, that I spent three hours at my toilet, and that I looked a hundred times at my clock and at my watch, which unfortunately went exactly alike.

"When half-past ten sounded, I said to myself that it was time to go.

"I lived at that period in the Rue de Provence ; I followed the Rue du Mont-Blanc, I traversed the Boulevard, took the Rue Louis-le-Grand, the Rue de Port-Mahon, and the Rue d'Antin. I looked up at Marguerite's windows.

"There was a light in them.

"I rang.

"I asked of the porter if Mademoiselle Gautier were at home.

"He replied that she never returned before eleven o'clock or a quarter past eleven.

"I looked at my watch.

"I thought I had come very slowly, I had taken only five minutes to come from the Rue de Provence to Marguerite's house.

"Then I walked about in this street without shops, and deserted at this hour.

"At the end of a half-hour Marguerite arrived. She descended from her coupé looking around her, as if she were seeking some one.

"The carriage went off at a walk, the stables and the carriage-house not adjoining the building. At the moment when Marguerite was about to ring, I approached and said to her :

"'Good-evening !'

"'Ah! it is you?' she replied, in a tone not very reassuring as to the pleasure she felt in finding me there.

"'Did you not give me permission to come and pay you a visit to-day?'

"'That is true ; I had forgotten it.'

"This word overthrew all my reflections of the morning, all my hopes of the day. However, I was beginning to get accustomed to these manners and I did not go away, as I would undeniably have done formerly.

"We entered.

"Nanine had opened the door in advance.

"'Has Prudence returned?' asked Marguerite.

"'No, madame.'

"'Go and say that, as soon as she returns, she must come here. Before that, extinguish the lamp in the salon, and, if any one comes, say that I have not returned and that I shall not return.'

" It was evidently a case of a woman preoccupied with something and perhaps annoyed by some importunate person. I did not know what countenance to assume, nor what to say. Marguerite went towards her bed-chamber; I remained where I was.

" ' Come,' she said to me.

" She took off her bonnet, her velvet mantle, and threw them upon her bed, then she let herself fall in a great easy-chair, before the fire which she caused to be kept up even till the commencement of the summer, and said to me, playing with the chain of her watch :

" ' Well, what have you to tell me that is new ? '

" ' Nothing, excepting that I was wrong to come this evening.'

" ' Why ? '

" ' Because you seem vexed and because, doubtless, I annoy you.'

" ' You do not annoy me ; only, I am sick, I have been suffering all day, I have not slept and I have a frightful headache.'

" ' Would you like me to retire so that you may go to bed ? '

" ' Oh ! you can stay ; if I wish to go to bed, I will do so before you.'

" At that moment there was a ring at the door.

" ' Who is coming now ? ' she said with an impatient movement.

"A few minutes later the bell rang again.

"'There is then no one to open the door? I shall be obliged to open it myself.'

"In fact she rose, saying to me:

"'Wait here.'

"She traversed the apartment, and I heard the entrance door open.

"I listened.

"He to whom she had opened the door stopped in the dining-room. At the first words I recognized the voice of the young Comte de N——.

"'How do you feel this evening?' he said.

"'Badly,' replied Marguerite, dryly.

"'Do I disturb you?'

"'Perhaps.'

"'How you receive me! What have I done to you, my dear Marguerite?'

"'My dear friend, you have done nothing to me. I am sick, I must go to bed; therefore you will give me the pleasure of going away. It is abominable that I cannot come home in the evening without seeing you appear five minutes afterwards. What is it that you wish? that I should be your mistress? Well, I have already told you no a hundred times, that you bore me horribly and that you can go elsewhere. I repeat it to you to-day for the last time: "I do not want you, that is understood; adieu." Wait, here is Nanine coming back; she will light you out. Good-evening.'

"And, without another word, without listening to the young man's stammering excuses, Marguerite came back into her chamber and closed the door violently, through which door Nanine in her turn almost immediately entered.

"'Do you hear me,' said Marguerite to her, 'you will tell that imbecile every time that I am not in, or that I do not wish to receive him. I am weary to death of seeing ceaselessly men who come to ask of me the same thing, who pay me and who think themselves quits with me. If those who were commencing in our shameful trade knew what it was, they would make themselves ladies' maids sooner. But no, the vanity of having dresses, carriages, diamonds, carries us away; you believe what you hear, for prostitution has its faith, and you use up, little by little, your hearts, your bodies, your beauty; you are dreaded like a wild beast, scorned like a pariah, you are surrounded only by those who always take from you more than they give you, and you go some fine day and end like a dog, after having ruined others and ruined yourself.'

"'Come now, madame, calm yourself,' said Nanine; 'you are very nervous this evening.'

"'This dress worries me,' replied Marguerite, tearing open the clasps of her corsage; 'give me a dressing-gown. Well, and Prudence?'

"'She has not yet returned, but they will send her in to madame as soon as she comes in.'

" 'And there is another,' continued Marguerite, taking off her dress and putting on a white dressing-gown—'and there is another who knows very well how to find me when she has need of me, and who cannot render me a service willingly.   She knows that I am waiting for that answer this evening, that it is necessary for me to have it, that I am anxious about it, and I am certain that she has gone off running about without thinking of me.'

" 'Perhaps she has been detained ?'

" 'Get us some punch.'

" ' You are going to make yourself worse again,' said Nanine.

" 'So much the better !   Bring me also some fruits, a pâté or the wing of a chicken, something immediately; I am hungry.'

"To convey to you the impression which this scene had on me is useless; you can imagine it, can you not ?

" 'You will have supper with me,' she said to me ; 'meanwhile, take a book, I am going into my dressing-room for a moment.'

" She lit the candles in a branched candlestick, opened a door at the foot of her bed, and disappeared.

"For my part, I fell into reflections on this woman's life, and my love was augmented by pity.

"I was walking about hastily in this chamber, buried in thought, when Prudence entered.

" 'Well, you here ?' she said to me ; 'where is Marguerite ?'

" ' In her dressing-room.'

" ' I will wait for her. I say, she finds you charming; did you know that ?'

" ' No.'

" ' She did not tell it to you a little ?'

" ' Not at all.'

" ' How do you come to be here?'

" ' I came to pay her a visit.'

" ' At midnight ?'

" ' Why not ?'

" ' You joker !'

" ' She even received me very badly.'

" ' She will receive you better.'

" ' You think so ?'

" ' I bring her a piece of good news.'

" ' That is not bad ; so she spoke to you of me ?'

" ' Yesterday evening, or, rather, this night, after you had gone off with your friend —— Apropos, how is he, your friend? his name is Gaston R——, I think ?'

" ' Yes,' I said, unable to repress a smile in recalling the confidence which Gaston had made to me, and in seeing that Prudence scarcely knew his name.

" ' He is very nice, that young fellow ; what does he do ?'

" ' He has twenty-five thousand francs of income.'

" ' Ah ! truly ! well, to return to you, Marguerite questioned me about you ; she asked me who you were, what you did, what mistresses you had had ; in short, everything that could be asked concerning a man of your age. I told her all that I knew, adding that you were a charming fellow, and there you are.'

" ' I am obliged to you; but now, tell me, with what commission did she charge you yesterday?'

" ' With none; it was to make the count go away, that which she said, but she charged me with one to-day, and it is the reply to that that I bring her this evening.'

" At that moment Marguerite came out of her dressing-room, coquettishly arrayed in her night-cap ornamented with bows of yellow ribbons, technically known as ' cabbages.'

" She was ravishing thus.

" Her naked feet were in satin slippers, and she was finishing the toilet of her finger-nails.

" ' Well,' she said when she saw Prudence, ' have you seen the duke?'

" ' Parbleu ! '

" ' And what did he say to you?'

" ' He gave me.'

" ' How much ?'

" ' Six thousand.'

" ' You have them?'

" ' Yes.'

" ' Did he seem vexed?'

" ' No.'

" ' Poor man !'

"This 'poor man!' was said in a tone impossible to render. Marguerite took the six notes of a thousand francs each.

" 'It was time,' she said. 'My dear Prudence, are you in need of money?'

" 'You know, my child, that it is within two days of the 15th; if you could lend me three or four hundred francs, you would do me a service.'

" 'Send for them to-morrow morning, it is too late now to make change.'

" 'Do not forget.'

" 'Rest assured. Will you sup with us?'

" 'No, Charles is waiting for me at home.'

" 'You are then still crazy over him?'

" 'Insane, my dear! Till to-morrow. Adieu, Armand.'

" Madame Duvernoy departed.

" Marguerite opened her étagère and threw into it the bank-notes.

" 'You will permit me to get into bed!' she said, smiling and going toward her couch.

" 'Not only will I permit it, but I even entreat you to do so.'

" She threw back on the foot of the bed the lace covering and lay down inside.

" 'Now,' she said, 'come and sit near me and we will talk.'

" Prudence was right; the response which she had brought to Marguerite had cheered her.

"'You will forgive me my bad humor this evening?' she said, taking my hand.

"'I am ready to forgive you a great many other things.'

"'And you love me?'

"'Madly.'

"'Notwithstanding my bad character?'

"'Notwithstanding everything.'

"'You will swear it to me?'

"'Yes,' I said to her in a low voice.

"Nanine then entered, carrying some plates, a cold chicken, a bottle of Bordeaux, strawberries, and two covers.

"'I have not had any punch made for you,' said Nanine, 'the Bordeaux is better for you. Is it not, monsieur?'

"'Certainly,' I replied, still under the influence of the emotion caused in me by Marguerite's last words and with my eyes ardently fixed upon her.

"'Very well,' she said, 'put all that on the little table, bring it up to the bed; we will serve ourselves. You have been up now for three nights, you must want to sleep, go to bed; I will need nothing more.'

"'Shall I double lock the door?'

"'Yes, indeed! and above all say that no one is to be admitted to-morrow before noon.'

XII

"At five o'clock in the morning, when the daylight began to appear through the curtains, Marguerite said to me :

"'Forgive me if I drive you away, but it is necessary. The duke comes every morning ; they will tell him that I am asleep when he comes, and he will wait perhaps till I awaken.'

"I took in my hands Marguerite's head, the loosened hair of which streamed around her, and I gave her a last kiss, saying :

"'When shall I see you again.'

"'Listen,' she replied, 'take that little gilded key which is on the mantel-piece, open that door with it ; bring the key here, and go away. In the course of the day you will receive a letter and my orders, for you know that you are to obey blindly.'

"'Yes, and if I ask already for something?'

"'What is it?'

"'That you let me keep this key.'

"'I have never done for any one that which you ask.'

" 'Well, do it for me, for I swear to you that I, I do not love you as the others loved you.'

" 'Very well, keep it ; but I warn you that it depends entirely upon me as to whether that key shall be of any service to you.'

" 'Why ?'

" 'There are bolts on the inside of the door.'

" 'Wicked one !'

" 'I will have them taken off.'

" 'You love me then a little ?'

" 'I do not know how it happens, but it seems to me that I do.   But now, go away ; I am dead with sleep.'

" We remained for a few moments in each other's arms, and I departed.

" The streets were deserted, the great city was still sleeping, a soft freshness pervaded these quarters which the noise of men would invade a few hours later.

" It seemed to me that this sleeping city belonged to me ; I sought in my memory the names of those whose happiness up to this time I had envied, and I could not recall one than whom I did not think myself more fortunate.

" To be loved by a chaste young girl, to reveal to her the first this strange mystery of love, certainly, that is a great felicity, but it is the most simple thing in the world.   To capture a heart which is not used to attacks, that is to enter into a city open and ungarrisoned. Education, the sentiment of duty and of the family, are very efficient sentinels; but there are no sentinels so vigilant that they will not betray a maid of sixteen, to whom, by the voice of the man whom she loves, Nature communicates her first counsels of love which are all the more ardent as they appear the more pure.

"The more the young girl believes in the good, the more readily she abandons herself, if not to the lover, at least to love, for, being without suspicions, she is without strength, and to make himself beloved by her is a triumph that any man of twenty-five can give himself whenever he desires. And that is so true that we see how the young girls are surrounded by ramparts and constant surveillance! The convents have not walls high enough, the mothers, locks strong enough, religion, duties sufficiently continuous, to secure all these charming birds in their cages, which are not even strewn with flowers. Therefore is it small wonder that they should desire this world which is hidden from them, that they should believe that it is tempting, that they should listen to the first voice which, through the bars, comes to relate to them the secrets, and that they should bless the hand which is the first to lift a corner of the mysterious veil!

"But to be really loved by a courtesan, that is a victory much more difficult to win. With them, the body has worn out the soul, the senses have burned out the heart, debauchery has enclosed the sentiments in armor. The words which are said to them they have known for a long time ; the methods which are employed they are acquainted with ; even the love which they inspire they have sold. They love by trade, and not by impulse. They are better guarded by their calculations than a virgin by her mother and her convent ; thus they have invented the word caprice for those loves without traffic which they allow themselves from time to time as a repose, as an excuse, or as a consolation ; after the manner of those usurers who levy contributions on a thousand individuals, and who think that they have redeemed everything by lending some day twenty francs to some poor devil who is dying of hunger ; without requiring any interest and without demanding a receipt from him.

"Then, when God permits a courtesan to love, this love, which seems at first a pardon, becomes almost always for her a chastisement. There is no absolution without repentance. When a creature who has all her past to reproach her feels herself suddenly filled with a love profound, sincere, irresistible, of which she would never have thought herself capable ; when she has avowed this love, how the man thus loved rules over her ! How strong he feels himself with the cruel right to say to her : ' You do no more for love than you have done for money.'

"Then she does not know what proofs to give. A child, as the fable relates, after having long amused himself in a field by crying : ' Help !' in order to distract the travelers, was one day devoured by a bear, because those whom he had so often deceived did not this time believe in the real cries of distress which he uttered. It is the same with these unfortunate women when they love seriously. They have lied so many times that no one is willing to believe them, and they are devoured by their love in the midst of their remorse.

" From this come those grand devotions, those austere retreats, of which some of them have given the example.

" But, when the man who inspires this redeeming love has a soul sufficiently generous to accept it without remembering the past, when he gives himself up to it, when he loves, in short, as he is loved, this man exhausts at one stroke all the terrestrial emotions, and after this love his heart will be closed to all others.

" I did not make these reflections on the morning on which I returned to my lodgings. They would have been only the presentiment of that which was going to happen to me, and, notwithstanding my love for Marguerite, I did not foresee any such consequences; it is to-day that I make them. Everything being irrevocably finished, they result naturally from that which has happened.

" But let us return to the first day of this liaison. When I re-entered, I was in a state of unreasoning gayety. When I reflected that the barriers placed by my imagination between Marguerite and myself had disappeared, that I possessed her, that I occupied a share in her thoughts, that I had in my pocket the key to her apartment and the right to make use of that key, I was content with life, proud of myself, and I loved God who permitted all this.

" One day a young man is walking through a street, he brushes against a woman, he looks at her, he turns round, he passes on. He is not acquainted with this woman, she has pleasures, griefs, loves, in which he has no part. He does not exist for her, and perhaps if he spoke to her she would make a mock of him as Marguerite had done of me. Weeks, months, years roll away, and suddenly, when they have followed each one his own destiny in a different order of things, the logic of chance brings them face to face with each other. This woman becomes the mistress of this man and loves him. How? why? their two existences no longer make but one ; scarcely is their intimacy established than it seems to have lasted forever, and everything that preceded is effaced from the memory of the two lovers. It is curious, we must admit it.

" As for myself, I no longer remembered how I had lived before the day before. All my being was exalted with joy at the memory of some words exchanged during this first night. Either Marguerite was skillful in deceiving, or she had conceived for me one of those sudden passions which reveal themselves in the first kiss, and which die sometimes, for that matter, as they were born.

"The more I reflected upon it, the more I said to myself that Marguerite had no reason for feigning a love which she did not feel, and I said to myself also that women have two manners of loving which may result the one from the other,—they love with the heart or with the senses. Frequently a woman takes a lover in obedience to the will of the senses alone, and learns, without expecting it, the mystery of immaterial love and no longer lives but by her heart; frequently a young girl, seeking in marriage only the reunion of two pure affections, receives this sudden revelation of the physical love, this energetic conclusion of the chastest impressions of the soul.

"I fell asleep in the midst of these reflections. I was awakened by a letter from Marguerite, a letter containing these words:

"'These are my orders: this evening, at the Vaudeville. Come during the third entr'acte.

"'M. G.'

"I locked this note up in a drawer, so as to have the reality always under my hand, in case I should doubt, as I did at certain moments.

"She did not tell me to come to see her during the day, I did not dare to present myself in her apartments; but I had so great a desire to see her before the evening that I went to the Champs Élysées; where, as on the day before, I saw her drive out and return.

"At seven o'clock I was at the Vaudeville.

"Never had I entered a theatre so early.

"All the boxes were filled one after the other.   One only remained empty,—the stage proscenium box.

"At the commencement of the third act I heard the door of this box, on which I had almost constantly kept my eyes fixed, open; Marguerite appeared.

"She came immediately into the front of the box, looked through the orchestra seats, saw me, and thanked me by a glance.

"This evening she was marvellously beautiful.

"Was I the cause of this coquetry?   Did she love me enough to believe that the more beautiful I found her, the happier I should be?   I was still ignorant; but if such had been her intention, she succeeded, for when she showed herself the heads undulated, one toward another, and the actor then on the stage himself looked at her who thus affected the spectators by her mere appearance.

"And I had in my possession the key to the apartments of this woman, and in three or four hours she would again belong to me.

"Those who ruin themselves for actresses and kept women are blamed; that which surprises me is that they do not commit for them twenty times more follies. It is necessary to live, as I have done, in this life to know how strongly the little daily gratifications of his vanity which they give their lover cement strongly in his heart, since we have no other word, the love which he has for his mistress.

" Prudence took her place afterwards in the box, and a man whom I recognized as the Comte de G—— seated himself at the back.

" When I saw him, a cold passed over my heart.

" Doubtless Marguerite perceived the impression produced upon me by the presence of this man in her box, for she smiled at me again, and, turning her back on the count, she appeared to be very attentive to the play. At the third entr'acte she turned round, said two words to the count, who left the box, and Marguerite made me a sign to come to see her.

" 'Good-evening,' she said to me when I entered, offering me her hand.

" 'Good-evening,' I replied, addressing her and Prudence.

" 'Sit down.'

" 'But I am taking some one's place. Will not Monsieur le Comte de G—— return?'

" 'Yes, I have sent him to get some bonbons for me so that we can talk alone for a moment. Madame Duvernoy has been taken into confidence.'

" 'Yes, my children,' said the latter ; 'but be easy, I will say nothing.'

" 'What troubles you this evening?' said Marguerite, rising and coming into the shadow of the box to kiss me on the forehead.

" ' I have been somewhat unwell.'

" ' You should go to bed,' she went on, with that little air of irony which became so well her fine and *spirituelle* countenance.

" ' Where ? '

" ' In your own house.'

" ' You know very well that I should not sleep.'

" ' Then it is not necessary to come here to make faces because you have seen a man in my box.'

" ' That is not the reason.'

" ' Yes it is, I know all about it, and you are wrong ; therefore we will talk no longer of that. You will come home after the theatre with Prudence, and you will stay there till I call you. Do you understand ? '

" ' Yes.   Could I disobey you ? '

" ' You love me still ? '

" ' Can you ask me ? '

" ' You have thought of me ? '

" ' All day long.'

" ' Do you know that I decidedly am afraid of falling in love with you.   Ask Prudence.'

" ' Ah ! ' replied that plump person, ' it is idiotic.'

" ' Now, you can go back to your seat; the count is coming back, and it is not necessary that he should find you here.'

" ' Why ? '

" ' Because it is disagreeable to you to see him here.'

" 'No; only if you had said to me that you desired to come to the Vaudeville this evening, I could have sent you this box as well as he.'

"'Unfortunately, he brought it to me without my asking him for it, and offering to accompany me here. You know very well that I could not refuse. All that I could do was to write to you where I was going, so that you could see me, and because I myself would have pleasure in seeing you again so soon; but since it is in this manner that you thank me, I will profit by the lesson.'

" 'I am in the wrong, forgive me.'

" 'That is all very well, return politely to your place, and, above all, don't be jealous.'

"She kissed me again, and I went out.

"In the corridor I met the count returning.

"I went back to my seat.

"After all, the presence of Monsieur de G—— in Marguerite's box was the most simple thing in the world. He had been her lover, he brought her a box, he accompanied her to the theatre, all that was very natural, and, when I took for mistress a girl like Marguerite, it became quite necessary for me to accept her habits.

"I was none the less very unhappy the rest of the evening, and it was very mournfully that I went off, after having seen Prudence, the count, and Marguerite get into a calash which was waiting for them at the door.

"Nevertheless, a quarter of an hour later, I was in Prudence's rooms. She had but just returned herself.

XIII

"'You came almost as quickly as we did,' said Prudence to me.

"'Yes,' I replied mechanically. 'Where is Marguerite?'

"'At home.'

"'Alone?'

"'With Monsieur de G——.'

"I walked about in the salon in an agitated manner.

"'Well, what is it that disturbs you?'

"'Do you think that I find it amusing to wait here until Monsieur de G—— leaves Marguerite's apartments?'

"'You are perfectly unreasonable. You must understand that Marguerite cannot put the count out the door. Monsieur de G—— was with her a long time, he has always given her a great deal of money; he still does so. Marguerite expends more than a hundred thousand francs a year; she has a great many debts. The duke sends her whatever she asks for, but she does not always dare to ask him for all that she wants. She must not quarrel with the count, who gives her at least ten

155

thousand francs a year. Marguerite really loves you, my
dear friend ; but your liaison with her, in her interest
and in your own, must not be taken seriously. It is not
with your seven or eight thousand francs of yearly allowance that you could support that girl's luxury; it would
not be enough to keep up her carriage. Take Marguerite for what she is, for a nice girl, clever and pretty;
be her lover for a month, two months; give her bouquets, bonbons, and theatre boxes; but do not get anything else into your head, and do not make scenes of
ridiculous jealousy with her. You know very well with
whom you have to do ; Marguerite is not all virtue. You
please her, you love her well ; do not worry yourself
about the rest. It seems to me very fine that you should
take offence ! you have the most charming mistress in
Paris ! She receives you in a magnificent apartment,
she is covered with diamonds, she will not cost you a
sou if you wish, and you are not satisfied ! What the
devil ! you ask too much.'

" 'You are quite right, but it is stronger than I am,
the thought that that man is her lover gives me frightful
pain.'

" 'In the first place,' said Prudence, 'is he still her
lover ? He is a man she has use for, that is all.

" ' For the last two days she has shut her door to him ;
he came this morning, she could not do otherwise than
accept his box and allow him to accompany her. He
has brought her back, he went up to her apartment a

moment, he will not remain there, since you are waiting here. All that is very natural, it seems to me. Moreover, you accept the duke well enough.'

"'Yes, but he is an old man, and I am very sure that Marguerite is not his mistress. Then, you are often able to accept one liaison and not to accept two. This facility resembles too much a mercenary calculation, and brings the man who consents, even through love, too near those who on a lower stage make a trade of this consent and a profit from this trade.'

"'Ah! my dear, how much behind the times you are! How many have I seen, and of the most noble, the most elegant, the richest, do that which I advise you to do, and that without any effort, without shame, without remorse! Why, you can see that every day. But how do you suppose the kept women of Paris could manage to keep up the style they do if they did not have three or four lovers at once? There is no fortune, however considerable it might be, that could alone provide for the expenses of a woman like Marguerite. A fortune of five hundred thousand francs of income is an enormous fortune in France; well, my dear friend, an income of five hundred thousand francs would not be enough, and for this reason,—a man who has such a revenue has an establishment set up, horses, servants, carriages, hunting, friends; frequently he is married, he has children, he goes about, he plays, he travels, I don't know what! All these habits are considered so much a

matter of course that he cannot abandon them without
being thought to be ruined and making a scandal.
Everything taken into consideration, with five hundred
thousand francs a year, he cannot give to a woman more
than forty or fifty thousand francs a year, and even that
is a great deal. Well, the other loves come in to complete the woman's annual expenditure. With Marguerite, it is still more convenient,—she fell, by a miracle
from Heaven, on an old man worth ten millions, whose
wife and whose daughter are dead, who has no longer
any relatives but nephews who are rich themselves, who
gives her all that she wants without asking of her anything in exchange; but she cannot ask of him more
than seventy thousand francs a year, and I am certain
that if she did ask more of him, notwithstanding his
fortune and the affection which he has for her, he would
refuse her.

"'All those young men who have twenty or thirty
thousand livres of income in Paris, that is to say,
scarcely enough to live on in the world which they
frequent, know very well, when they are the lovers of a
woman like Marguerite, that she could not even pay for
her apartment, and her servants with what they give her.
They do not tell her that they know it, they appear to see
nothing, and when they have had enough of her, they go
away. If by chance they should have the vanity of paying for everything, they ruin themselves like fools and
go off to be killed in Africa, leaving a hundred thousand

francs worth of debts in Paris. Do you think that the woman is grateful to them for it? Not the least in the world. On the contrary, she says that she has sacrificed her position to them, and that, whilst she was with them, she lost money. Ah! you think all these details shameful, do you not? they are true. You are a charming young man whom I love with all my heart; I have lived for twenty years among kept women, I know what they are and what they are worth, and I would not wish to see you take seriously the caprice which a pretty girl of the town has for you.

" 'Then, in addition to all that, we will admit,' continued Prudence, 'that Marguerite loves you enough to renounce the count and the duke, in case the latter should perceive your liaison and tell her to choose between you and him, the sacrifice which she would make to you would be enormous, that is incontestable. What similar sacrifice could you make, on your part? When satiety comes, when you wish her no longer, in short, what would you do to recompense her for that which you had made her lose! Nothing. You would have isolated her from the world in which lay all her fortune and her future, she would have given you the finest years of her life, and she would be forgotten. Either, you would be an ordinary man, then, throwing her past into her face, you would say to her in leaving her that you acted only as her other lovers had done, and you would abandon her to certain misery; or, you

would be an honest man, and, believing yourself compelled to keep her near you, you would deliver yourself
up to inevitable unhappiness, for this liaison, excusable
in a young man, is no longer so in a man of mature
age.   It becomes an obstacle to everything, it permits
you neither family nor ambition, these second and last
loves of a man.   Believe me, then, my friend, take
things for what they are worth, women for what they
are, and do not give to a kept woman the right to call
herself your creditor in anything whatever.'

" It was very wisely reasoned, and with a logic of which
I would have thought Prudence incapable.   I found no
reply to make to her, excepting that she was right ; I
took her hand and thanked her for her counsels.

" ' Come, come,' she said to me, ' drive away these
evil theories and laugh ; life is charming, my dear, it is
according to the glass through which you look at it.
See now, consult your friend Gaston, and there is one
now who, it seems to me, understands love as I understand it.   That of which you may be convinced, without which you will become a very insipid sort of a
fellow, is that there is near here a pretty girl who is
waiting impatiently for the man who is with her to go
away, who thinks of you, who keeps her night for you,
and who loves you, I am certain of it.   At present,
come and take your place at the window with me, and
let us watch the count go away, he will not be long in
leaving his place to you.'

"Prudence opened her window, and we leaned on our elbows side by side on the balcony.

"She looked at the rare passers-by, I was dreaming.

"Everything that she had said to me was humming in my head, and I could not help admitting that she was right; but the genuine love which I bore to Marguerite could with difficulty accommodate itself to this reasoning. Thus I gave vent from time to time to sighs which made Prudence turn to look at me, and shrug her shoulders like a physician who despairs of his patient.

"'How easily it is to be seen that life should be brief,' I said to myself, 'by the rapidity of sensations! I have only known Marguerite for two days, she has been my mistress only since yesterday, and she has already taken such possession of my thoughts, my heart and my life, that the visit of this Comte de G—— is an unhappiness to me.'

"Finally the count came out, took his seat in his carriage and disappeared. Prudence closed the window.

"At the same moment Marguerite called us.

"'Come quickly, the table is being set,' she said; 'we are going to have supper.'

"When I entered her apartment, Marguerite ran to me, threw herself on my neck, and embraced me with all her strength.

"'Are we still sulky?' she said to me.

"'No, that is over,' replied Prudence, 'I have preached to him, and he has promised to be good.'

" ' Excellent ! '

" I cast my eyes upon the bed in spite of myself, it was not disarranged ; as to Marguerite, she was still in her white dressing-gown.

" We sat down at the table.

" Charm, sweetness, expansion, Marguerite had them all, and I was indeed forced from time to time to recognize that I had no right to ask anything else of her ; that very many men would be happy in my place, and that, like the shepherd of Virgil, I had only to enjoy the pleasures which a god, or, rather, a goddess, gave me.

" I endeavored to put Prudence's theories into practice, and to be as gay as my two companions ; but that which was natural with them was an effort for me, and the nervous laugh which I had, and with which they were deceived, was very near to tears.

" Finally the supper was over, and I remained alone with Marguerite.   She went and sat down on her carpet before the fire, according to her custom, and looked at the flame on the hearth with a thoughtful air.

" She was thinking ! Of what ? I did not know, for my part, I looked at her with love and almost with terror, as I thought of what I was ready to suffer for her sake.

" ' Do you know of what I am thinking ? '

" ' No. '

" ' Of a combination which I have found. '

" ' And what is that combination?'

" ' I cannot confide it to you as yet, but I can tell you what will result from it. It will result from it that in a month I shall be free, that I shall no longer owe anything, and we will go and spend the summer together in the country.'

" ' And you cannot tell me by what means?'

" ' No, it is necessary only that you shall love me as I love you, and everything will succeed.'

" ' And it is you alone who have found this combination?'

" ' Yes.'

" ' And you will execute it alone?'

" ' I alone will have the trouble,' she said with a smile which I shall never forget; 'but we will share the benefits.'

" I could not help reddening at this word 'benefits;' I recalled Manon Lescaut sharing with Desgrieux the money of Monsieur de B——.

" I replied in a somewhat hard tone, and rising:

" ' You will permit me, my dear Marguerite, to partake of the benefits only of the enterprises which I conceive and which I carry out myself.'

" ' What does that mean?'

" ' That means that I strongly suspect Monsieur le Comte de G—— of being your associate in this happy combination of which I will accept neither the charges nor the benefits.'

"'You are a child. I thought that you loved me, I was deceived, it is well.'

"And, at the same time, she rose, opened her piano and commenced to play the *Invitation à la valse*, up to the famous passage in major which always checked her.

"Was it through force of habit, or to recall to me the evening in which we had first met ? All that I know is, that with this melody my remembrances came back to me and, going up to her, I took her head between my hands and kissed her.

"'You forgive me?' I said to her.

"'You know it very well,' she replied ; 'but notice that we are only at the second day, and that already I have something to forgive you. You keep very badly your promises of blind obedience.'

"'What could you expect, Marguerite, I am too much in love with you, and I am jealous of the least of your thoughts. That which you have just proposed to me should render me wild with joy, but the mystery which precedes the execution of this project constricts my heart.'

"'Come now, let us reason it out a little,' she replied, taking my two hands and looking at me with a charming smile which it was impossible for me to resist ; 'you love me, do you not ? and you would be happy to pass three or four months in the country alone with me ; I also, I should be happy in this solitude with another, not only should I be happy in it, but it is necessary for my health. I cannot leave Paris for such a length of time without putting my affairs in order and the affairs of a woman such as I are always very much in confusion ; well, I have found a means of arranging everything, my affairs and my love for you, yes, for you, do not laugh, I am foolish enough to love you ! and here you are taking on great airs and saying great words to me. You child, you child three times over, remember only that I love you, and do not disquiet yourself about anything —— Is that agreed, come now ?'

" ' Everything that you wish is agreed to, as you know very well.'

" ' Well, then, before the end of a month we shall be in some village, taking walks along the shore and drinking milk. That seems strange to you, that I should be talking in this way, I, Marguerite Gautier ; that comes, my friend, from the fact that when this Parisian life, which seems to render me so happy, does not consume me, it wearies me, and that then I have sudden aspirations towards a calmer existence which should recall to me my childhood. Everybody has had a childhood once, whatever he may have become later. Oh ! be easy, I am not going to tell you that I am the daughter of a retired colonel and that I was brought up at Saint-Denis. I am a poor country girl, and I could not write my own name six years ago. Now you are reassured, are you not ? Why is it that it is to you first that I address myself to have shared the pleasure of the desire which

has come to me?   Doubtless because I have recognized
that you loved me for myself and not for your own sake,
whereas the others never loved me but for themselves.

"'I have often been in the country, but never as I
would have wished to go there.   It is on you that I
count for this easy happiness, do not be wicked, then,
and grant it to me.   Say this to yourself,—she will not
live to be old, and I shall repent some day of not having
done for her the first thing that she asked of me, and
which was so easy to do.'

"What reply could I make to such words, above all
in the remembrance of a first night of love, and in the
expectation of a second?

"An hour later, I clasped Marguerite in my arms,
and if she had asked me to commit a crime, I would
have obeyed her.

"At six o'clock in the morning I left her, and before
going I said to her:

"'Until this evening?'

"She embraced me still more strongly, but she did
not reply.

"In the course of the day I received a letter which
contained these words:

"'My dear boy, I am somewhat unwell, and the
doctor orders me quiet.   I am going to bed early this
evening and shall not see you.   But, to recompense you,
I shall expect you to-morrow at noon.   I love you.'

" My first words were : 'She is deceiving me !'

"A cold sweat broke out on my forehead, for already I loved this woman too much not to be overwhelmed by this suspicion.

"And yet I must expect this occurrence almost daily with Marguerite, and it had often happened to me with my other mistresses without my concerning myself much about it. Whence, then, came the empire which this woman assumed over my life?

"Then I reflected, since I had the key of her apartment, that I could go to see her as usual. In this way I should quickly know the truth, and, if I found a man there, I would slap his face.

"Meanwhile, I went to the Champs-Élysées. I remained there four hours. She did not appear. In the evening I went to all the theatres in which she was accustomed to appear. She was in none of them.

"At eleven o'clock I went to the Rue d'Antin.

"There was no light in Marguerite's windows. Nevertheless I rang. The porter asked me whom I wished to see.

" ' Mademoiselle Gautier,' I said to him.

" 'She has not returned.'

" 'I will go up and wait for her.'

" 'There is no one in her apartment.'

"There was evidently here an arrangement, which I could disregard since I had the key; but I feared to make a ridiculous scene, and I went out.

" But I did not return home, I could not leave the
street and did not lose sight of Marguerite's house.   It
seemed to me that I had still something to learn, or, at
least, that my suspicions were about to be confirmed.

" Near midnight a coupé which I knew very well
stopped near No. 9.

" The Comte de G—— descended from it and entered
the house, after having dismissed his carriage.

" For a moment I hoped that, like myself, he would
be told that Marguerite was not at home and that I
should see him come out ; but at four o'clock in the
morning I was still waiting for him.

" I have suffered a great deal for the last three weeks,
but it is as nothing, I think, in comparison with what I
suffered that night.

XIV

"When I returned home I took to weeping like a child. There is no man who has not been deceived at least once, and who does not know what it is to suffer.

"I said to myself, under the influence of those feverish resolutions which we always think ourselves strong enough to keep, that I must absolutely break off with this love, and I waited impatiently for the daylight that I might secure my place in the diligence and return to my father and my sister, in whose double love, which would never deceive me, I could confide.

"However, I did not wish to depart without Marguerite's knowing well why I went. Only a man who decidedly no longer loves his mistress can leave her without writing to her.

"I wrote and rewrote twenty letters in my head.

"I had to do with a woman who was just like all the other kept women, I had idealized her much, too much, she had treated me like a school-boy, by making use, to deceive me, of a trick of an insulting simplicity, that was clear. My self-love took the upper hand. It was necessary to leave this woman without giving her the satisfaction of knowing what this rupture made me suffer, and this is what I wrote to her in my most elegant hand-writing, and with tears of rage and pain in my eyes :

"'My Dear Marguerite: I hope that your indis-position of yesterday was but slight. I went to inquire after you at eleven o'clock last night, and was informed that you had not returned. Monsieur de G—— was more fortunate than I, for he presented himself a few minutes later, and at four o'clock this morning he was still in your house.

"'Forgive me the few wearisome hours that I have caused you to pass, and be assured that I shall never forget the happy moments which I owe to you.

"'I should certainly go to-day to inquire after your health, but I intend returning to my father.

"'Adieu, my dear Marguerite; I am neither rich enough to love you as I should like, nor poor enough to love you as you would like. Let us forget, then, you, a name which must be almost indifferent to you, and I, a happiness which becomes impossible to me.

"'I send you back your key, of which I have never availed myself, and which may be of use to you, if you are often ill as you were yesterday.'

"As you see, I had not the strength to finish this letter without an impertinent irony, which proved how much I was in love.

"I read and reread this letter ten times, and the idea that it would cause Marguerite pain quieted me a little. I endeavored to harden myself in the sentiments which it affected, and when, at eight o'clock, my servant entered, I gave it to him to be delivered immediately.

"'Shall I wait for an answer?' asked Joseph (my servant was named Joseph, like all other servants).

"'If you are asked if there is an answer, you will say that you do not know, and you will wait.'

"I clung to this hope that she would reply to me.

"Poor and feeble things that we are!

"All the time that my servant was gone, I was a prey to an extreme agitation. At times, when I recalled how Marguerite had given herself to me, I asked myself by what right I had written her an impertinent letter, when she could reply to me that it was not Monsieur de G—— who deceived me, but I who deceived Monsieur de G——; a line of reasoning which permits many women to have several lovers. At times, when I recalled this girl's promises, I wished to convince myself that this letter was still too mild, and that there were no expressions strong enough to brand a woman who amused herself at the expense of a love as sincere as mine. Then I said to myself that I would have done better not to have written to her, but to have gone to see her in the course of the day, and that, by this means, I might have derived pleasure from the tears which I should have caused her to shed.

"Finally I asked myself what she would reply, already ready to accept the excuses which she would give me.

"Joseph returned.

"'Well?' I said to him

"'Monsieur,' he replied, 'Madame was in bed and was still asleep; but as soon as she rings, the letter will be given her, and, if there is any answer, they will bring it.'

"She was sleeping!

"Twenty times I was on the point of sending for the letter again, but I always thought:

"'They have perhaps already given it to her, and I should appear to have repented.'

"The nearer the hour approached at which it was probable that she would reply, the more I regretted having written.

"Ten o'clock, eleven o'clock, noon sounded.

"At midday I was on the point of going to the rendezvous, as if nothing had happened. In short, I could not conceive of any way of issuing from the circle of iron which was compressing me.

"Then I thought, with that superstition of people who are expecting, that if I should go out for a little while, I would find when I returned that an answer had arrived. The replies impatiently awaited always arrive when you are not at home.

"I went out under the pretext of going to déjeuner.

"Instead of breakfasting in the Café Foy, on the corner of the boulevard, as I was in the habit of doing, I preferred to go and take déjeuner at the Palais-Royal and pass by the Rue d'Antin. Every time that I saw a woman approaching in the distance, I thought it was Nanine bringing me a reply. I passed through the Rue d'Antin without having even met a street porter. I arrived at the Palais-Royal, I went in Véry's. The waiter made me eat, or, rather, he brought me whatever he wished, for I did not eat.

"In spite of myself, my eyes were constantly fixed on the clock.

"I returned home, convinced that I should find a letter from Marguerite.

"The porter had received nothing. I still had a hope in my servant. He had seen no one since I went out.

"If Marguerite had been going to reply to me, she would have answered long before this.

"Then, I took to regretting the terms of my letter; I should have kept complete silence, which would, doubtless, have caused some proceeding on her part brought about by her anxiety; for, not seeing me come to the rendezvous given the day before, she would have asked of me the reasons for my absence, and then only I should have given them to her. In this manner she could not have done otherwise than vindicate herself, and that which I wished was that she should vindicate herself. I felt already that, whatever reasons she might have offered me, I would have believed them, and that I would have liked anything better than not seeing her again.

"I even came to believe that she would come herself to see me; but the hours passed by and she did not come.

"Decidedly, Marguerite was not like other women, for there are very few who, on receipt of a letter like that which I had written, would not have made some reply.

"At five o'clock I hastened to the Champs-Élysées.

"'If I meet her,' I thought, 'I will affect an indifferent air, and she will be convinced that I no longer think of her.'

"At the corner of the Rue Royal I saw her passing in her carriage; the meeting was so sudden that I turned pale. I do not know if she perceived my emotion; for my part, I was so troubled that I only saw her carriage.

"I did not continue my promenade in the Champs-Élysées. I looked at the theatre posters, for I still had a chance of seeing her.

"There was to be a first representation at the Palais-Royal. Marguerite would certainly be present.

"I was in the theatre at seven o'clock.

"All the boxes filled up, but Marguerite did not appear.

"Then I left the Palais-Royal, and I went into every theatre which she was in the habit of frequenting, into the Vaudeville, the Variétés, the Opéra-Comique.

"She was not to be found anywhere.

"Either, my letter had given her too much pain for her to care for the theatre, or, she feared to meet me and wished to avoid an explanation.

"This is what my vanity was whispering to me on the boulevard, when I met Gaston, who asked me whence I came.

"'From the Palais-Royal.'

"'And I from the Opera,' he said to me; 'I thought I should see you there.'

"'Why?'

"'Because Marguerite was there.'

"'Ah! she was there?'

"'Yes.'

"'Alone?'

"'No, with one of her female friends.'

"'And that was all?'

"'The Comte de G—— came into her box a moment; but she went away with the duke. I thought every moment that I should see you appear. There was a seat beside me which remained empty all the evening, and I was certain that it had been taken by you.'

"'But why should I go wherever Marguerite does?'

"'Because you are her lover, *pardieu !*'

"'And who told you that?'

" 'Prudence, whom I met yesterday. I congratulate you, my dear fellow; she is a charming mistress, not to be had by any one who wishes her. Keep her, she will do you honor.'

"This simple observation of Gaston showed me the absurdity of my sensitiveness.

"If I had met him the night before and if he had spoken thus to me, I certainly would not have written that idiotic letter of the morning.

"I was for a moment on the point of going to Prudence's house and sending word to Marguerite that I wished to speak to her; but I feared that, to avenge herself, she would reply that she could not receive me, and I returned home, after having passed through the Rue d'Antin.

"I asked of my porter again if he had any letter for me.

"Nothing !

" 'She has wished to see if I would make some new demonstration and if I would retract my letter to-day,' I said to myself as I went to bed; 'but when she sees that I do not write to her, she will write to me to-morrow.'

"That evening above all I repented of what I had done. I was alone, in my own house, unable to sleep, devoured with anxiety and jealousy, when, simply by allowing things to take their natural course, I might have been by Marguerite's side and hearing again

charming words which I had only heard twice, and
which burned in my ears in my solitude.

"That which was most frightful in my situation was
that reason convinced me of my being in the wrong; in
fact, everything said to me that Marguerite loved me.
In the first place, this project of passing a summer alone
with me in the country; then this certainty that nothing
compelled her to be my mistress, since my fortune was
insufficient for her needs, and even for her caprices.
She had evidently been actuated only by the hope of
finding in me a sincere affection, one in which she
might repose from the mercenary loves in the midst of
which she lived, and on the second day only I had destroyed this hope, and I had repaid in impertinent irony
the love accepted during two nights. That which I had
done, then, was more than ridiculous, it was indecent.
Had I only paid this woman I might have had the right
to blame her life, and did I not seem, in withdrawing
on the second day, like a parasite of love who was afraid
that he would be presented with the bill for his dinner?
What! I had known Marguerite for thirty-six hours, I
had been her lover for twenty-four, and already I was
assuming airs of sensitiveness; and, instead of consider-
ing myself too happy that she was willing to share with
me, I wished to have all to myself and to constrain her
to break at one stroke with all the relations of her past
which were the revenues of her future. What had I to
reproach her with? Nothing. She had written me that

she was unwell, when she might have told me quite
brutally, with the hideous frankness of certain women,
that she had to receive a lover; and, instead of believing in her letter, instead of going to walk in all the
streets of Paris except the Rue d'Antin; instead of passing the evening with my friends and presenting myself
on the next day at the hour she indicated, I had played
the Othello, I had spied on her, and I had thought to
punish her by seeing her no more. But, on the contrary,
she must have been delighted at this separation; but she
must have found me supremely idiotic, and her silence
was not even rancor; it was contempt.

"I should then have made to Marguerite some gift
which would leave her in no doubt as to my generos-
ity, and which would have permitted me, in treating her
simply like a kept woman, to consider myself at quits
with her; but I would have considered the slightest appearance of trafficking as an offence, if not to the love
she had for me, at least to the love which I had for her,
and, since this love was so pure that it admitted of no
sharing with another, it could not repay by any gift, no
matter how costly, the happiness which had been given
it, however brief that happiness might have been.

"This is what I repeated to myself that night, and what
I was ready to go and say at any moment to Marguerite.

"When the day broke, I had not yet fallen asleep, I
was in a fever; it was impossible for me to think of
anything but Marguerite.

"As you will readily understand, it was necessary to take some decisive step and come to some conclusion either with the woman or with my scruples, if, however, she would still consent to receive me.

"But, as you know, a decisive step is always postponed; therefore, not being able to remain in my own rooms, not daring to present myself in Marguerite's, I undertook a method of approaching her, a method which my self-respect would permit me to set down to chance, in case it succeeded.

"It was nine o'clock; I hastened to Prudence, who asked me to what she owed this matinal visit.

"I did not dare to say to her frankly what had brought me. I told her that I had come out early to secure a place in the diligence to G——, where my father lived.

"'You are very fortunate,' she said to me, 'to be able to leave Paris in this fine weather.'

"I looked at her, asking myself if she were laughing at me.

"But her countenance was serious.

"'Are you going to say good-bye to Marguerite?' she continued, still seriously.

"'No.'

"'You are right.'

"'You think so?'

"'Naturally. Since you have broken with her, what use to see her again?'

" ' You know, then, of our rupture ? '

" ' She showed me your letter.'

" ' And what did she say to you ? '

" ' She said to me : " My dear Prudence, your pro-
tégé is not civil ; you think such letters as that, but you
do not write them ! " ' '

" ' And in what manner did she say that to you ? '

" ' Laughingly, and she added :

" ' " He has supped twice in my house, and he does
not even pay his digestion call." '

" This was all the effect that my letter and my jeal-
ousies had produced ! I was cruelly humiliated in the
vanity of my love.

" ' And what did she do yesterday evening ? '

" ' She went to the Opera.'

" ' I knew it.   And afterwards ? '

" ' She had supper in her own apartments.'

" ' Alone.'

" ' With the Comte de G——, I believe.'

" Thus my rupture had produced no change in Marguerite's habits.

" It is under such circumstances as these that certain
people say to you :

" ' It is not necessary to think longer of that woman,
she does not love you.'

" ' Well, I am pleased to see that Marguerite is not
breaking her heart for me,' I replied, with a forced
smile.

" 'And she is very right. You have done that which you should do, you have been more reasonable than she, for that girl loved you, she did nothing but talk about you and would have been quite capable of committing some folly.'

" ' Why did she not reply to me, since she loves me ?'

" ' Because she comprehended that she was doing wrong in loving you. Then, women permit their love to be deceived sometimes, but never their self-love to be wounded, and it is always wounding to the self-love of a woman to leave her two days after you have been her lover, whatever reasons you may give for this rupture. I know Marguerite, she will die rather than answer you.'

" ' What must I do, then ?'

" 'Nothing. She will forget you, you will forget her, and you will have nothing with which to reproach each other.'

" 'But if I should write to her to ask her forgiveness?'

" 'Be careful to do nothing of the kind, she would forgive you.'

" I was on the point of falling on Prudence's neck.

" A quarter of an hour later, I had returned to my room, and I wrote to Marguerite :

" 'Some one who repents of a letter which he wrote yesterday, who will go away to-morrow if you do not forgive him, would wish to know at what hour he can lay his repentance at your feet.

" 'When will he find you alone ? for, as you know, confessions should be made without witnesses.'

"I folded up this species of prose madrigal, and I sent it by Joseph, who gave the letter to Marguerite herself, and she told him that she would reply later.

"I did not go out but for a moment for dinner, and at eleven o'clock in the evening I still had no reply.

"I resolved then to suffer no longer and to depart in the morning.

"In consequence of this resolution, convinced that I could not sleep if I went to bed, I commenced to pack my trunks.

XV

"It was nearly an hour later, when Joseph and I were preparing everything for my departure, that my door-bell was violently rung.

"'Shall I open the door?' asked Joseph.

"'Open it,' I said, asking myself who could come at such an hour to see me, and not daring to believe that it was Marguerite.

"'Monsieur,' said Joseph to me returning, 'it is two ladies.'

"'It is us, Armand,' cried a voice which I recognized as that of Prudence.

"I issued from my chamber.

"Prudence, standing, was looking at the few curiosities in my salon; Marguerite, seated on the sofa, was reflecting.

"When I entered, I went straight to her, I knelt before her, I took her two hands, and, in great emotion, I said to her: 'Forgive me.'

"She kissed me on the forehead and said to me:

"'This makes the third time that I have forgiven you.'

" ' I was going to depart to-morrow.'

" 'Why should my visit alter your resolution? I do not come to prevent you leaving Paris. I come because I did not have during the day time to answer you, and because I did not wish to allow you to believe that I was irritated against you. Moreover, Prudence did not wish that I should come; she said that I would perhaps disturb you.'

" 'You disturb me, you, Marguerite! and how?'

" 'Goodness! you might have had a woman with you,' replied Prudence, 'and it would not have been amusing for her to see arrive two more.'

" While Prudence was making this observation, Marguerite looked at me attentively.

" 'My dear Prudence,' I replied, 'you do not know what you are saying.'

" 'It is very nice, your apartment,' she answered; 'can we see the bed-chamber?'

" 'Yes.'

" Prudence entered my chamber, less for the purpose of seeing it than to make amends for the foolish speech she had uttered, and to leave us alone, Marguerite and I.

" 'Why did you bring Prudence?' I then said to her.

" 'Because she was with me at the theatre, and because, on leaving here, I wished to have some one to accompany me.'

" 'Am I not here?'

"'Yes; but in addition to my not wishing to disturb you, I was very sure that, in coming as far as my door, you would ask to ascend to my apartment, and, as I could not permit you to do so, I did not wish that you should go away with the right to reproach me for a refusal.'

"'And why could you not receive me?'

"'Because I am very strictly watched, and the least suspicion might do me the greatest injury.'

"'Is that indeed the only reason?'

"'If there were another, I would tell it to you; we are not to have any more secrets from each other.'

"'Come now, Marguerite, I do not wish to take several roads to arrive at that which I wish to say to you. Frankly, do you love me a little?'

"'A great deal.'

"'Then, why did you deceive me?'

"'My friend, if I were Madame la Duchesse So-and-So, if I had two hundred thousand livres of income, if I were your mistress, and if I had another lover than you, you would have the right to ask me why I deceived you; but I am Mademoiselle Marguerite Gautier, I have forty thousand francs of debts, not one sou of fortune, and I spend a hundred thousand francs a year; your question becomes an idle one, and my reply useless.'

"'That is just,' I said, letting my head fall on Marguerite's knees; 'but I, I love you like a fool.'

" 'Well, my friend, it would be advisable to love me
a little less, or to comprehend me a little better.   Your
letter gave me much pain.   If I had been free, in the
first place, I would not have received the count night
before last, or, having received him, I would have come
to ask of you the pardon which you have just asked of
me, and I would have in the future no other lover but
you.   I thought for a moment that I could give myself
that happiness for six months; you were not willing;
you insisted upon knowing the means, well! Mon Dieu!
the means were easy enough to guess.   It was a sacrifice
much greater than you believe that I made in employing
them.   I could have said to you: "I need twenty thousand francs;" you were in love with me, you would
have found them, at the risk of reproaching me with it
later.   I preferred to owe nothing to you; you did not
comprehend this delicacy, for it was one.   We women,
when we have still a little heart left, we give to words
and things an extension and a development unknown
to other women; I repeat it to you, then, that on the
part of Marguerite Gautier, the method which she found
to pay her debts without asking of you the necessary
money was a delicacy by which you should have profited
without saying anything.   If you had known me only
to-day, you would be very happy at what I should promise
you, and you would not ask me what I had done day
before yesterday.   We are sometimes forced to purchase
a satisfaction for our souls at the expense of our bodies,

and we suffer still more when, after all, this satisfaction escapes us.'

"I listened and I looked at Marguerite with admiration. When I reflected that this marvellous creature, whose feet I had formerly so desired to kiss, consented that I should enter for something into her thoughts, that I should have a part in her life, and that I was not yet contented with that which she gave me, I asked myself if man's desire had any limits, when, satisfied as promptly as mine had been, it still extended to other things.

"'It is true,' she went on; 'we creatures of chance, we entertain fantastic desires and inconceivable loves. We give ourselves, sometimes for one thing, sometimes for another. There are men who ruin themselves without obtaining anything from us, there are others who have us with a bouquet. Our hearts have caprices; it is their sole distraction and their sole excuse. I have given myself to you more quickly than to any other man, I swear it; why? because, seeing me spit blood, you took my hand, because you wept, because you are the only human creature who was willing to pity me. I am going to say a foolish thing, but I used to have a little dog that looked at me sorrowfully when I coughed; it was the only creature that I have loved.

"'When it died, I wept more than I did at the death of my mother. It is true that she had beaten me during twelve years of her life. Well, I loved you immediately as much as my dog. If men but knew what they could obtain with a tear, they would be more loved and we should be less ruinous.

"'Your letter contradicted you, it revealed to me that you had not all the intelligence of the heart, it injured you more in the love which I had for you than anything else that you could have done. It was jealousy, it is true, but ironical and impertinent jealousy. I was already very sad when I received that letter, I counted on seeing you at noon, taking breakfast with you, effacing—in short—by the sight of you an importunate thought which troubled me, and which, before I knew you, I admitted without effort.

"'Then,' continued Marguerite, 'you were the only person before whom I had thought that I had recognized immediately that I could think and speak freely. All those who surround women like myself have an interest in scrutinizing their slightest words, in drawing a consequence from their most insignificant actions. We naturally have no friends. We have egotistical lovers who expend their fortunes not for us, as they say, but for their vanity.

"'For these, we are obliged to be gay when they are joyous, very interesting when they wish to sup, sceptical, as they are. We are forbidden to have any heart under penalty of being derided, and of ruining our credit.

"'We do not belong to ourselves. We are no longer beings, but things. We are the first in their self-love, the last in their esteem. We have female friends, but they are friends like Prudence, women formerly kept who have still the extravagant tastes which their age no longer permits them to gratify. Then they become our friends, or, rather, our messmates. Their friendship goes as far as servitude, never as far as disinterestedness. Never do they give us any but counsel that is profitable for themselves. Little it matters to them that we have ten lovers the more, provided that they gain thereby gowns or a bracelet, and that they can from time to time procure a ride in our carriages and go to our boxes in the theatres. They receive our bouquets of the night before, and borrow our cashmeres. They never render us a service, no matter how slight, without getting paid for it the double of what it is worth. You saw yourself, on the evening on which Prudence brought me the six thousand francs which I had asked her to go and request for me from the duke, she borrowed from me five hundred francs which she will never return me, or which she will pay back in bonnets that will never be taken out of their band-boxes.

"'We can then have, or at least I could then have, only one happiness, that is, sorrowful as I am often, ill as I am always, to find a man sufficiently superior not to demand of me an account of my life, and to be the lover of my impressions much more than of my body. This man I had found in the duke; but the duke is old,

and age neither protects nor consoles. I had thought
myself able to accept the life which he offered me; but,
what would you expect? I was perishing of ennui, and,
when it comes to being consumed, you might as well
throw yourself into a conflagration as asphyxiate yourself with charcoal.

"'Then I met you, you, young, ardent, happy, and
I endeavored to make of you the man whom I had
longed for in the midst of my boisterous solitude. That
which I loved in you, it was not the man who was, but
he who was going to be. You do not accept this role,
you reject it as unworthy of you, you are a commonplace
lover; do as the others, pay me and we will speak of it
no more.'

"Marguerite, whom this long confession had fatigued,
threw herself backward in the sofa, and to repress a
slight attack of coughing, carried her handkerchief to
her lips and even to her eyes.

"'Forgive me, forgive me,' I murmured, 'I had comprehended all that, but I wished to hear you say it,
my adored Marguerite. Let us forget the rest and
remember only one thing,—that is, that we belong to
each other, that we are young and that we love each
other.

"'Marguerite, make of me whatever you wish, I am
your slave, your dog; but, in the name of Heaven, tear
up the letter which I wrote you and do not allow me to
go away to-morrow; I shall die if I do.'

" Marguerite drew my letter from the corsage of her dress and, handing it to me, said with a smile of ineffable softness:

" 'There it is, I brought it back to you.'

" I tore up the letter, and I kissed with tears the hand that restored it to me.

" At that moment Prudence reappeared.

" ' What do you say, Prudence, do you know what he asks of me?' said Marguerite.

" ' He asks your forgiveness.'

" ' Exactly so.'

" 'And you forgive him?'

" 'I have to ; but he wishes something more.'

" 'What is it?'

" ' He wishes to take supper with us.'

" 'And you consent?'

" ' What do you think about it ?''

" 'I think that you are both two children, who neither of you have any head. But I think also that I am very hungry, and that the sooner you consent, the sooner we will sup.'

" ' Come,' said Marguerite, ' we will go, all three, in my carriage. Now,' she added, turning toward me, ' Nanine will have gone to bed, you will open the door, take my key, and try not to lose it again.'

" I embraced Marguerite as though I would suffocate her.

" Thereupon Joseph entered.

"'Monsieur,' he said to me with the air of a man delighted with himself, 'the trunks are all packed.'

"'Entirely?'

"'Yes, monsieur.'

"'Well, unpack them; I am not going.'

XVI

"I could have recounted the beginning of this liaison to you in a few words," said Armand to me, "but I wished you to see by what events and by what gradations we had arrived at this point, I, to consent to whatever Marguerite desired, Marguerite, to be able to live only with me.

"It was the morning after the evening on which she came for me that I sent her *Manon Lescaut*.

"From this moment, as I could not change the life of my mistress, I changed my own. I wished, above all, not to leave myself the time to reflect on the role which I had accepted, for, despite myself, it affected me very greatly. Thus my habits of life, usually so calm, suddenly assumed the appearance of confusion and disorder. Do not think that, however disinterested it may be, the love which a kept woman has for you does not cost anything. Nothing is so expensive as the thousand caprices of flowers, theatre boxes, suppers, country excursions, which you can never refuse your mistress.

"As I have told you, I had no fortune. My father was, and is still, receiver-general at G—— He enjoys
193

a great reputation for honesty, thanks to which he
found the security which he was obliged to furnish
before he could enter upon the discharge of his func-
tions. This office gives him forty thousand francs a
year, and in the ten years he has held it he had reim-
bursed his bondsman and has been putting aside a sum
for my sister's dot. My father is the most honorable
man that you could meet. My mother, at her death,
had left six thousand francs of income, which he divided
between my sister and myself on the day on which he
obtained the post which he had been soliciting ; then,
when I arrived at the age of twenty-one, he added to
this little income an annual allowance of five thousand francs, assuring me that with eight thousand francs
I could be very comfortable in Paris, if I wished, in
addition to this income, to create a position for myself,
either at the bar or in medicine. I accordingly came to
Paris, I pursued my legal studies, I was admitted to the
bar, and, like a great many other young men, I put my
diploma in my pocket and allowed myself to drift somewhat into the idle life of Paris. My expenses were very
modest ; nevertheless, I expended my year's income in
eight months and I passed the four months of summer
in my father's house, which gave me, in fact, about twelve
thousand livres of income and the reputation of a good
son. For the rest, not a sou of debts.

"This was my condition when I made Marguerite's
acquaintance.

"You will understand that, in spite of myself, my living expenses increased. Marguerite's nature was a very capricious one, and it constituted her one of those women who never consider as a serious outlay the thousand distractions of which their existence is made up. From this it resulted that, wishing to spend as much time with me as possible, she would write me in the morning that she would dine with me, not in her own apartments, but at some restaurant, either in Paris or in the country. I would go for her, we would dine, we would go to the theatre, we would have supper frequently, and I had spent in the course of the evening four or five louis, which made twenty-five hundred or three thousand francs a month, which reduced my year to three months and a half, and placed me under the necessity of either running into debt or of leaving Marguerite.

"Now I was willing to accept everything except this last eventuality.

"Pardon me all these details, but you will see that they were the cause of the events that followed. This which I am relating to you is a true story and a simple one, and in which I leave all the frankness of the details and all the simplicity of the developments.

"I comprehended, then, that, as nothing in the world would have sufficient influence over me to make me forget my mistress, it would be necessary for me to find some means of meeting the expenses which she caused me. Then, this love had so completely changed me that every moment which I passed away from Marguerite seemed to me a year, and that I felt the necessity of consuming these moments in the fire of some passion, and of living through them so quickly that I should not perceive that I was living in them.

"I began by borrowing five or six thousand francs on my little capital, and I took to play, for, since they have destroyed the gambling houses, you can play anywhere. Formerly, when you entered the game at Frascati's, you had a chance of making a fortune,—you played against good money, and, if you lost, you had the consolation of saying to yourself that you might have won; whilst now, excepting in the clubs where there is still a certain severity in requiring payment, you have almost the certainty, whenever you win an important sum, that you will not receive it. You can readily comprehend why.

"Gambling is only followed by young men in great need, and who have not a fortune sufficient for the life which they lead; they take to play, then, and there results from it naturally this—perhaps they win, and then the losers serve to pay for the horses and the mistresses of these messieurs, which is highly disagreeable. Debts are contracted, relations commenced around the green cloth end in quarrels in which honor or life always suffers more or less; and, when you are an honest man, you find yourself ruined by very honest young men who

have no other fault than that of not possessing two
hundred thousand livres of income.

"I do not need to speak of those who cheat at play,
and of whom, some day, you hear of the obligatory
departure and the tardy condemnation.

"I launched myself, then, in this life, rapid, noisy,
volcanic, which formerly terrified me when I thought of
it, and which had become for me the inevitable complement to my love for Marguerite. What could you
expect me to do?

"Those nights which I did not spend in the Rue
d'Antin, if I had spent them in my own rooms, I would
not have slept. Jealousy would have kept me awake,
and would have set my thoughts and my blood on fire;
whilst gambling turned aside for a moment the fever
which would have taken possession of my heart and
transferred it to a passion the absorbing interest of
which seized me, despite myself, until the hour sounded
in which I should repair to my mistress. Then, and it
is in this that I recognized the violence of my love,
whether I were winning or losing, I quitted the table
pitilessly, sorry for those whom I left there, and who
were not, like myself, going to find happiness in quitting it.

"For the greater number, gambling is a necessity;
for myself, it was a remedy.

"Cured of Marguerite, I should have been cured of
play.

"Moreover, in the midst of all this, I maintained a sufficient composure; I lost that only which I could pay, and I won only that which I would have been able to lose.

"For the rest, fortune favored me. I did not make any debts, and I expended three times as much money as when I did not play. It was not easy to resist a mode of life which permitted me to satisfy, without inconveniencing myself, the thousand caprices of Marguerite. As for her, she loved me always quite as much, and even more.

"As I have said to you, I had commenced at first by being received only from midnight to six o'clock in the morning, then I was admitted from time to time into her boxes at the theatre, then she came sometimes to dine with me. One morning I did not go away before eight o'clock, and there came a day on which I did not go away till noon.

"While waiting for the moral metamorphosis, a physical metamorphosis had taken place in Marguerite. I had undertaken her cure, and the poor girl, divining my object, obeyed me in order to prove to me her gratitude. I had succeeded, without disturbances and without effort, in causing her to forsake her former habits. My physician, whom I had consulted concerning her, told me that repose and quiet alone could preserve her health, so that for the late suppers and the sleeplessness I had succeeded in substituting a healthful régime

and regular sleep. In spite of herself Marguerite became accustomed to this novel existence, of which she
experienced the salutary effects. Already she had fallen
into the habit of occasionally spending an evening in
her own apartment, or indeed, if the weather was fine,
she enveloped herself in a cashmere, put a veil over her
head, and we went on foot like two children, to traverse in the evenings the sombre alleys of the Champs-
Élysées. She returned fatigued, took a light supper,
went to bed after a little music, or after having read,
something which she had never done before. Her
cough, which, every time I heard it, gave me a pang,
had almost completely disappeared.

"At the expiration of the six weeks there was no
longer any question of the count, definitely sacrificed;
the duke alone compelled me still to conceal my liaison with Marguerite, and even he had been often sent
away while I was there, under the pretext that madame
was sleeping and had desired not to be awakened.

"It resulted from the habit, and even the necessity,
which Marguerite had fallen into, of seeing me, that I
always left the gaming table just about the time that a
skillful player would have quitted it. When everything
was reckoned up, I found myself in consequence of my
winnings possessed of some ten thousand francs, which
seemed to me an inexhaustible capital.

"The period at which I usually went to rejoin my
father and my sister had arrived, and I did not go; so

that I frequently received letters from both of them, asking me to come to them.

"To all these requests I replied in the best manner I could, always repeating that I was well and that I was not in need of money, two circumstances which, I thought, would console my father a little for the delay in paying my annual visit.

"In the meanwhile, it came to pass that, one morning, Marguerite, having been awakened by a brilliant sunshine, leaped out of bed and asked me if I would take her to spend the day in the country.

"Prudence was sent for, and we set off, all three, after Marguerite had directed Nanine to say to the duke that she had wished to take advantage of the fine weather and that she had gone to the country with Madame Duvernoy.

"In addition to the presence of the Duvernoy being necessary to pacify the old duke, Prudence was one of those women who seem to be made expressly for these excursions to the country. With her unalterable gayety and her eternal appetite, she could not leave a moment of ennui to those whom she accompanied, and she knew perfectly how to order the eggs, the cherries, the milk, the rabbit *sauté*, and everything which comprises, in short, the traditional déjeuner in the environs of Paris.

"It only remained for us to decide where to go.

"It was Prudence again who delivered us from this embarrassment.

" ' Is it to the real country that you want to go?' she asked.

" ' Yes.'

" ' Well, let us go to Bougival, to the Point-du-Jour, to the widow Arnould's.   Armand, go and get a calash.'

" An hour and a half later, we were at the widow Arnould's.

" Perhaps you know this inn, a hotel on week-days, a public-house on Sundays.   From the garden, which is at the height of an ordinary first floor, you discover a magnificent view.   At the left, the aqueduct of Marly closes the horizon ; to the right, the view extends over an infinity of hills; the river, almost without any current in this locality, unrolls itself like a great white watered ribbon, between the plain of the Gabillons and the island of Croissy, forever lulled by the shivering of its tall poplars and the murmur of its willows.

" In the background, in a broad patch of sunlight, rise little white houses with red roofs and factories which, losing in the distance their hard and commercial character, complete the landscape admirably.

" In the extreme distance, Paris in the mists.

" As Prudence had said to us, it was the real country, and, I must say it, it was a real déjeuner.

" It is not through gratitude for the happiness which I owe it that I say all this, but Bougival, notwithstanding its frightful name, is one of the prettiest countries that can be imagined.   I have traveled a great deal,

I have seen greater things, but none more charming than this little village lying smiling at the foot of the hill which protects it.

" Madame Arnould proposed to us to go boating, which Marguerite and Prudence accepted joyfully.

" The country has always been associated with love, and very justly;—nothing so sets off the woman whom you love as the blue sky, the paths, the flowers, the breezes, the resplendent solitude of the fields or the woods. However strongly you may love a woman, whatever confidence you may have in her, whatever certainty in the future may be given you by her past, you are always more or less jealous. If you have ever been in love, seriously in love, you must have felt that necessity of isolating from the world the being in which you would wish to live entirely. It seems that, however indifferent she may be to her surroundings, the beloved woman loses something of her perfume and her unity by the contact with men and things. I experienced this much more strongly than any other. My love was not an ordinary love ; I was in love as much as an ordinary creature could be, but with Marguerite Gautier, that is to say, that in Paris at every step I might elbow a man who had been the lover of this woman, or who would be to-morrow. Whilst in the country, surrounded by those who had never seen us and who were not concerned with us, in the midst of nature all adorned with her springtime, this annual forgiveness, and far removed from the noise of the town, I could conceal my love and love without shame and without fear.

"The courtesan in her disappeared, little by little. I had by my side a woman, young and beautiful, whom I loved, by whom I was loved, and who was called Marguerite,—the past had no more evil shapes, the future no more clouds. The sunshine lit up my mistress as it would have lighted the chastest fiancée. We walked together in those charming spots which seem to be contrived expressly to recall the verses of Lamartine or to sing the melodies of Scudo. Marguerite wore a white dress; she leaned on my arm, she repeated to me in the evening under the starry sky the words which she had said the night before, and in the distance the world continued its life without soiling with its shadow the smiling picture of our youth and our love.

"Such were the thoughts that were communicated to me by the ardent sun of that day, through the leaves, while, stretched at my length on the grass of the little island on which we had landed, free from all the human ties which had formerly retained it, I allowed my imagination to run wild, and to gather all the hopes that it encountered.

"Add to this that, from the spot where I lay, I could see on the bank a charming little house with two stories, with an iron railing in the shape of a hemicycle; through the railing, in front of the house, a green lawn, smooth as velvet, and behind the building a little wood, full of mysterious retreats, and which would efface each morning under its moss the footpath made the night before.

" Some climbing flowers concealed the flight of steps that led up to the entrance of this uninhabited house and covered the whole of the first story.

" Through contemplating this house steadily I ended by convincing myself that it belonged to me, so completely did it correspond with the plan I had been forming. I saw there Marguerite and myself, in the day-time in the wood which covered the hill, in the evening seated on the lawn, and I asked myself whether terrestrial creatures had ever been as happy as we.

" ' What a pretty house ! ' said Marguerite to me, she having followed the direction of my eyes, and perhaps of my thoughts.

" ' Where ? ' asked Prudence.

" ' Over there.'   And Marguerite indicated with her finger the building.

" ' Oh ! ravishing,' replied Prudence, ' does it please you ? '

" ' Very much.'

" ' Well, ask the duke to lease it for you ; he will do it, I am sure of it. I will take charge of it, I will, if you wish.'

" Marguerite looked at me, as though to ask me what I thought of this advice.

" My dream had suddenly flown away at the sound of Prudence's last words, and had thrown me so brutally

back into the reality that I was still confused from the
fall.

"'In fact, it is an excellent idea,' I stammered, without knowing what I said.

"'Well, I will arrange that,' said Marguerite, clasping
my hand and interpreting my words according to her
desire. 'Let us go immediately and see if it is to let.'

"The house was vacant and to let for two thousand
francs.

"'Will you be happy here?' she said to me.

"'Am I certain of coming here?'

"'And for whom, then, would I come to bury myself
here, if it were not for you?'

"'Well, then, Marguerite, let me hire this house
myself.'

"'Are you crazy? not only would that be useless, but
it would be dangerous; you know very well that I have
no right to accept anything but from one man; let things
be, then, you great child, and say nothing.'

"'That being done, when I have two days free, I will
come and spend them with you,' said Prudence.

"We left the house and took the road back to Paris,
discussing the new resolution. I clasped Marguerite in
my arms, so closely that when we descended from the
carriage I was already beginning to contemplate my mistress's combination with a less scrupulous mind.

XVII

"The next morning Marguerite dismissed me at an early hour, telling me that the duke was coming betimes, and promising to write to me as soon as he departed, to give me the rendezvous for the evening as usual.

"In fact, in the course of the day, I received this note:

"'I am going to Bougival with the duke; be at Prudence's house this evening at eight o'clock.'

"At the indicated hour Marguerite had returned, and came to rejoin me at Madame Duvernoy's.

"'Well, everything is arranged,' she said on entering.

"'The house is taken?' asked Prudence.

"'Yes; he consented immediately.'

"I did not know the duke, but I was ashamed to deceive him as I was doing.

"'But that is not all!' resumed Marguerite.

"'What else is there?'

"'I was anxious about a lodging-place for Armand.'

"'In the same house?' asked Prudence, laughing.

"'No, but at the Point-du-Jour, where we break-fasted, the duke and I. While he was looking at the

view, I asked Madame Arnould—for her name is
Madame Arnould, is it not?—I asked her if she had a
comfortable apartment. She has one exactly, with a
salon, antechamber, and bed-chamber. It is everything that is necessary, I think. Sixty francs a month.
Everything furnished in a style that would divert a
hypochondriac. I took the apartment. Did I do well?'

"I fell on Marguerite's neck.

"'That will be charming,' she continued, 'you
shall have a key to the little gate, and I have promised
the duke a key to the main gate which he will not take,
since he will only come in the day-time, when he does
come. I think, between ourselves, that he is delighted
with this caprice which will get me out of Paris for some
time, and silence his family a little. Nevertheless, he
asked me how it was that I, so fond of Paris, could
bring myself to burying myself thus in this country
place ; I answered him that I was unwell and that it was
in order to obtain some repose. He appeared to believe
me only with difficulty. That poor old man is always
suspicious. We will therefore take a great many pre-
cautions, my dear Armand ; for he will have me watched,
down there, and it is not enough that he rents a house
for me, he must also pay my debts, and unfortunately I
have a few. Will all that suit you?'

"'Yes,' I replied, endeavoring to suppress the scruples which this manner of living awoke in me from time
to time.

Chapter XVI

————

" *Marguerite wore a white dress; she leaned on my arm, she repeated to me in the evening under the starry sky the words which she had said the night before, and in the distance the world continued its life without soiling with its shadow the smiling picture of our youth and our love.*"

" 'We went all over the house, we shall be exceedingly comfortable in it. The duke was concerned about everything. Ah! my dear,' she added impulsively, embracing me, 'you are not unlucky, it is a millionaire who makes your bed for you.'

" 'And when will you move in?' asked Prudence.

" 'As soon as possible.'

" 'Will you take your carriage and horses?'

" 'I will take my whole establishment. You will have charge of my apartment during my absence.'

" A week later Marguerite had taken possession of the country house, and I was installed at the Point-du-Jour.

" 'Then began an existence which I should have great difficulty in describing to you.

" In the commencement of her sojourn at Bougival Marguerite was unable to break off all at once with her usual habits, and, as the house was always open to them, all her female friends came to see her; for the space of a month there was not a day on which she did not have eight or ten guests at her table. On her side, Prudence brought all the people whom she knew, and did the honors of the house for them, quite as if this house belonged to her

" The duke's money paid for all that, as you may well believe, and nevertheless it happened at times that Prudence came to ask of me a thousand-franc note, ostensibly in Marguerite's name. You know that I had won some money at play; I therefore hastened to give to Prudence what Marguerite had asked of me through her, and in the fear that she might be in need of more than I had, I borrowed in Paris a sum equal to that which I had formerly borrowed, and which I had scrupulously returned.

"I thus found myself again possessed of some ten thousand francs, without counting my allowance.

"However, the pleasure which Marguerite experienced in receiving her friends diminished somewhat before the expense which this pleasure led to, and above all before the necessity in which she found herself sometimes of asking me for money. The duke, who had taken this house so that Marguerite might have some quiet in it, no longer appeared, fearing always to meet there some joyful and numerous company by whom he did not care to be seen. This he felt all the more strongly because, coming one day to dine tête-à-tête with Marguerite, he fell into the midst of a déjeuner of fifteen persons who had not yet finished breakfasting at the hour at which he expected to sit down to dinner. When, doubting nothing, he had opened the door of the dining-room, a general shout of laughter welcomed his entrance and he had been obliged to retire hastily before the impertinent gayety of the young women there assembled.

"Marguerite rose from the table, sought the duke in the adjoining room and endeavored to make him overlook this incident, but the old man, wounded in his self-respect, had resented the affront,—he stated, cruelly

enough, to the poor girl that he was weary of supporting the follies of a woman who did not know how even
to make herself respected in her own house, and he
departed, highly incensed.

"From that day nothing more had been heard from
him. Marguerite had been quite promptly obliged to
dismiss her guests, to change her habits, the duke sending her no word. What I had gained was, that my
mistress belonged to me more completely, and that my
dream was finally realized. Marguerite could no longer
do without me. Without disturbing herself as to the
results, she proclaimed our liaison openly, and I had
come to that point that I lived in her house. The servants called me monsieur, and considered me as officially
their master.

"Prudence had indeed delivered to Marguerite a
comprehensive lecture on the subject of this new mode
of life ; but the latter replied to her that she loved
me, that she could not live without me, and that, come
what might, she would not renounce the happiness of
having me always at her side, adding that all those who
were not pleased with this arrangement were at full
liberty not to return.

"This is what I heard one day when Prudence had
said to Marguerite that she had something very important to communicate to her, and when I listened at the
door of the chamber in which they had shut themselves up.

"A short time afterwards, Prudence returned.

"I was in the back of the garden when she entered; she did not see me. I suspected, from the manner in which Marguerite went to meet her, that a conversation similar to that which I had already overheard would take place between them, and I wished to hear this also.

"The two women shut themselves up in a boudoir, and I stationed myself where I could hear.

" 'Well?' asked Marguerite.

" 'Well! I have seen the duke.'

" 'What did he say to you?'

" 'That he would forgive you freely the first scene, but that he has since learned that you are living publicly with M. Armand Duval, and that that he will not forgive. Let Marguerite leave this young man, he said to me, and I will give her all that she wishes, as formerly, but if not, she must not expect to ask me for anything whatever.'

" 'You replied to him?'

" 'That I would communicate to you his decision, and I promised him to make you hear reason. Reflect, my dear child, on the position which you are losing and which Armand can never give you back. He loves you with all his soul, but he has not a sufficient fortune to provide for all your needs, and he will certainly be obliged some day to leave you, when it will be too late and when the duke will no longer do anything for you. Do you wish that I should speak to Armand?'

"Marguerite appeared to reflect, for she did not reply. My heart beat violently while I waited for her response.

"'No,' she answered, 'I will not leave Armand, and I will not hide myself to live with him. It is perhaps folly, but I love him! what would you have? And then, moreover, he has fallen into the habit of loving me without any obstacle; he would suffer too much to be obliged to leave me, were it only for an hour every day. Moreover, I have not so much time to live as to make myself unhappy and do the will of an old man, the sight alone of whom makes me old. Let him keep his money; I will do without it.'

"'But how will you manage?'

"'I don't know.'

"Prudence doubtless was about to make some reply, but I suddenly burst into the room and hastened to throw myself at Marguerite's feet, covering her hands with the tears which the joy of being thus loved caused me to shed.

"'My life is all yours, Marguerite, you have no more need of that man, am I not here? shall I ever abandon you, and could I pay enough for the happiness which you give me? No more constraints, my Marguerite, we love each other, what does the rest matter to us?'

"'Oh! yes, I love you, my Armand!' she murmured, twining her two arms around my neck, 'I love you as I never thought I could love. We shall be happy, we will live together peacefully, and I will bid an eternal adieu to that life at which I now blush. Never will you reproach me with the past, will you?'

"The tears stifled my voice. I could only reply by pressing Marguerite against my heart.

"'There now,' she said, turning towards Prudence and in a voice of emotion, 'you will carry this scene to the duke, and you will add that we have no more need of him.'

"From that day, there was no more question of the duke. Marguerite was no longer the girl whom I had known. She avoided everything which could recall to me the life in the midst of which I had found her. Never did wife, never did sister, have for her husband or her brother the love and the care which she had for me. This sickly, delicate nature was sensitive to all impressions, accessible to all sentiments. She had broken with her former friends as with her old habits, with her manner of speech as with her former expenditures. When we were seen issuing from the house to go on the river in a charming little boat which I had bought, no one would have thought that this woman in a white dress and a broad straw hat, carrying on her arm the simple silk pelisse which was to protect her against the freshness of the air on the water, was that Marguerite Gautier who, four months previously, had been notorious for her luxury and her scandals.

"Alas! we hastened to be happy, as if we had felt that we should not be so long.

"For the last two months we had not even been to Paris. No one had come to see us except Prudence and that Julie Duprat of whom I have spoken to you, and to whom Marguerite was to give later the touching recital which I have here.

"I passed entire days at the feet of my mistress. We opened the windows which looked out on the garden, and, contemplating the summer descend joyfully on the flowers which it caused to open, and, under the shadow of the trees, we inspired, side by side, that true life which neither Marguerite nor I had comprehended up to this time.

"The least things served to give this young woman childish delights and astonishments. There were days in which she ran around the garden like a little girl of ten, chasing a butterfly or a dragon-fly. This courtesan, who had expended in bouquets more money than would be required to keep an entire family living in comfort, sat on the lawn sometimes for an hour examining the simple flower whose name she bore.

"It was at this time that she read so often *Manon Lescaut*. I have frequently surprised her making annotations in the book, and she always said to me that when a woman loves she cannot do that which Manon did.

"On two or three occasions the duke wrote to her. She recognized his handwriting, and handed the letters to me without reading them.

"Sometimes the expressions in these letters brought the tears into my eyes.

"He had thought, when he closed his purse to Marguerite, that he would bring her back to him; but, when he saw the inutility of this measure, he could not contain himself; he wrote her, asking again, as formerly, permission to return, whatever conditions she might impose with this permission.

"I read, then, these pressing and reiterated letters, and I tore them up, without imparting their contents to Marguerite, and without advising her to see the old man again, although a sentiment of pity for the sorrow of the poor man moved me to do so; but I feared that she would see in this advice only the wish, in causing the duke to renew his visits, to have him assume again the expenses of the household; I feared, above all, that she should think me capable of avoiding in any way all the responsibilities of her life in all the consequences to which her love for me might have for her.

"From this it resulted that the duke, receiving no reply, ceased to write, and that Marguerite and I continued to live together without concerning ourselves about the future.

XVIII

"To give you the details of our new life would be difficult. It was made up of a series of childish things, charming for us, but quite insignificant for those to whom I might recount them. You know what it is to love a woman, you know how the days shorten, and in what amorous idleness you allow yourself to be carried on to the morrow. You are not ignorant of that forgetfulness of all things which is born of a strong love, partaken and confiding. Every being which is not the beloved woman seems to be a useless being in creation. You regret having formerly thrown portions of your heart to other women, and you cannot foresee the possibility of ever pressing another hand than that which you now hold between your own. The brain admits neither of labor or memory, nothing, in short, of anything that might distract it from the only thought that is constantly offered it. Every day you discover in your mistress a new charm, an unknown voluptuousness. Existence is no longer anything but the reiterated accomplishment of a continuous desire, the soul is no longer anything but the vestal charged with keeping alive the sacred fire of love.

"Frequently, when the night fell, we went to seat ourselves in the little wood which overlooked the house. There we listened to the cheerful harmonies of the evening, thinking, each of us, of the approaching hour which would leave us until the morrow clasped in each other's arms. At other times we remained in bed the entire day, without allowing even the sun to penetrate into our chamber. The curtains were hermetically closed, and the outside world arrested its course a moment for us. Nanine alone had the right to open our door, but only for the purpose of bringing us our meals; we even took them without rising, and constantly interrupting them with laughter and follies. To this succeeded a slumber of a few moments, for, disappearing in our love, we were like two obstinate divers who return to the surface only to take breath.

"However, I occasionally surprised Marguerite in moments of sadness, and even of tears; I asked her the cause of this sudden grief, and she replied:

"'Our love is not an ordinary love, my dear Armand. You love me as though I had never belonged to any one, and I tremble lest, later, repenting of your love and accounting my past as a crime, you should force me to throw myself again into the existence from the midst of which you took me. Reflect that now that I have tasted of a new life, I should die in resuming the other. Tell me, then, that you will never leave me.'

"'I swear it to you!'

"At this word she looked at me as though to read in my eyes the sincerity of my oath, then she threw herself into my arms, and, hiding her head on my breast, she said to me:

"'Indeed, you do not know how much I love you!'

"One evening, we were leaning on the balcony of the window, we looked at the moon which seemed to issue with difficulty from her couch of clouds, and we listened to the wind agitating noisily the trees, we held each other's hands and for a full quarter of an hour we had not spoken when Marguerite said to me: 'Here is the winter; shall we go away?'

"'And to what place?'

"'To Italy.'

"'You are wearied, then?'

"'I fear the winter, I fear, above all, our return to Paris.'

"'Why?'

"'For a great many reasons.'

"And she resumed suddenly, without giving me any reason for her fears: 'Do you wish to depart? I will sell everything that I have, we will go to live down there, nothing will remain to me of what I was, no one will know who I am. Do you wish it?'

"'Let us go away, if that will give you pleasure, Marguerite; let us go on a journey,' I said to her; 'but where is the necessity of selling the things which you will be glad to find again on your return? I have not a large enough fortune to accept such a sacrifice, but I have enough to enable us to travel in great style for five or six months, if that will amuse you the least in the world.'

"'In fact, no,' she continued, leaving the window and going to seat herself on the sofa in the shadow of the room; 'what would be the use of spending money in that way? I cost you already enough here.'

"'You reproach me with it, Marguerite, that is not generous.'

"'Forgive me, friend,' she said, offering me her hand, 'this stormy weather affects my nerves; I do not say what I mean.'

"And, after having embraced me, she fell into a long reverie.

"On several occasions there were scenes similar to this, and, if I was ignorant of their origin, I none the less discovered in Marguerite a feeling of anxiety concerning the future. She could not doubt of my love, for each day it augmented, and yet I often saw her sad, without her ever explaining to me the occasion of her sadness, otherwise than by a physical cause.

"Fearing that she was growing weary of a too monotonous life I proposed to her to return to Paris; but she always rejected this proposition, and assured me that she could be happy nowhere as she was in the country.

"Prudence came but rarely; but, as in revenge, she wrote letters which I never asked to see, although on every occasion they threw Marguerite into profound meditation.   I could only conjecture.

"One day Marguerite remained in her chamber.   I entered.   She was writing.

"'To whom are you writing?' I asked her.

"'To Prudence ; do you wish that I should read what I have written?'

"I had a horror of everything which might look like suspicion, I therefore replied to Marguerite that I had no need to know what she had written, and yet, I was certain of it, that letter would have informed me of the true cause of her sadness.

"The next day the weather was superb.   Marguerite proposed to me to take the boat and go to visit the Isle of Croissy.   She seemed very gay ; it was five o'clock when we returned.

"'Madame Duvernoy was here,' said Nanine as she saw us enter.

"'Has she gone?' asked Marguerite.

"'Yes, in madame's carriage ; she said that that had been arranged.'

"'Very good,' said Marguerite quickly; 'let us be served.'

"Two days later arrived a letter from Prudence, and, for two weeks, Marguerite appeared to have lost her mysterious melancholies, for which she did not cease to ask my forgiveness since they had disappeared.

"However, the carriage did not come back.

" ' How comes it that Prudence does not send back to you your coupé?' I asked one day.

" ' One of the horses is sick, and there are some repairs to be made to the carriage. It is better that all that should be attended to while we are still here, where we have no need of a carriage, than to wait till we return to Paris.'

" Prudence came to see us a few days later and confirmed to me what Marguerite had said.

" The two women were walking together in the garden, and when I joined them they changed the conversation.

" In the evening, when she went away, Prudence complained of being cold, and asked Marguerite to lend her a cashmere.

" A month passed in this manner, during which Marguerite was more joyful and more loving than she had ever been.

" However, the carriage did not come back, the cashmere had not been returned; all this puzzled me, despite myself, and, as I knew in what drawer Marguerite put Prudence's letters, I profited by a moment during which she was at the back of the garden to hasten to this drawer and to endeavor to open it; but my attempt was in vain, it was double locked.

" Then I searched in these which usually contained the jewels and the diamonds. These opened without resistance, but the cases had all disappeared,—with their contents, be it understood.

"A poignant fear contracted my heart.

"I thought I would require from Marguerite the truth concerning these disappearances, but she certainly would not have admitted it to me.

"'My good Marguerite,' I then said to her, 'I come to ask of you permission to go to Paris. My family do not know where I am, and there must have arrived letters from my father; he is doubtless anxious, and I should answer him.'

"'Go, my friend,' she said to me, 'but be back here early.'

"I set off. I hastened immediately to see Prudence.

"'Come now,' I said to her without any preliminaries, 'answer me frankly, where are Marguerite's horses?''

"'Sold.'

"'The cashmere?'

"'Sold.'

"'The diamonds?'

"'Pawned.'

"'And who sold and pawned them?'

"'I.'

"'Why did you not notify me of it?'

"'Because Marguerite forbade me.'

"'And why did you not ask me for money?'

"'Because she did not wish it.'

"'And to what use has this money been put?'

"'To pay her debts.'

"'She, then, owes a great deal?'

"'Thirty thousand francs still, or nearly so. Ah! my dear, I told you so, you would not believe me; well, now, you are convinced. The upholsterer whom the duke had engaged was shown the door when he presented himself at the duke's house, and the old man wrote him the next day that he would do nothing for Mademoiselle Gautier. This man wanted his money, he was given something on account, which were the few thousand francs which I asked of you; then, certain charitable souls notified him that his debtor, abandoned by the duke, was living with a youth who had no fortune; the other creditors were similarly notified, they demanded their money and made seizures. Marguerite wished to sell everything, but it was too late, and, moreover, I should have opposed it. It was necessary to pay, and, to avoid asking you for money, she sold her horses, her cashmeres, and pawned her jewels. Would you like to see the receipts of the purchasers and the tickets of the Mont-de Piété?'

"And Prudence, opening a drawer, showed me these papers.

"'Ah! you think,' she continued, with that persistence of the woman who has the right to say: 'I told you so!'—'Ah! you think that it is sufficient to love each other and to go to live in the country a pastoral and ethereal life? No, my friend, no. By the side of the ideal life there is the material life, and the most chaste resolutions are attached to the earth by threads which are ridiculous, but of iron, and which are not easily broken. If Marguerite has not deceived you twenty times, it is because she is of an exceptional nature. It is not because I have not advised her to it, for that vexes me, to see the poor girl deprive herself of everything. She would not do so! she replied to me that she loved you and would not deceive you for anything in the world. All this is very pretty, very poetic; but it is not with that money that creditors are paid, and to-day she cannot clear herself with less than thirty thousand francs, I repeat.it.'

"'Very well, I will give her that amount.'

"'You will borrow it?'

"'Good Lord! yes.'

"'You will do a fine thing; you will embroil yourself with your father, fetter your own resources, and thirty thousand francs are not to be found thus between one day and the next. Believe me, my dear Armand, I know the women better than you do; do not commit this folly of which you will repent some day. Be reasonable. I do not tell you to leave Marguerite, but live with her as you did at the commencement of the summer. Let her find the means to get out of her embarrassments. The duke will return to her little by little. The Comte de N——, if she will accept him, as he told me again yesterday, will pay all her debts and will give her four or five thousand francs a month. He has two hundred thousand livres of income. That will

give her a position, while as for you, you will have to
leave her some time ; do not wait till you are ruined, all
the more that this Comte de N—— is an imbecile, and
that nothing will prevent you from being Marguerite's
lover. She will weep a little at the commencement,
but she will end by becoming accustomed to it, and
will thank you one day for what you have done. Just
suppose that Marguerite is married, and deceive the
husband, that is all.

"'I told you all this before; only, at that time, it
was only an advice, and to-day it is almost a necessity.'

" Prudence was cruelly right.

"'This is how it is,' she continued, putting away the
papers which she had just shown me, 'the kept women
always foresee that they will be loved, never that they
will love themselves,—were it not for that they would
put money away, and at thirty they could give themselves the luxury of having a lover for nothing. If I
had only known what I now know, I myself! In short,
say nothing of all this to Marguerite, and bring her back
to Paris. You have lived four or five months with her,
that is very reasonable ; now, close your eyes, that is all
that is asked of you. At the end of a couple of weeks
she will take the Comte de N——, she will practise
economies this winter, and next summer you will begin
again. That is how to do it, my dear !'

" And Prudence appeared to be delighted with her
advice, which I indignantly rejected.

"Not only would my love and my self-respect not permit me to act in this manner, but, moreover, I was quite convinced that, at the point which she had now reached, Marguerite would die rather than admit of this sharing.

"'That is jesting enough,' I said to Prudence ; 'how much is definitely required for Marguerite?'

"'I have told you, thirty thousand francs.'

"'And when will this amount be required?'

"'Before two months.'

"'She shall have it.'

"Prudence shrugged her shoulders.

"'I will send it to her,' I continued ; 'but you will swear to me that you will not tell Marguerite that I sent it to her.'

"'Be easy.'

"'And if she send you anything else to sell or to pawn, let me know.'

"'There is no danger, she has nothing more.'

"Then I went to my own apartment to see if there were any letters from my father.

"There were four.

XIX

"In the first three letters my father expressed his anxiety because of my silence, and asked me the reason of it; in the last, he allowed me to perceive that he had been informed of the change in my mode of life, and announced to me his approaching arrival.

"I have always had a great respect and a sincere affection for my father. I therefore replied to him that a short journey had been the cause of my silence, and I asked him to let me know in advance the day of his arrival, so that I might go to meet him.

"I gave to my servant my address in the country, directing him to bring me the first letter which arrived stamped with the postmark of the city of G——, then I immediately set out for Bougival.

"Marguerite was waiting for me at the garden gate.

"Her looks betrayed her uneasiness. She threw herself on my neck and could not forbear saying to me:

"'Did you see Prudence?'

"'No.'

"'You were a long time in Paris.'

"'I found some letters from my father to which it was necessary to reply.'

"A few minutes later, Nanine entered, all out of breath. Marguerite rose and went to speak to her in a low tone of voice.

"When Nanine had gone out again, Marguerite said to me, seating herself by my side and taking my hand:

"'Why did you deceive me? You went to see Prudence.'

"'Who told you?'

"'Nanine.'

"'And how did she know it?'

"'She followed you.'

"'You told her, then, to follow me.'

"'Yes. I thought there must be some powerful motive to take you to Paris in this manner, you who have not left me before in four months. I feared that some misfortune had happened to you, or perhaps that you were going to see another woman.'

"'You child!'

"'I am reassured now, I know what you have done, but I do not know yet what has been said to you.'

"I showed her my father's letters.

"'That is not what I ask you; what I want to know is, why you went to see Prudence.'

"'To pay her a visit.'

"'You lie, my friend.'

" 'Well, then, I went to ask her if the horse were better, and if she no longer needed your cashmere or your jewels.'

" Marguerite blushed, but she did not reply.

" 'And,' I continued, 'I learned the use to which you had put the horses, the cashmeres, and the diamonds.'

" ' And you are going to quarrel with me ? '

" 'I am going to quarrel with you for not having thought to ask me for that which you needed.'

" 'In a liaison such as ours, if the woman has preserved ever so little of her personal dignity, she should impose upon herself all possible sacrifices rather than ask money of her lover and give a venal side to her love. You love me, I am sure of it, but you do not know how slight is the thread which binds to the heart the love which is entertained for women like me. Who knows? perhaps on some day of vexation or of weariness you might come to see in our liaison a mercenary calculation skillfully arranged ! Prudence is a gossip. What use had I for those horses? I have practised economy by selling them; I can very well do without them, and I shall expend no more money on them ; provided only that you love me, that is all that I ask, and you will love me as well without horses, without cashmeres, and without diamonds.'

" All this was said in a tone so natural that there were tears in my eyes as I listened.

"'But, my good Marguerite,' I replied, pressing lovingly the hands of my mistress, 'you knew well that some day I should learn of this sacrifice, and that, on the day which I learned it, I would not allow it.'

"'Why not?'

"'Because, dear child, I do not comprehend why the affection which you have for me should deprive you even of one jewel. I also, I do not wish that in some moment of vexation or of weariness you should reflect that, if you were living with another man, these moments would not exist, and that you should repent, even for one moment, of living with me. In a few days your horses, your diamonds, and your cashmeres will be returned to you. They are as necessary to you as air and life, and, it is perhaps absurd, but I love you better sumptuous than simple.'

"'Then that is because you no longer love me.'

"'You foolish one!'

"'If you loved me, you would allow me to love you in my own fashion; on the contrary, you persist in seeing in me only a woman to whom this luxury is indispensable, and whom you will always feel yourself constrained to pay. You are ashamed to accept the proofs of my love. In spite of yourself, you think of leaving me some day, and you desire that your delicacy shall be removed from all shadow of suspicion. You are quite right, my friend; but I had hoped for something better.'

"And Marguerite made a movement to rise; I detained her, saying to her:

"'I desire that you should be happy and that you should have nothing to reproach me with, that is all.'

"'And we will separate!'

"'Why, Marguerite? Who can separate us?' I cried.

"'You, who are not willing to permit me to understand your position, and who have the vanity to wish to maintain mine; you, who in preserving for me the luxury in the midst of which I have lived, wish to preserve the moral distance which separates us; you, in short, who do not believe that my affection is sufficiently disinterested to permit you to share with me the fortune which you have, with which we might live together happily, and who prefer to ruin yourself, slave that you are to an absurd prejudice. Do you think, then, that I compare a carriage and jewels with your love? Do you think that happiness consists for me in the vanities with which you content yourself when you do not love, but which become very trivial when you do? You will pay my debts, you will discount your fortune, and you will maintain me, in short! How long time will all that last? two or three months, and then it will be too late to take up the life which I propose to you, for, then you would have to accept everything from me, and that is what a man of honor can never do. Whilst, at present, you have eight or ten thousand francs of income with

which we could live. I will sell the superfluities which
I have, and from this sale alone I will procure myself
two thousand livres a year. We will hire a pretty little
apartment, in which we will remain, both of us. In
the summer, we will come to the country, not to a house
like this one, but to a little house big enough for two
persons. You are independent, I am free, we are
young; in Heaven's name, Armand, do not throw me
back into the life which I was forced to lead formerly!'

"I could not reply, the tears of gratitude and love
inundated my eyes, and I threw myself into Marguerite's
arms.

"'I had wished,' she went on,'to arrange everything
without saying anything to you, to pay my debts and
prepare my new apartment. In the month of October
we should have returned to Paris, and everything would
have been ready; but, since Prudence has told you all,
you will have to consent before, instead of consenting
afterward. Do you love me enough for that?'

"It was impossible to resist so much devotion. I
kissed Marguerite's hand with emotion, and I said to
her:

"'I will do whatever you like.'

"That which she had decided upon was therefore
agreed to.

"Whereupon she became possessed of a wild gayety,
she danced, she sang, she made a festival for herself of
the simplicity of her new apartment, concerning the

locality and the disposition of which she already consulted me.

" I saw her happy and proud with this new resolution,
which seemed as though it should definitely bring us
nearer together.

"Therefore I did not wish to be outdone by her in
any way.

"I decided upon my future life in a moment. I took
into consideration the amount of my fortune and I
abandoned to Marguerite the income which came to me
from my mother, and which seemed to me to be very
insufficient to recompense the sacrifice which I accepted.

" There remained to me the five thousand francs of
allowance made me by my father, and, whatever might
happen, I should always have with this annual income
enough to live on.

" I did not tell Marguerite my resolve, convinced as
I was that she would refuse this donation.

" This income came from a mortgage of sixty thousand francs upon a house which I had never even seen.
All that I knew was that at the end of every quarter my
father's notary, an old friend of our family, remitted
to me seven hundred and fifty francs upon my simple
receipt.

" The day on which Marguerite and I went to Paris
to look for apartments, I went to this notary, and I
asked him what steps I should take to transfer to another
person this annual income.

"The honest man believed me ruined, and questioned me as to the cause of this decision. Then, as it would be necessary, sooner or later, that I should tell him in whose favor I was making this donation, I preferred to tell him the whole truth at once.

"He did not offer any of those objections which his position as notary and friend authorized him to make to me, and he assured me that he would charge himself with arranging everything for the best.

"I recommended to him, naturally, the greatest discretion as far as my father was concerned, and I went to rejoin Marguerite, who was waiting for me at the house of Julie Duprat, where she had preferred to stop, rather than to go and listen to Prudence's sermons.

"We set out on our quest of apartments. All those that we saw Marguerite thought too expensive and I thought them too simple. However, we ended by agreeing, and we decided upon a little pavilion, separated from the principal mansion, in one of the quietest quarters of Paris.

"Behind this little pavilion extended a charming garden, which belonged to it, and which was surrounded by walls sufficiently high to separate us from our neighbors, and not too high to shut off the view.

"It was better than we had hoped for.

"Whilst I returned to my own apartments to take leave of them, Marguerite went to see a business man who, as she said, had already executed for one of her friends that which she was going to ask him for herself.

"She rejoined me in the Rue de Provence delighted. This man had promised to pay all her debts, to give her a receipt in full, and to hand over to her some twenty thousand francs in consideration of the transfer to him of all her furniture.

"You have seen by the amount which the sale of her effects brought that this honest man would have made more than thirty thousand francs from his client.

"We departed quite joyfully to return to Bougival, still continuing to discuss our plans for the future, which, thanks to our light-heartedness, and, above all, to our love, we saw only in golden tints.

"A week later we were at déjeuner when Nanine entered to inform me that my servant was asking for me.

"I caused him to be brought in.

"'Monsieur,' he said to me, 'your father has arrived in Paris, and requests you to return immediately to your apartment, where he is waiting for you.'

"This information was the most simple thing in the world, and yet, as we heard it, Marguerite and I looked at each other.

"We foresaw a misfortune in this incident.

"Thus, before she had communicated to me her share of this mutual impression, I replied to it, giving her my hand :

"'Fear nothing.'

"'Return as quickly as you can,' murmured Marguerite as she embraced me, 'I will wait for you at the window.'

"I sent Joseph back to tell my father that I was coming.

"In fact, two hours later, I was in the Rue de Provence.

XX

"My father, in a dressing-gown, was seated, writing, in my salon.

"I comprehended immediately, from the manner in which he looked up at me as I entered, that grave questions would be discussed.

"I accosted him, however, as if I had divined nothing in his countenance, and I embraced him.

"'When did you arrive, father?'

"'Yesterday evening.'

"'You came directly here, as usual?'

"'Yes.'

"'I much regret that I was not here to receive you.'

"I expected to see these words produce immediately the sermon which was promised me by his cold countenance; but he made no reply, sealed the letter which he had just written, and gave it to Joseph to put in the post.

"When we were alone, my father rose, and, leaning against the chimney-piece, said to me :

"'My dear Armand, we have serious matters to talk about.'

"'I am ready to listen to you, father.'

"' You promise me to be frank.'

"'That is my usual custom.'

"' Is it true that you are living with a woman named Marguerite Gautier?'

"' Yes.'

"' Do you know what this woman was?'

"' A kept woman.'

"' It is for her that you have forgotten to come to see us this year, your sister and me?'

"' Yes, father, I admit it.'

"' You love this woman, then, very much?'

"' You can see it yourself, father, since she has caused me to fail in a sacred duty, for which I humbly ask your pardon to-day.'

"My father had doubtless not expected such categorical replies, for he appeared to hesitate a moment, after which he said to me :

"' You certainly understand that you cannot continue to live in this manner always.'

"' I have feared it, father, but I have not understood it.'

"' But you must have understood,' he continued in a somewhat harder tone, 'that I would not permit it.'

"' I said to myself that, so long as I did nothing which was contrary to the respect which I owe to your name and to the traditional probity of the family, I could continue to live as I am living, and this relieved me somewhat from my fears.'

"The passions give you strength against the feelings. I was ready for any combat, even against my father, to retain Marguerite.

"'Well, the time for living differently has come.'

"'Eh! why, father?'

"'Because you are on the point of doing things which are contrary to the respect which you believe you owe to your family.'

"'I cannot explain these words to myself.'

"'I will explain them to you. That you should have a mistress, that is all very well; that you should pay her as a gallant man should pay for the love of a kept woman, there is nothing better; but that you should forget the most sacred things for her, that you should permit the rumor of your scandalous life to penetrate to the depths of my province and throw the suspicion of a stain on the honorable name which I have given you, that is what cannot be, that is what shall not be.'

"'Permit me to tell you, father, that those who have communicated to you such stories concerning me have been misinformed. I am the lover of Mademoiselle Gautier, I live with her, it is the most simple thing in the world. I do not give to Mademoiselle Gautier the name which I received from you, I expend for her what my means permit me to expend, I have not made any debts, and I have not placed myself, in short, in any of those positions which authorize a father to say to his son what you have just said to me.'

"'A father is always authorized to withdraw his son from the evil path which he sees him pursuing. You have not yet done any evil, but you will do it.'

"'Father!'

"'Monsieur, I know life better than you. There are no sentiments entirely pure except in women entirely chaste. Every Manon may make a Des Grieux, and times and manners have changed. It would be useless for the world to grow older, if it did not grow better. You will leave your mistress.'

"'I am greatly grieved to disobey you, father, but that is impossible.'

"'I will compel you to do so.'

"'Unfortunately, father, there are no more Sainte-Marguerite islands to which the courtesans are shipped off, and if there were, I would follow Mademoiselle Gautier there, in case you should succeed in sending her. What would you have? I am perhaps in the wrong, but I can only be happy on the condition that I remain this woman's lover.'

"'Come now, Armand, open your eyes, think of your father who has always loved you and who wishes only your happiness. Is it honorable in you to continue to live in marital relations with a woman who has been had by everybody?'

"'What matters it, father, if no one ever has her again! What matters it, if this woman loves me, if she regenerates herself through the love which she has for me and through the love which I have for her! What matters it, in short, if there should be a conversion!'

"'Eh! do you think, then, monsieur, that the mission of a man of honor should be to convert courtesans? Do you think, then, that God has created life for this grotesque object, and that the heart should have no other enthusiasm but this? What will be the conclusion of this marvellous cure, and what will you think of what you are saying to-day when you come to the age of forty? You will laugh at your love, if it be permitted you still to laugh, if it has not left traces too deep in your past. What would you be at this hour, if your father had had your ideas and had abandoned his life to all these love fancies, instead of establishing it unshakably on considerations of honor and loyalty? Reflect, Armand, and utter no more such silliness. Come now, you will leave this woman, your father entreats you?'

"I made no reply.

"'Armand,' continued my father, 'in the name of your sainted mother, believe me, renounce this life which you will forget much more quickly than you think, and with which you entwine an impossible theory. You are only twenty-four, think of the future. You cannot love always this woman, who will no more always love you. You both of you exaggerate your love. You are closing your own career. One step further, and you will not be able to leave the road you are on, and you will have, for the rest of your life, remorse for your youth. Go away, come and pass a month or two with your sister. Repose, and the pious love of the family, will quickly cure you of this fever, for it is nothing else.

"'During this time your mistress will console herself; she will take another lover, and, when you see for whom you were on the point of displeasing your father and losing his affection, you will say to me that I did well to come to seek you, and you will bless me.

"'Come, you will go away, will you not, Armand?'

"I felt that my father was in the right as far as all other women are concerned, but I was convinced that he was wrong as to Marguerite. Nevertheless, the tone in which he had addressed his last words to me was so gentle, so supplicating, that I did not dare to answer him.

"'Well?' he said in a voice of emotion.

"'Well, father, I cannot promise you anything,' I said finally; 'that which you ask of me is beyond my strength. Believe me,' I continued, as I saw him make an impatient movement, 'you exaggerate to yourself the results of this liaison. Marguerite is not the woman you think. This love, far from launching me on a career of evil, is capable, on the contrary, of developing in me the most honorable sentiments. True love is always elevating, whatever may be the woman who inspires it. If you knew Marguerite, you would comprehend that I expose myself to nothing. She is as noble as the most noble women. As much cupidity as you find in the others, so much disinterestedness is there in her.'

"'Which will not prevent her from accepting your entire fortune, for the sixty thousand francs which come to you from your mother, and which you give her, are, remember well what I say to you, your entire fortune.'

"My father had probably reserved this peroration and this menace to give me the finishing-stroke.

"I was stronger before his menaces than before his prayers.

"'Who told you that I was about to transfer this money to her?' I asked.

"'My notary. Would an honest man have committed such an act without notifying me? Well, it was to prevent your ruining yourself for a woman of the town that I came to Paris. Your mother left you in dying means with which to live honorably, and not to be generous to your mistresses.'

"'I swear to you, father, Marguerite is ignorant of this donation.'

"'And why, then, did you make it?'

"'Because Marguerite, this woman whom you calumniate and whom you wish that I should abandon, makes the sacrifice of everything that she possesses so that she may live with me.'

"'And you accept this sacrifice? What sort of a man are you, then, monsieur, to permit a Mademoiselle Marguerite to sacrifice anything for you? Come now,

246 THE LADY OF THE CAMELLIAS

we have had enough of this! You will leave this woman.
A moment ago, I entreated you; now, I order you; I
do not wish any such dirty business in my family. Pack
your trunks and get ready to follow me.'

"'Pardon me, father,' I then said, 'but I am not
going! ——'

"'Because? ——'

"'Because I am already of an age at which one no
longer obeys an order.'

"My father turned pale at this reply.

"'It is well, monsieur,' he returned, 'I know what
there remains for me to do.'

"He rang.

"Joseph appeared.

"'Have my trunks sent to the Hotel de Paris,' he
said to my servant. And at the same time he passed
into his chamber, where he completed his toilet.

"When he came out again, I went to meet him.

"'You will promise me, father,' I said to him, 'to
do nothing which could give pain to Marguerite?'

"He stopped, looked at me contemptuously, and contented himself by replying:

"'I think you are a fool.'

"After which, he went out, closing the door violently
behind him.

"I left in my turn, took a cabriolet, and set out for
Bougival.

"Marguerite was waiting for me at the window.

XXI

" ' At last!' she cried, throwing herself on my neck. 'Here you are! How pale you are!'

" Then I related to her my scene with my father.

" ' Ah, Mon Dieu! I was afraid of it,' she said. 'When Joseph came to announce to us the arrival of your father, I shuddered as at the news of a calamity. Poor friend! and it is I who cause you all these troubles. You would perhaps do better to leave me than to quarrel with your father. However, I have done nothing to him. We are living very quietly, we are going to live still more quietly. He knows very well that you must have a mistress, and he should be glad that it was I, since I love you and have no ambitions for anything more than your position will permit. Did you tell him how we have arranged for the future?'

" ' Yes, and it was that which irritated him the most, for he saw in this determination the proof of our mutual love.'

" ' What is to be done, then?'

" ' Stay together, dear Marguerite, and let this storm pass over.'

247

"'Will it pass over?'

"'It will have to.'

"'But your father will not stop there.'

"'What do you think he will do?'

"'How do I know? everything that a father can do to have his son obey him. He will call to your attention all my past life, and will perhaps do me the honor to invent some new stories to persuade you to leave me.'

"'You know very well that I love you.'

"'Yes; but I know also this, that it is always necessary, sooner or later, to obey a father, and you will end, perhaps, by allowing yourself to be convinced.'

"'No, Marguerite, it is I who will convince him. It is only the antics of some of his friends which have put him in such a rage; but he is good, he is just, and he will get over his first impressions. Then, after all, what difference does it make to me!'

"'Do not say that, Armand; I should prefer anything rather than that it should be said that I had caused you to quarrel with your family; let this day go by and to-morrow return to Paris. Your father will have reflected on his side, as you have on yours, and perhaps you will come to a better understanding. Do not offend his principles, have the appearance of being willing to make some concessions to his wishes; do not seem to be so firmly attached to me, and he will allow things to remain as they are. Have hopes, dear friend, and be very certain of one thing, that is, that whatever happens, your Marguerite will remain to you.'

" ' You swear it to me?'

" ' Have I need to swear?'

" How sweet it is to allow yourself to be persuaded by the voice that you love ! Marguerite and I passed the rest of the day in talking over our projects, as if we had comprehended the necessity of realizing them more quickly. We expected at each moment some new incident, but fortunately the day passed without bringing anything new.

" The next morning I set off at ten o'clock, and I arrived at the hotel about noon.

" My father had already gone out.

" I went to my own apartment, where I hoped that he had gone perchance. No one had been there. I went to the notary's. No one !

" I went back to the hotel, and I waited till six o'clock. M. Duval did not return.

" I took the road back to Bougival.

" I found Marguerite, not waiting for me as on the evening before, but seated at the corner of the fire which the season already required.

" She was so deeply buried in her thoughts as to allow me to approach her easy-chair without being heard and without causing her to turn round. When I touched her

forehead with my lips,• she shuddered, as if this kiss had
suddenly awakened her.

" ' You frightened me,' she said. ' And your father?'

" ' I have not seen him. I do not know what that
means. I did not find him, neither at his hotel nor at
any of the places where there was a possibility of his
being.'

" ' Well, we will have to begin again to-morrow.'

" ' I have a great mind to wait until he sends for me.
I have done, I think, all that I should do.'

" ' No, my friend, that is not enough, you must go
back to your father, above all, to-morrow.'

" ' Why to-morrow rather than another day ? '

" ' Because,' said Marguerite, who seemed to me to
blush a little at this question, ' because this insistence
on your part will thus more quickly be shown and our
forgiveness will take place more promptly.'

" All the rest of the day Marguerite was preoccupied,
thoughtful, sad. I was obliged to repeat everything I
said to her a second time in order to get a response.
She attributed this preoccupation to the fears for the
future which had been inspired in her by the events of
the last two days.

" I passed my night in reassuring her, and she made
me go off in the morning with an anxious insistence
which I could not explain to myself.

" As on the day before, my father was absent ; but,
on going out, he had left this note for me :

" 'If you come back to see me to-day, wait for me until four o'clock ; if at four o'clock I have not returned, come back to dine with me to-morrow ;—it is necessary that I should see you.'

" I waited for him until the hour indicated.   He did not appear.   I departed.

" On the evening before, I had found Marguerite sad and thoughtful ; this time she was feverish and agitated. When she saw me enter, she threw herself on my neck, but she wept a long time in my arms.

" I questioned her on this sudden grief, the rapid gradations of which alarmed me.   She gave me no positive reason, saying everything that a woman can say when she does not wish to admit the truth.

" When she was a little calmer, I related to her the results of my journey ; I showed her my father's letter, observing to her that we could hope for the better from it.

" At the sight of this letter and at my observation, her tears redoubled to such a degree that I summoned Nanine, and that, fearing a nervous attack, we put the poor girl to bed, she crying all the time without saying a syllable, but holding my hands and kissing them every minute.

" I asked Nanine if, during my absence, her mistress had received any letter or visit that could have occasioned the state in which I found her ; but Nanine answered that no one had come and that nothing had been brought to the house.

"However, there had happened since the day before something all the more disquieting that Marguerite concealed it from me.

"She appeared to be somewhat more calm in the course of the evening; and, making me take my seat at her bedside, she renewed to me, over and over, the assurances of her love. Then she smiled upon me, but with an effort, for, despite herself, her eyes filled with tears.

"I employed every means to cause her to admit the true cause of this grief, but she resolutely refused to give me any other than the vague reasons of which I have already told you.

"She finally went to sleep in my arms, but with that sleep that wearies the body instead of resting it; at intervals she would utter a cry, awake suddenly, and, after having assured herself that I was indeed by her side, she would make me swear to love her always.

"I could not understand this intermittent sorrow, which was prolonged until the morning. Then she fell into a sort of stupor. For the last two nights she had not slept.

"This repose was not of long duration.

"About eleven o'clock Marguerite awoke, and, seeing that I was already up, she looked around her, exclaiming:

"'Are you going away already?'

" ' No,' I said, taking her hands, ' but I wished to let you sleep. It is still early.'

" ' At what time are you going to Paris?'

" ' At four o'clock.'

" ' So early? Until then you will remain with me, will you not?'

" ' Certainly. Is not that my usual custom?'

" ' What happiness!'

" ' We are going to have déjeuner?' she went on, with an absent air.

" ' If you wish it.'

" ' And then you will embrace me, well up to the time you go away?'

" ' Yes, and I will return as soon as possible.'

" ' You will return?' she said, looking at me with haggard eyes.

" ' Naturally.'

" ' That is right, you will return this evening, and I, I will wait for you, as usual, and you will love me, and we shall be happy as we have been ever since we have known each other.'

"All these words were said in such an abrupt tone, they seemed to conceal some trouble so insistent, that I trembled lest I should see her at any moment fall into delirium.

" ' Listen,' I said to her, ' you are sick, I cannot leave you in this state. I am going to write to my father not to wait for me.'

" ' No, no,' she cried quickly, ' do not do that. Your
father would accuse me again of preventing you from
going to him when he wishes to see you; no, no, you
must go, you must. Besides, I am not sick, I am very
well. It is only because I had a bad dream, and was
not wide awake.'

" From this moment Marguerite endeavored to appear
more cheerful. She no longer wept.

" When the hour came at which I should go, I embraced her and asked her if she would accompany me
as far as the railway station; I hoped that the little
journey would serve to distract her thoughts, and that
the air would do her good.

" I was desirous, above all, of remaining with her as
long as possible.

" She accepted, took a cloak, and accompanied me
with Nanine, so as not to have to return alone.

" Twenty times I was on the point of not going at
all. But the hope of returning quickly, and the fear of
irritating my father still further against me, sustained
me, and the train bore me away.

" ' Until this evening,' I said to Marguerite on leaving her.

" She made no reply to me.

" Once before she had not replied to me, in the same
way, and the Comte de G——, as you will remember,
had passed the night with her; but that occasion was so
distant in point of time that it seemed to be effaced

from my memory, and, if I feared anything, it certainly was no longer that Marguerite would deceive me.

"When I arrived in Paris, I hastened to Prudence's apartment to ask her to go out to see Marguerite, hoping that her liveliness and her cheerfulness would serve to entertain her. I entered without being announced, and found Prudence at her toilet.

"'Ah!' she said to me with an uneasy air. 'Is Marguerite with you?'

"'No.'

"'How is she?'

"'She is unwell.'

"'Is she not coming?'

"'Was she expected to come?'

"Madame Duvernoy flushed and replied, with a certain embarrassed air:

"'What I meant to say was: "Since you have come to Paris, is she not coming to rejoin you"?'

"'No.'

"I looked at Prudence; she lowered her eyes, and on her countenance I thought I perceived a fear that my visit would be prolonged.

"'I came purposely to ask you, my dear Prudence, if you have nothing to do, if you would not go out to see Marguerite this evening; you will keep her company, and you can pass the night out there. I have never seen her before as she has been to-day, and I tremble lest she should fall ill.'

"'I am dining out to-night,' replied Prudence, 'and I cannot go see Marguerite this evening; but I will see her to-morrow.'

"I took my leave of Madame Duvernoy, who seemed to me almost as much preoccupied as Marguerite, and I hastened to my father, whose first look studied me attentively.

"He offered me his hand.

"'Your two calls gave me pleasure, Armand,' he said, 'they led me to hope that you had reflected, on your side, as I have reflected, I, on mine.'

"'May I be permitted to inquire, father, what has been the result of your reflections?'

"'It has been, my son, that I had exaggerated to myself the importance of the stories which had been told me, and that I have promised myself to be somewhat less severe with you.'

"'What do you say, father!' I cried joyfully.

"'I say, my dear son, that it is necessary that every young man should have a mistress, and that, because of my new information, I should prefer to know you rather the lover of Mademoiselle Gautier than of any other.'

"'My excellent father! how happy you make me!'

"We conversed thus for a few moments, then we took our places at the table. My father was charming all through the dinner.

"I was in a hurry to return to Bougival to relate to Marguerite this happy change in the state of affairs. Every minute I looked at the clock.

" 'You are watching the hour,' said my father, 'you are impatient to leave me. Oh! young people! you will always sacrifice sincere affections for doubtful ones.'

" 'Do not say that, father. Marguerite loves me, I am sure of it.'

" My father did not reply; he had the appearance neither of disbelieving nor of believing.

" He insisted strongly on my spending the night with him and not going back till the next day, but I had left Marguerite ill, I told him, and I asked his permission to go to rejoin her at an early hour, promising him to return the next day.

" The weather was fine ; he wished to accompany me as far as the station. Never had I been so happy. The future appeared to me such as I had long hoped to see it.

" I loved my father more than I had ever loved him.

" As I was about to leave, he insisted for the last time that I should stay; but I refused.

" 'You love her, then, very much ?' he asked me.

" 'Madly.'

" 'Go, then !' and he passed his hand over his forehead as if he sought to drive away an uneasy reflection, then he opened his mouth as if to say something to me ; but he contented himself with clasping my hand, and he left me suddenly, saying :

" 'Till to-morrow, then.'

XXII

"It seemed to me that the train crawled along.

"I was at Bougival at eleven o'clock.

"Not one window in the house was lit up, and I rang without any one answering me.

"It was the first time that such a thing had happened to me. Finally the gardener appeared. I entered.

"Nanine came to me with a light. I reached Marguerite's chamber.

"'Where is madame?'

"'Madame has gone to Paris,' replied Nanine.

"'To Paris?'

"'Yes, monsieur.'

"'When?'

"'An hour after you left.'

"'She gave you nothing for me?'

"'Nothing at all.'

"Nanine left me alone.

"'She was quite capable of having fears,' I thought, 'and of having gone to Paris to assure herself that the visit which I said I was going to pay to my father was not merely a pretext for securing a day of liberty.'

259

" ' Perhaps Prudence wrote to her about some important affair,' I said to myself when I was alone ; but I had seen Prudence on my arrival in the city, and she had said nothing to me that could lead me to suppose that she had written to Marguerite.

"Suddenly I thought of that question which Madame Duvernoy had put to me : 'She is not then coming in to-day?' when I had told her that Marguerite was ill. I recalled at the same time the embarrassed air of Prudence when I looked at her after this speech which seemed to betray a rendezvous. To this memory was added that of Marguerite's tears during the course of the day, tears which my father's welcome had almost made me forget.

"From that moment all the incidents of the day grouped themselves around my first suspicion and fixed it so solidly in my mind that everything tended to confirm it, even the paternal clemency.

"Marguerite had almost insisted upon my going to Paris ; she had pretended to be calm when I had proposed to stay with her. Had I fallen into a trap? Was Marguerite deceiving me? Had she counted upon being able to return sufficiently early to prevent my discovering her absence, and had she been detained by some accident? Why had she said nothing to Nanine, or why had she not written to me? What was the meaning of all these tears, this absence, this mystery?

" This is what I asked myself in fright, in this empty chamber and with my eyes fixed on the clock, which, marking midnight, seemed to say to me that it was too late for me to hope to see my mistress return.

" However, after all the arrangements which we had made, after the sacrifice offered and accepted, was it probable that she would deceive me? No. I endeavored to reject my first suppositions.

" 'The poor girl has found a purchaser for her furniture, and she has gone to Paris to conclude the bargain. She has not wished to notify me, for she knows that, although I accept it, this sale, necessary to our future happiness, is painful to me, and she would have thought it wounding to my self-respect and my delicacy to speak of it to me. She would prefer to appear only when everything was consummated. Prudence was evidently expecting her for that purpose, and betrayed herself before me ; Marguerite has not been able to conclude her sale to-day and is sleeping in Prudence's apartment, or perhaps, even, she may arrive at any moment, for she must know that I would be anxious, and would certainly not be willing to leave me so long.

" 'But, then, why those tears? Doubtless, notwithstanding her love for me, the poor girl could not bring herself without weeping to abandon all the luxury in which she has lived up to the present, and which made her happy and envied.'

"I forgave her very readily these regrets. I waited impatiently for an opportunity to say to her, while covering her with kisses, that I had divined the cause of her mysterious absence.

"However, the night advanced and she did not appear.

"Anxiety contracted little by little its iron circle, and compressed my head and my heart. Perhaps something had happened to her! Perhaps she was wounded, sick, dead! Perhaps I was about to see a messenger arrive announcing to me some tragic accident! Perhaps the morning would find me still a prey to the same anxieties and the same fears!

"The thought that Marguerite might be deceiving me at the hour in which I was waiting for her in the midst of the terrors caused by her absence did not occur to me again. It must have required some cause outside of her will to detain her away from me, and, the more I thought of it, the more I was convinced that this cause could be none other than some misfortune. Oh, vanity of man! you appear under all possible forms.

"One o'clock sounded. I said to myself that I would wait an hour longer, but that, if at two o'clock Marguerite had not appeared, I would set out for Paris.

"While waiting, I looked for a book, for I dared not think.

"*Manon Lescaut* lay open upon the table. It seemed to me that in certain places the pages were dampened, as if with tears. After turning them over awhile, I closed the book, the words of which appeared to me void of sense through the veil of my doubts.

"The hour passed very slowly. The sky was cloudy. An autumn rain was whipping against the windows. The empty bed appeared to me at moments to take on the aspect of a tomb. I was afraid.

"I opened the door. I listened, and I heard nothing but the noise of the wind in the trees. Then a carriage passed upon the road. The half-hour sounded mournfully from the steeple of the church.

"I had arrived at such a point as to fear that some one would enter. It seemed to me that only a misfortune could come to find me at such an hour and in such sombre weather.

"Two o'clock sounded. I waited a little longer. The clock alone troubled the silence with its monotonous and measured ticking.

"Finally, I left this chamber the least objects in which had taken on that mournful aspect which the unquiet solitude of the heart gives to everything that surrounds it.

"In the adjoining room I found Nanine asleep over her work. At the sound of the opening of the door she awoke, and asked me if her mistress had returned.

" 'No; but if she returns you will say to her that I could no longer resist my anxiety, and that I have gone to Paris.'

" ' At this hour ? '

" ' Yes.'

" ' But how? you cannot find a carriage.'

" ' I will go on foot.'

" ' But it is raining.'

" ' What does that matter ? '

" ' Madame will come back, or, if she does not, it will still be time enough in the morning to go to see what has detained her. You will get yourself assassinated on the road.'

" ' There is no danger, my dear Nanine ; good-bye till to-morrow.'

" The honest girl went to get my cloak, threw it over my shoulders, offered to go and waken the Mère Arnould and to inquire of her whether it were possible to get a carriage; but I declined, convinced that I should lose in this probably unsuccessful attempt more time than I should require to accomplish half my journey.

" Then, I felt the need of the fresh air and of the physical fatigue which might diminish the over-excitement to which I was a prey.

" I took the key of the apartment in the Rue d'Antin, and, after having bade adieu to Nanine, who went with me to the gate, I set out.

"At first I began to run, but the earth was recently moistened and I doubly fatigued myself. At the end of a half-hour of this course, I was obliged to stop, I was drenched in perspiration. I recovered my breath and I continued on my road. The night was so dark that I trembled lest, at any moment, I should run against one of the trees of the road, which, presenting themselves suddenly to my eyes, had the appearance of great phantoms hastening toward me.

"I overtook one or two of the carrier's wagons, which I soon left behind me.

"A calash passed at a rapid trot, going in the direction of Bougival. At the moment in which it passed me the hope suddenly came to me that Marguerite might be inside.

"I stopped, crying: 'Marguerite! Marguerite!'

"But no one replied, and the calash continued on its way. I watched it disappear in the distance, and I set out again.

"I took two hours to arrive at the barrier de l'Étoile.

"The sight of Paris gave me new strength, and I descended almost running the long Allée which I had traversed so many times.

"On this night, no one was passing.

"You would have thought it the public promenade of a dead city.

"The day was commencing to dawn.

"When I arrived at the Rue d'Antin, the great city was already moving a little before awakening altogether.

"Five o'clock was sounding from the church of Saint-Roch at the moment I entered Marguerite's house.

"I threw my name to the porter, who had received enough twenty-franc pieces from me to know that I had the right to come at five o'clock in the morning to see Mademoiselle Gautier.

"I therefore passed in without hindrance.

"I could have asked him if Marguerite were at home, but he might have answered me that she was not, and I preferred to doubt two minutes longer, for, while doubting, I still hoped.

"I put my ear to the door, endeavoring to discover some noise, some movement.

"Nothing. The silence of the country side seemed to prevail even here.

"I opened the door, and I entered.

"All the curtains were closely drawn.

"I drew open those of the dining-room, and directed my steps towards the bed-chamber, the door of which I opened.

"I leaped to the cords of the curtains and pulled them violently.

"The curtains parted; a feeble light entered, I ran to the bed.

"It was empty!

"I opened the doors, one after another, I explored all the rooms.

"No one.

"It was enough to make one go mad.

"I went into the dressing-room, the window of which I opened, and I called Prudence several times.

"Madame Duvernoy's window remained closed.

"Then I went down to the porter again, and I asked him if Mademoiselle Gautier had been to her house on the day before.

"'Yes,' this man replied, 'with Madame Duvernoy.'

"'She said nothing for me?'

"'Nothing.'

"'Do you know what they did afterwards?'

"'They got into a carriage.'

"'What kind of a carriage?'

"'A hired coupé.'

"What did all that mean?

"I rang at the neighboring door.

"'Whom do you wish to see, monsieur?' asked the concierge after he had opened the door.

"'Madame Duvernoy.'

"'She has not yet returned.'

"'You are sure of it?'

"'Yes, monsieur; here is even a letter for her which was brought yesterday evening, and which I have not yet handed to her.'

"And the porter showed me a letter, on which I mechanically turned my eyes.

"I recognized Marguerite's handwriting.

"I took the letter.

"The address was in these words:

"'For Madame Duvernoy, to be handed to M. Duval.'

"'This letter is for me,' I said to the porter, and I showed him the address.

"'You are Monsieur Duval?' he inquired.

"'Yes.'

"'Ah! I recognize you, you come often to see Madame Duvernoy.'

"As soon as I was in the street, I broke the seal of this letter.

"The thunder might have broken at my feet without terrifying me more than did this reading:

"'At the hour at which you read this letter, Armand, I shall already be the mistress of another man. Everything is therefore ended between us.

"'Return to your father, my friend, go to see again your sister, that young girl, chaste and ignorant of all our miseries, and by whose side you will soon forget all that you have been made to suffer by that lost woman who is called Marguerite Gautier, whom you were willing to love for a moment, and who owes to you the only happy hours in a life which, she hopes, will not last much longer.'

"When I had read the last word, I thought that I was going mad.

"For a moment I was really afraid of falling on the pavement of the street. A cloud passed before my eyes, and the blood hammered in my temples.

"Finally, I recovered myself a little, I looked around me, quite surprised to see the life of others continuing around me without ceasing at my misfortune.

"I was not strong enough to support alone the blow which Marguerite had dealt me.

"Then I remembered that my father was in the same city, that in ten minutes I could be with him, and that, whatever might be the cause of my trouble, he would share it with me.

"I ran like a crazy man, like a thief, to the hotel de Paris ; I found the key in the door of my father's apartment. I entered.

"He was reading.

"At the slight degree of surprise which he manifested on seeing me, you would have said that he was expecting me.

"I threw myself into his arms without saying a word, I gave him Marguerite's letter, and, letting myself sink down before his bed, I wept scalding tears.

XXIII

"When all the ordinary things of life had resumed their usual course, I could not believe that the day which rose was not the same for me as those which had preceded it. There were moments in which it seemed to me that a circumstance, which I did not recall, had caused me to pass the night away from Marguerite, but that, if I returned to Bougival, I would find her anxious, as I had been, and that she would ask me what had thus detained me from her side.

"When daily existence has contracted such a habit as that of this love, it seems impossible that this habit should be broken without breaking at the same time all the other springs of life.

"I was thus forced from time to time to reread Marguerite's letter, to thoroughly convince myself that I had not dreamed.

"My body, succumbing under the mortal stroke, was incapable of a movement. The anxiety, the night walk, the news of the morning, had exhausted me. My father took occasion of this total prostration of my forces to require of me a formal promise to depart with him.

"I promised everything that he wished. I was incapable of sustaining any discussion, and I felt the need of real affection to aid me to live after that which had left me.

"I was too well pleased that my father was willing to console me for such a grief.

"All that I recall is, that on that day, about five o'clock, he caused me to take my place with him in a post-chaise. Without saying anything to me, he had caused my trunks to be packed, he had them attached with his own behind the vehicle, and he carried me off.

"I was not conscious of what I was doing until the city had disappeared, and until the solitude of the route recalled to me the void in my heart.

"Then my tears came again.

"My father understood that words, even from him, would not console me, and he allowed me to weep without speaking to me, contenting himself with clasping my hand from time to time, as if to recall to me the fact that I had a friend beside me.

"That night I slept a little. I dreamed of Marguerite.

"I awoke with a start, not comprehending why I was in a vehicle.

"Then the reality returned to my consciousness, and I let my head fall on my chest.

"I did not dare to hold converse with my father, I feared constantly that he would say to me:

" ' You see that I was right when I denied the love of this woman.'

" But he did not abuse his advantage, and we arrived at G—— without his having said to me anything connected in the slightest way with the event which had led to my departure.

" When I embraced my sister, I recalled the words concerning her in Marguerite's letter, but I immediately comprehended that, however good she might be, my sister would be quite insufficient to make me forget my mistress.

" The hunting season was open, my father thought that it might be a distraction for me. He therefore organized hunting parties with neighbors and friends. I went to them without repugnance as without enthusiasm, with that sort of apathy which characterized all my actions since my departure.

" The game was driven up to us by beaters. I was stationed at my post. I would set my empty gun down beside me, and I would fall into reverie.

" I looked at the passing clouds. I allowed my thoughts to wander in solitary plains, and, from time to time, I could hear myself called to by some hunter who would show me a hare within ten feet of me.

" None of these details escaped my father's observation, and he did not allow himself to be deceived by my calm exterior. He comprehended perfectly that, however overwhelmed it might be, my heart would experience one day a terrible reaction, a dangerous one perhaps, and, while carefully avoiding appearing to console me, he did his utmost to find me distraction.

" My sister, naturally, had not been informed of all these events; she therefore could not understand how it was that I, formerly so cheerful, had suddenly become so thoughtful and so melancholy.

" Sometimes, aware in the midst of my grief of my father's anxious look, I extended to him my hand and clasped his own as if to tacitly ask his forgiveness for the trouble which, in spite of myself, I caused him.

" A month passed in this manner, but it was all that I could endure.

" The thought of Marguerite incessantly pursued me. I had loved too much and I still loved too much this woman for her to become indifferent to me all at once. It was necessary that I should love her or that I should hate her. It was necessary, above all, whatever sentiment I might entertain for her, that I should see her again, and that immediately.

" This desire entered into my soul and lodged itself there with all the violence of the will which finally reappears in a body that has long been inert.

" It was not at some time within the future, in a month, in a week, that I required Marguerite, it was the day after the very day on which this idea had come to me ; and I went to my father to say to him that I was about to leave him because of some affairs that recalled me to Paris, but that I would quickly return.

" He doubtless suspected the reason of my departure, for he insisted that I should remain; but, seeing that the failure to carry out this desire, in the irritable state in which I was, might have fatal consequences for me, he embraced me and entreated me, almost with tears, to soon return to him.

" I did not sleep before I arrived in Paris.

" Once there, what was I going to do? I was quite ignorant; but it was necessary, above all, that I should concern myself about Marguerite.

" I went to my own rooms to change my costume, and, as the weather was fine, and as there was still time, I took my way to the Champs-Élysées.

" At the end of half an hour I saw coming in the distance, and from the Rond-point to the Place de la Concorde, Marguerite's carriage.

" She had repurchased her equipage, for the carriage was the same; only, she was not in it.

" Scarcely had I remarked this absence when, casting my eyes around me, I saw Marguerite walking on foot accompanied by a woman whom I had never seen before.

" As she passed by me, she grew pale, and a nervous smile moved her lips. As for me, the violent beating of my heart shook my chest; but I succeeded in assuming a cold expression, and I saluted coldly my former mistress, who immediately rejoined her carriage and took her seat in it accompanied by her friend.

"I knew Marguerite's nature. The unexpected meeting with me must have thrown her into great confusion. She had doubtless heard of my departure, which had tranquilized her fears as to the consequences of our rupture; but, seeing that I had returned and finding herself face to face with me, pale as I was, she had comprehended that my return had some object, and she must have asked herself what was going to take place.

"If I had found her unhappy, if, to avenge myself on her, I had been able to go to her aid, I might perhaps have pardoned her and certainly would not have thought of doing her ill; but I found her happy, at least in appearance; another had restored to her the luxury which I had not been able to continue to her; our rupture, brought about by her, took on consequently the most mercenary character; I was humiliated in my self-love as in my love, it followed necessarily that she must pay for what I had suffered.

"I could not be indifferent to whatever this woman did; consequently, what would wound her the most would be my indifference; it was, then, this sentiment that I must feign, not only in her eyes, but in the eyes of others.

"I endeavored to assume a smiling countenance, and I went to see Prudence.

"The femme de chambre announced me and made me wait a few moments in the salon.

"Madame Duvernoy finally appeared and introduced me into her boudoir; as I took a seat I heard the door of the salon open, and the floor creaked under a light footstep; then the door on the landing was violently closed.

"'I disturb you?' I asked of Prudence.

"'Not at all, Marguerite was there. When she heard your name announced, she took flight; that was she who just went out.'

"'I make her afraid then, now?'

"'No, but she fears that it might be disagreeable to you to see her again.'

"'Why should it be,' I said, making an effort to breathe freely, for my emotion was suffocating me; 'the poor girl left me that she might see again her carriage, her furniture, and her diamonds, she did well, and I should not quarrel with her. I met her to-day,' I continued in a negligent manner.

"'Where?' asked Prudence, who was looking at me and seemed to be asking herself if this man were indeed he whom she had known so very loving.

"'On the Champs-Élysées, she was with another woman, a very pretty one. Who is that other woman?'

"'What is she like?'

"'A blonde, slender, thin, wearing ringlets like the English; blue eyes, very elegant.'

"'Ah! that is Olympe; a very pretty girl, in fact.'

" 'With whom does she live?'

" 'With no one, with everybody.'

" 'And she lives?'

" 'Rue Tronchet, No. ——. Ah! there, do you want to make love to her?'

" 'No one knows what may happen.'

" 'And Marguerite?'

" 'To say to you that I no longer think of her at all, that would be to lie; but I am one of those men with whom the manner of breaking off counts for a great deal. Now, Marguerite gave me my dismissal in so off-hand a fashion that I find myself to be very much of a fool to have loved her as I did, for I was truly very much in love with that girl.'

"You can imagine in what kind of a tone I endeavored to make these statements;—the sweat came out on my forehead.

" 'She loved you very much, come now, and she loves you still,—the proof of it is that after having met you to-day she came immediately to tell me about this meeting. When she got here she was all trembling, on the point of being ill.'

" 'Well, what did she say to you?'

" 'She said to me: "Doubtless he will come to see you," and she entreated me to implore you to pardon her.'

" 'I have pardoned her, you can tell her so. She is a very nice girl of the town, but she is a girl of the

town; and that which she did to me, I should have expected it. I am even grateful to her for her resolution,
for to-day I ask myself what my idea of living entirely
with her would have brought us to. It was folly.'

" 'She will be very well pleased to learn that you
have appreciated the necessity in which she found herself. It was high time that you left each other, my
dear. That scoundrel of a business man whom she had
procured to sell her furniture for her had been to see
her creditors to learn how much she owed them,—
they took fright, and everything was to have been sold
in two days.'

" 'And now it is all paid?'

" 'Nearly.'

" 'And who furnished the funds?'

" 'The Comte de N——. Ah! my dear! there are
men made expressly for these things. In short, he gave
twenty thousand francs; but he has attained his ends.
He knows very well that Marguerite is not in love with
him, which does not prevent him from being very nice
with her. As you have seen, he has bought her horses
for her again, he has redeemed her jewels, and gives her
as much money as the duke gave her; if she will live
quietly, that man will remain with her a long time.'

" 'And what is she doing? is she living altogether in
Paris?'

" 'She never wanted to go back to Bougival after
you had left. It was I who went there to settle up her

affairs, and also yours, of which I made a package
which you can send and get here. There is everything
in it, excepting a little portfolio with your monogram.
Marguerite wished to take it and has it with her. If
you want it, I will ask her for it again.'

"'Let her keep it,' I stammered, for I felt the tears
come into my eyes at the thought of this village where
I had been so happy, and at the idea that Marguerite
wished to keep something that had belonged to me and
that recalled me to her.

"If she had entered the room at that moment, my
resolutions of vengeance would have all disappeared, and
I should have fallen at her feet.

"'For the rest,' continued Prudence, 'I have never
seen her as she is now; she scarcely sleeps at all, she
runs to all the balls, she takes suppers, she even gets
tipsy. Not long ago, after a supper, she remained in
her bed a week; and when the doctor gave her permission to get up, she commenced again, at the risk of
killing herself. Shall you go to see her?'

"'Of what use would it be! I came to see you, you,
because you were always very considerate to me, and
because I knew you before I knew Marguerite. I owe
it to you that I have been her lover, as it is to you I
owe that I am no longer so, do I not?'

"'Ah! Goodness! I did all that I could to induce
her to leave you, and I believe that, later, you will not
quarrel with me about it.'

" ' I owe you a double gratitude,' I said, rising, for my contempt was growing for this woman who could thus take seriously all that I said to her.

" ' You are going?'

" ' Yes.'

" I had learned enough.

" ' When shall we see you?'

" ' Soon. Adieu.'

" ' Adieu.'

" Prudence conducted me to the door, and I returned home with tears of rage in my eyes and a thirst for vengeance in my heart.

" Thus it appeared that Marguerite was decidedly a courtesan like all the others; thus it was evident that that deep love which she had for me had not struggled against the desire to resume her former mode of life, and against the necessity of having a carriage and participating in orgies.

" This is what I said to myself in my wakeful nights, whereas, if I had reflected as coolly as I affected to be doing, I would have seen in this new dissolute life of Marguerite the hope on her part of silencing a persistent thought, an incessant memory.

" Unfortunately, the evil passion dominated in me, and I sought only for a means of torturing this poor creature.

" Oh! man is very little and very vile when one of his small passions is wounded.

"This Olympe, with whom I had seen her, was, if not Marguerite's friend, at least the person with whom she associated the most since her return to Paris. She was about to give a ball, and, as I supposed that Marguerite would be there, I endeavored to procure an invitation for myself, and I succeeded.

"When I arrived at this ball filled with my painful feelings, it was already very animated. They were dancing, they were even crying out, and, in one of the quadrilles, I perceived Marguerite dancing with the Comte de N——, who appeared to be very proud to display her and who seemed to say to all the world :

"'This woman is mine !'

"I went to lean against a chimney-piece, just opposite Marguerite, and I watched her dance. As soon as she perceived me, she was troubled. I met her look and I saluted her in an absent manner with my hand and my eyes.

"When I reflected that, after the ball, it would be no longer with me but with that rich imbecile that she would go away, when I represented to myself that which in all probability would follow their return to her apartment, the blood mounted to my face, and I felt the necessity of troubling their amours.

"After the quadrille, I went to speak to the mistress of the house, who displayed to her guests magnificent shoulders and the half of a dazzling breast.

" This girl was beautiful, and, from the point of view of form, more beautiful than Marguerite. I comprehended this even better from certain looks which the latter threw upon Olympe while I was conversing with her. The man who was the lover of this woman might be as proud as was Monsieur de N——, and she was beautiful enough to inspire a passion equal to that with which Marguerite had inspired me.

" She had no lover at this period. It would not be difficult to become that man. All that was necessary was to show enough gold.

" My resolution was taken. This woman should be my mistress.

" I commenced my role of suitor by dancing with Olympe.

" A half-hour later, Marguerite, pale as death, put on her pelisse and left the ball.

XXIV

"This was already something, but it was not enough. I understood the power which I had over this woman, and I abused it like a blackguard.

"When I reflect that, now, she is dead, I ask myself if God will ever pardon me the wrong which I did her.

"After the supper, which was of the noisiest, they commenced to play.

"I seated myself at the side of Olympe and I risked my money with such recklessness that she could not but notice it. In a moment I had gained a hundred and fifty or two hundred louis, which I spread out before me, and upon which she fixed ardent eyes.

"I was the only one who was not completely absorbed by the play and who paid attention to her. All the rest of the night I won, and it was I who gave her the money with which to play, for she had lost all that she had before her, and probably all that she had in the house.

"At five o'clock in the morning, every one went away.

"I had gained three hundred louis.

"All the players had already descended the stairs, I alone had remained behind without being noticed, for I was the friend of none of these messieurs.

"Olympe herself was lighting the stairway, and I was about to descend like the others when, turning back to her, I said to her:

"'I must speak to you.'

"'To-morrow,' she said to me.

"'No, now.'

"'What have you to say to me?'

"'You will see.'

"And I re-entered the apartment.

"'You have lost?' I said to her.

"'Yes.'

"'All that you had in the house?'

"She hesitated.

"'Be frank.'

"'Well, that is true.'

"'I have gained three hundred louis, here they are, if you will keep me here.'

"And, at the same time, I threw the gold upon the table.

"'And why do you make this proposition?'

"'Because I love you, *pardieu!*'

"'No, but because you are in love with Marguerite, and because you wish to revenge yourself on her by becoming my lover. You cannot deceive a woman like me, my dear friend; unfortunately, I am still too young

and too handsome to accept the role which you propose
to me.'

"'Therefore, you refuse?'

"'Yes.'

"'Do you prefer to love me for nothing? It would
be I who would not accept then. Reflect, my dear
Olympe; I might have sent you any person whatsoever
to offer to you these three hundred louis from me on the
conditions which I state, you would have accepted. I
liked better to treat directly with you. Accept, without
seeking for the causes of my action; say to yourself that
you are beautiful, and that there is nothing surprising in
the fact that I am in love with you.'

" Marguerite was a kept woman, like Olympe, and yet
I would never have dared to have said to her, the first
time that I had met her, that which I had just said to
this woman. It was because I loved Marguerite, it was
because I had divined in her instincts which were want-
ing in this other creature, and that, at the very moment
at which I proposed this bargain, she with whom I was
concluding it, notwithstanding her extreme beauty, dis-
gusted me.

"She ended by accepting, be it understood, and at
noon I left her house as her lover; but I quitted her bed
without carrying away any souvenir of the caresses and
the words of love of which she had felt herself obliged
to be prodigal in return for the six thousand francs
which I had left with her.

"And yet men have ruined themselves for this woman.

"From that day, I made Marguerite endure an incessant persecution. Olympe and she ceased to see each other, you will readily understand why. I gave to my new mistress a carriage, jewels, I gambled, I perpetrated, in short, all the follies that might be expected of a man in love with a woman like Olympe. The news of my new passion spread rapidly.

"Prudence herself allowed herself to be deceived, and ended by believing that I had completely forgotten Marguerite. The latter, whether it were that she had divined the motive which prompted my conduct, whether it were that she was deceived like the others, met only with great dignity the daily affronts which I offered her. But she appeared to suffer, for, wherever I encountered her I saw her always paler, sadder. My love for her, exalted to that point that it thought itself become hate, rejoiced at the sight of this daily torture. Several times, when my conduct had been of an infamous cruelty, Marguerite lifted to me such supplicating looks that I blushed at the role which I had undertaken and that I was on the point of asking her pardon.

"But these repentances were of the duration only of the lightning flash, and Olympe, who had ended by putting all self-respect aside, and who comprehended that by injuring Marguerite she would obtain from me all that she wished, constantly excited me against her,

Chapter XXIII

"*I felt the necessity of troubling their amours.*

"*After the quadrille, I went to speak to the mistress of the house, who displayed to her guests magnificent shoulders and the half of a dazzling breast.*

*   *   *   *   *   *   *   *   *   *

"*I commenced my role of suitor by dancing with Olympe.*

"*A half-hour later, Marguerite, pale as death, put on her pelisse and left the ball.*"

and insulted her on every occasion with that cowardly
persistence of a woman authorized by a man.

"Finally, it.came to pass that Marguerite no longer
went either to balls or to the theatre through fear of
meeting Olympe and me. Then anonymous letters
succeeded to direct impertinences, and there was no
shameful thing that I did not put my mistress up to
relating, and that I did not relate myself, concerning
Marguerite.

"I must have been mad to have arrived at this point.
I was like a man who, having intoxicated himself with
bad wine, passes into one of those states of nervous
exaltation in which the hand is capable of committing a
crime without the will being in any way implicated. In
the midst of all this, I was suffering martyrdom. The
calmness without disdain, the dignity without contempt,
with which Marguerite met all my attacks, and which in
my own eyes made her superior to me, irritated me still
more against her.

"One evening, Olympe had gone to some place, I
have forgotten where, and had met Marguerite, who this
time had not yielded to the insolent girl who insulted
her, so that the latter had been forced to give way
before her. Olympe returned furious, and Marguerite
had been carried away fainting.

"On returning, Olympe related to me what had passed,
said to me that Marguerite, seeing her alone, had wished
to be avenged on her for being my mistress, and that

I must immediately write to her that she must respect, whether I were present or absent, the woman I loved.

"I need not tell you that I consented, and that everything that I could find of shameful, bitter and cruel I put in this letter, which I sent the same day to her.

"This time the blow was too heavy for the unhappy one to endure it without reply.

"I suspected that some reply would be returned; therefore I resolved not to leave my rooms during the day.

"About two o'clock there was a ring at the door, and I saw Prudence enter.

"I endeavored to assume an indifferent air in order to ask her the object of her visit; but this time Madame Duvernoy was not smiling, and in a tone of serious emotion she said to me that, since my return, that is to say about three weeks, I had not let an occasion pass of injuring Marguerite; that she was ill in consequence, and that the scene of the evening before and my letter of the morning had caused her to take to her bed.

"Briefly, without addressing any reproaches to me, Marguerite had sent to ask mercy of me, saying to me that she had neither the mental nor the physical strength to support my attacks.

"'That Mademoiselle Gautier should dismiss me from her house,' I said to Prudence, 'that was within her rights; but that she should insult a woman whom I love, under the pretext that this woman is my mistress, that is what I shall never permit.'

" 'My friend,' said Prudence to me, 'you are under the influence of a girl without either heart or intelligence; you are in love with her, that is true, but that is no reason for torturing a woman who cannot defend herself.'

" 'Let Mademoiselle Gautier send me her Comte de N——, and the game will then be equal.'

" 'You know very well that she will not do that. Therefore, my dear Armand, let her alone; if you should see her, you would be ashamed of the manner in which you have conducted yourself toward her. She is pale, she coughs, she will not last much longer.'

" And Prudence offered me her hand, adding :

" 'Come to see her, your visit would make her very happy.'

" 'I have no desire to meet Monsieur de N——.'

" 'Monsieur de N—— is never in her house. She cannot endure him.'

" 'If Marguerite wishes to see me, she knows where I live, let her come here; but, for my part, I will not set foot in the Rue d'Antin.'

" 'And you will receive her well?'

" 'Certainly.'

" 'Well, I am sure that she will come.'

" 'Let her come.'

" 'Shall you go out to-day?'

" 'I shall be at home all the evening.'

" 'I will tell her so.'

"Prudence departed.

"I did not even write to Olympe that I was not coming to see her. I did not put myself out in any degree with that girl. I scarcely passed one night a week with her. She consoled herself, I believe, with an actor of I know not what theatre on the boulevard.

"I went out to dine and returned almost immediately. I caused fires to be lit in every room, and I sent Joseph away.

"I would not be able to give you any account of the various impressions which agitated me during an hour of waiting; but when, about nine o'clock, I heard the door-bell ring, they accumulated in an emotion so strong that, in going to open the door, I was obliged to lean against the wall so as not to fall.

"Fortunately, the antechamber was in obscurity, and the alteration of my features was less visible.

"Marguerite entered.

"She was all in black, and veiled. I could scarcely recognize her face under the lace.

"She passed into the salon and lifted her veil.

"She was pale as marble.

" 'Here I am, Armand,' she said ; 'you wished to see me, I came.'

"And, letting her head fall into her two hands, she broke into tears.

"I approached her.

"'What is it that troubles you?' I said to her in an altered voice.

"She clasped my hand without replying, for the tears still suppressed her voice. But, a few moments later, having recovered a little calmness, she said to me :

"'You have done me a great deal of harm, Armand, and I, I have done nothing to you.'

"'Nothing?' I replied with a bitter smile.

"'Nothing but what circumstances have caused me to do to you.'

"I do not know if, in the course of your life, you have ever experienced or if you will ever experience that which I felt at the sight of Marguerite.

"On the last occasion on which she had come to see me, she had seated herself in the place where she was now sitting ; only, since that time, she had been the mistress of another ; other kisses than mine had touched her lips, to which my own were attracted, despite myself, and nevertheless I felt that I loved this woman as much and perhaps more than I had ever loved her.

"Meanwhile I found it difficult to open the conversation upon the subject which had brought her here. Marguerite doubtless comprehended this, for she went on :

"'I am going to weary you, Armand, for I have two things to ask of you,—forgiveness for that which I said yesterday to Mademoiselle Olympe, and mercy with

regard to that which you are perhaps ready to do to me
further. Willingly or not, since your return you have
done me so much harm that I am incapable now of
supporting the fourth part of the emotions which I
have supported up to this morning.   You will have
pity on me, will you not? and you will understand
that there are for a man with a heart more noble
things to do than to avenge himself on a woman ill
and sorrowful as I am. See now, feel my hand. I
have a fever, I have left my bed to come to ask of
you, not your friendship, but your indifference.'

" In fact, I took Marguerite's hand.   It was burning,
and the poor woman shivered under her cloak of furs.

"I rolled up to the fire the easy-chair in which she
was seated.

"'Do you think, then, that I did not suffer,' I replied, 'on that night when, after having waited for you
in the country house, I came to seek you in Paris where
I found only that letter, which almost drove me mad?

"'How could you deceive me so, Marguerite, I who
loved you so much!'

"'Do not speak of that, Armand, I have not come to
talk of it. I have wished to see you otherwise than as
an enemy, that is all, and I have wished to grasp your
hand once more. You have a mistress, young, pretty,
whom you love, it is said;—be happy with her, and
forget me.'

"'And you, you are happy, doubtless?'

" ' Have I the countenance of a happy woman, Armand? Do not mock at my sorrow, you who know better than any one its cause and extent.'

" ' It depended only upon yourself to be never unhappy, if, indeed, you were as you said.'

" ' No, my friend, circumstances were stronger than my will. I obeyed, not my instincts as a courtesan, as you seem to say, but as a serious necessity and certain reasons which you will know one day, and which will cause you to forgive me.'

" ' Why do you not tell me those reasons to-day?'

" ' Because they would not re-establish an impossible reconciliation between us, and because they would perhaps separate you from those from whom you should not separate.'

" ' Who are those from whom I should not separate?'

" ' I cannot tell you.'

" ' Then you lie.'

" Marguerite rose and walked towards the door.

" I could not see this mute yet expressive sorrow without being moved when I compared to myself this pale and weeping woman with that reckless girl who had mocked me at the Opéra-Comique.

" ' You are not going away,' I said, putting myself before the door.

" ' Why not?'

" ' Because, notwithstanding all that you have done to me, I love you still, and I wish to keep you here.'

" ' So that you may drive me away to-morrow, is it not ? No, it is impossible. Our two destinies have separated, do not endeavor to reunite them; you might come to despise me, whereas at present you can only hate me.'

" ' No, Marguerite,' I cried, feeling all my love and all my desires reawaken at the touch of this woman. ' No, I will forget everything, and we shall be happy as we promised ourselves that we should be.'

" Marguerite shook her head in sign of doubt, and said :

" ' Am I not your slave, your dog? do with me whatever you like, take me, I am yours.'

" And, taking off her cloak and her bonnet, she threw them upon the sofa, and began to unclasp hurriedly the corsage of her dress, for, by one of those reactions so frequent in her malady, the blood mounted from her heart to her head and was suffocating her.

" A dry and harsh cough followed.

" ' Tell my coachman to take my carriage away,' she said.

" I went down-stairs myself to send the man away.

" When I returned, Marguerite was extended before the fire, and her teeth were chattering with cold.

" I took her in my arms, I undressed her without her making a movement, and I carried her, icy cold, to my bed.

"Then I seated myself beside her, and I endeavored to warm her again under my caresses. She did not say a word to me, but she smiled at me.

"Oh! this was a strange night. All of Marguerite's life seemed to have passed into the kisses with which she covered me, and I loved her so much that in the midst of the transports of her feverish love I asked myself if I were not going to kill her, so that she might never belong to another.

"One month of a love like this, and, in body as in heart, there would be nothing left but a corpse.

"The daylight found us still both awake.

"Marguerite was livid. She did not say a word. Great tears rose from time to time in her eyes and stopped on her cheeks, brilliant as diamonds. Her exhausted arms opened from time to time to clasp me, and fell back without strength on the bed.

"At one moment I thought that I could forget what had passed since my departure from Bougival, and I said to her :

"'Do you wish that we should go away, that we should leave Paris?'

"'No, no,' she said to me, almost in terror, 'we should be too unhappy, I can no longer serve for your happiness ; but, so long as I retain breath, I will be the slave of your caprices. At whatever hour of the day or night you wish me, come, I shall be yours ; but associate no more your future with mine, you would

be too unhappy, and you would render me too unhappy.

"'I shall be for some little time yet a pretty girl,
profit by it, but do not ask of me anything else.'

"When she had gone, I was affrightened at the solitude in which she had left me. Two hours after her
departure I was still seated on the bed which she had
just left, looking at the pillow which preserved the impress of her form, and asking myself what I was going
to become, between my love and my jealousy.

"At five o'clock, without knowing what I was going
to do there, I repaired to the Rue d'Antin.

"It was Nanine who opened the door to me.

"'Madame cannot receive you,' she said to me with
embarrassment.

"'Why not?'

"'Because Monsieur le Comte de N—— is with her,
and he understood that I was to allow no one to enter.'

"'That is right,' I stammered. 'I had forgotten.'

"I returned to my own rooms like a drunken man,
and, do you know what I did during the moment of delirious jealousy which sufficed for the shameful action
which I was about to commit, do you know what I did?
I said to myself that this woman was making sport of
me, I represented her in her inviolable tête-à-tête with
the count as repeating the same words that she had said
to me during the night, and, taking a five-hundred-franc
note, I sent it to her with these words:

" ' You went away so quickly this morning that I forgot to pay you.

" ' Enclosed find the price of your night.'

"Then, when this letter had gone, I went out, as if to avoid the instantaneous remorse for this infamy.

"I went to see Olympe, whom I found trying on dresses, and who, when we were alone, sang obscene songs to distract me.

"This was, indeed, the type of the courtesan without shame, without heart, and without mind, for me at least, for perhaps some man had entertained for her the same dream that I had had for Marguerite.

"She asked me for money, I gave it to her, and, then free to go away, I returned home.

"Marguerite had not replied to me.

"It is useless to tell you in what a state of agitation I passed the next day.

"At half-past six a messenger brought me an envelope containing my letter and the five-hundred-franc note, not a word more.

" ' Who gave you this ? ' I said to the man.

" ' A lady who was going off with her femme de chambre in the Boulogne mail, and who directed me not to bring it until the coach was outside the court.'

" I hastened to Marguerite's house.

" ' Madame left for England, to-day at six o'clock,' replied the porter to my inquiries.

" Nothing retained me longer in Paris, neither hatred nor love. I was exhausted by so many emotions. One of my friends was going to take a journey to the East ; I expressed to my father the desire which I had to accompany him ; my father gave me drafts on foreign houses, letters of recommendation, and eight or ten days later I embarked at Marseilles.

" It was at Alexandria that I learned from an attaché of the embassy whom I had met a few times at Marguerite's, of the illness of the poor girl.

" I wrote to her then the letter to which she made the reply that you have seen, and which I received at Toulon.

" I set out immediately, and you know the rest.

" Now there is nothing left but for you to read the few sheets which Julie Duprat gave to me, and which are the indispensable complement of that which I have related to you."

XXV

Armand, fatigued by this long recital often interrupted by his tears, carried his two hands to his forehead and closed his eyes, either to reflect or to endeavor to sleep, after having handed me the pages written by Marguerite.

A few moments later, a slightly more rapid respiration showed that he was sleeping, but with that light slumber which the slightest sound will dissipate.

This is what I read, and which I transcribe here without adding or retracting a syllable :

"To-day is the 15th of December. I have been ill for three or four days. This morning I took to my bed; the weather is sombre, I am sad; no one is with me, I am thinking of you, Armand. And you, where are you at the hour at which I write these lines? Far from Paris, very far, I have been told, and perhaps you have already forgotten Marguerite. In any case, may you be happy, you to whom I owe the only moments of joy in my life.

"I have not been able to resist the desire to give you an explanation of my conduct, and I have written you a letter; but, written by a woman such as I, such a letter might be regarded as a falsehood, at least unless its authority were sanctified by death, and unless, instead of a letter, it were a confession.

" To-day, I am ill; I may well die of this illness, for I have always had a presentiment that I shall die young. My mother died of a pulmonary disease, and the manner in which I have lived up to the present can only have aggravated this affection, the only heritage which she left me; but I do not wish to die without putting you in possession of the facts concerning me, if indeed, when you return, you are still interested in the poor girl whom you loved before you went away.

" This is what that letter contained, and I am happy to write it over again, to give myself a new proof of my justification :

" You remember, Armand, how the news of the arrival of your father surprised us at Bougival; you remember the involuntary terror which this arrival caused me, the scene which took place between you and him, and which you related to me that evening.

" The next day, while you were in Paris and were waiting for your father who did not return, a man presented himself at my house and handed me a letter from M. Duval.

" This letter, which I herewith enclose, requested me, in the gravest terms, to send you away the next day under some pretext or other, and to receive your father;

he wished to speak with me, and recommended me, above all, to say nothing to you of his action.

"You remember with what insistence I advised you, on your return, to go back to Paris the next day.

"You had been gone about an hour when your father presented himself. I spare you an account of the impression which his severe countenance produced upon me. Your father was imbued with the old theories which held that every courtesan was a being without heart, without reason, a species of machine to swallow gold, always ready, like iron machinery, to crush the hand that offers her anything, and to tear without pity, without discernment, even that which causes her to live and act.

"Your father's letter was conceived in terms very well calculated to cause me to consent to receive him; but he did not present himself before me at all in the spirit in which he had written. There was enough of haughtiness, of impertinence, and even of threats in his first words to cause me to give him to understand that I was in my own house and that I was under no obligations to give an account of my life to him excepting only through the sincere affection which I had for his son.

"M. Duval calmed down a little, and yet proceeded to say to me that he could no longer allow his son to ruin himself for me; that I was beautiful, it was true, but that, however beautiful I might be, I should not

make use of my beauty to ruin the future of a young
man by such expenditures as I was making.

"To this, there was only one reply to make, was there
not? that was, to show the proofs that, since I had been
your mistress, there was no sacrifice that I had not made
to remain faithful to you, without asking of you more
money than you could give. I showed him the pawn
tickets of the Mont-du-Piété, the receipts from purchasers to whom I had sold articles that I had not been
able to pawn; I imparted to him my resolution to dis-
pose of all my furniture in order to pay my debts and
to be able to live with you without being to you a too
heavy charge. I described our happiness to him, the
revelation which you had made to me of a more tranquil and more happy life, and he ended by yielding
to the evidence presented and offering me his hand,
asking my pardon for the manner in which he had
first presented himself.

"Then he said to me:

"'Then, madame, it is no longer by remonstrances
and menaces, but by prayers, that I must endeavor to
obtain from you a sacrifice greater still than all those
which you have so far made for my son.'

"I trembled at this preamble.

"He drew nearer to me, took my two hands in his,
and continued in an affectionate tone:

"'My dear child, do not take ill what I am going to
say to you; comprehend only that life has sometimes

cruel necessities for the heart, but that it is necessary
to submit to them. You are good, and your soul has
generous instincts unknown to very many women who
perhaps despise you and who are not worthy of you.
But reflect, that by the side of the mistress, there is
the family; that outside of love, there are duties; that
to the age of the passions succeeds the age in which a
man, to be respected, must be solidly established in a
serious position. My son has no fortune, and yet he
is ready to transfer to you his mother's heritage. If
he should accept from you the sacrifice which you are
on the point of making, it will be a matter of his honor
and his dignity to make to you, in exchange, this transfer which will secure you forever against complete ad-
versity. But this sacrifice, he cannot accept it, because
the world, which you do not know, would attribute
this consent to an unworthy reason which should not
attaint the name we bear. It would not be considered
whether Armand loved you, whether you loved him,
whether this double love were a happiness for him and a
rehabilitation for you; only one thing would be considered, that is, that Armand Duval had permitted a
kept woman—forgive me, my child, all that I am forced
to say to you—to sell her property for his benefit. Then
the day of reproaches and of regrets would arrive, of
that you may be sure, for you as for all others, and you
would both of you be carrying a chain that you could
not break. What would you do then? Your youth

would have been lost, my son's future would have been destroyed ; and I, his father, I should have from only one of my children the recompense which I expect from two.

" ' You are young, you are beautiful, life will console you ; you have a noble nature, and the remembrance of a good action will acquit you for many past things. Within the six months that he has known you, Armand has forgotten me. I wrote to him four times without his thinking to reply once. I might have died without his knowing it !

" ' Whatever might be your resolution to live otherwise than as you have been doing, Armand, who loves you, would not consent to the seclusion to which the modesty of his position would condemn you, and which would not be suitable for your beauty. Who knows what he would do then ! He has been gambling, that I have learned ; without saying anything to you about it, that I know also ; but in a moment of intoxication, he might have lost a part of that which I have been saving, for so many years, for my daughter's dot, for him, and to secure the tranquillity of my old days. That which might have happened, may happen yet.

" ' Are you certain, moreover, that the life which you leave for him would not attract you again? Are you certain, you have loved him, not to love another? Would you not suffer, in short, from the complications which your liaison would bring into your lover's life, and for which, perhaps, you would not be able to console him if, with advancing years, ideas of ambition should succeed the dreams of love? Reflect on all that, madame; you love Armand, prove it to him by the sole means which still remains to you to prove it,—by making to his future the sacrifice of your love. No misfortune has yet arrived, but one might arrive, and perhaps even greater ones than those I have foreseen. Armand might become jealous of some man whom you have loved; he might provoke him, there might be a duel, he might be killed, in short, and think of what you would suffer before that father who would demand of you an account for the life of his son.

" 'Finally, my dear child, you must know all, for I have not yet told you all; know, then, what it was that brought me to Paris. I have a daughter, as I have told you, young, beautiful, pure as an angel. She loves, and she also has made of this love the dream of her life. I have written all this to Armand, but, entirely occupied with you, he has not replied. Well, my daughter is about to be married. She marries the man she loves, she is entering an honorable family which desires that everything should be honorable in mine. The relatives of the man who is about to become my son-in-law have learned how Armand is living in Paris, and have declared to me that they would withdraw their consent if Armand continues this life. The future of a young girl who has done you no harm, and who has the right to look forward to the future, is in your hands.

" ' Have you the right, and do you feel yourself strong enough, to destroy it? In the name of your love and of your repentance, Marguerite, grant me my daughter's happiness.'

"I wept silently, my dear friend, before all these reflections which I had often made myself, and which, in your father's mouth, acquired a still more serious reality. I said to myself all that which your father did not venture to say to me, and which had been twenty times on the point of his tongue,—that I was, after all, only a kept woman, and that, whatever reason I might give to our liaison, it would always have the appearance of a mercenary transaction; that my past life gave me no right to dream of such a future, and that I was accepting responsibilities for which my habits and my reputation would give no guarantee. Finally, I loved you, Armand. The paternal manner in which M. Duval spoke to me, the chaste sentiments which he evoked in me, the esteem of this honorable old man which I would acquire, yours, which I was sure to gain later, all this awoke in my heart noble thoughts which elevated me in my own eyes and which spoke to me of a holy pride, unknown till then. When I thought that one day, this old man, who implored me for his son's future, would tell his daughter to mingle my name in her prayers, as the name of a mysterious friend, I felt myself transformed, and I was proud of myself.

"The exaltation of the moment exaggerated perhaps the force of these impressions; but this was what I experienced, dear friend, and these new sentiments silenced the counsels given me by the souvenirs of the happy hours passed with you.

"'It is well, monsieur,' I said to your father, wiping my eyes. 'Do you believe that I love your son?'

"'Yes,' answered M. Duval.

"'With a disinterested love?'

"'Yes.'

"'Do you believe that I have made of this love the hope, the dream, and the pardon of my life?'

"'Sincerely.'

"'Well, monsieur, embrace me once as you would embrace your daughter, and I swear to you that this kiss, the only one really chaste that I have ever received, will make me strong against my love, and that before the end of a week, your son will have returned to you, unhappy perhaps for a time, but cured forever.'

"'You are a noble young woman,' replied your father, kissing me on the forehead, 'and you undertake a thing for which God will give you credit; but I very much fear that you will obtain nothing from my son.'

"'Oh! you may be easy, monsieur, he will hate me.'

"It was necessary that there should be an unsurmountable barrier between us, for one as for the other.

"I wrote to Prudence that I would accept the propositions of M. le Comte de N——, and that she could go to tell him that I would sup with her and with him.

"I sealed the letter, and, without informing him of the contents, I asked your father to send it to its address as soon as he returned to Paris.

" He asked me, nevertheless, what it contained.

" ' It is your son's happiness,' I replied to him.

" Your father embraced me a last time. I felt on my forehead two tears of gratitude which were, as it were, the baptism of my former faults, and, at the moment when I had just consented to deliver myself to another man, I was dilated with pride in thinking of what I purchased by this new fault.

" It was very natural, Armand; you had told me that your father was the most honest man that could be met.

" M. Duval took his seat in his carriage again, and departed.

" Nevertheless, I was a woman, and when I saw you again, I could not keep from weeping, but I did not weaken.

" Did I do well? that is what I ask myself to-day when I lie ill in a bed which I shall not leave perhaps till death.

" You were a witness of all that I experienced as the hour of our inevitable separation drew near ; your father was no longer there to sustain me, and there was a moment in which I was on the point of avowing everything to you, so much was I appalled at the thought that you would hate me and despise me.

"One thing which you will not perhaps believe, Armand, is that I prayed God to give me strength, and, that which proves that he accepted my sacrifice, is that he gave me the strength which I implored.

"At this supper I had still need of aid, for I did not wish to know what I was about to do, so much I feared that my courage would forsake me!

"Who would have said this to me, Marguerite Gautier, that I would suffer so much at the mere thought of a new lover?

"I drank that I might forget, and when I woke the next morning, I was in the count's bed.

"This is the whole truth, dear friend, judge me and forgive me, as I have forgiven you all the harm which you have done me since that day.

XXVI

" That which followed that fatal night, you know it as
well as I ; but that which you do not know, that which
you cannot suspect, is, what I have suffered since our
separation.

" I had heard that your father had carried you off,
but I doubted greatly whether you could long live
away from me, and, the day on which I met you
on the Champs-Élysées, I was affected but not astonished.

" Then commenced that series of days of which each
one brought me a new insult from you, insults which I
received almost with joy, for, in addition to the fact that
they were proofs that you loved me still, it seemed to
me that, the more you persecuted me, the greater would
I be in your eyes on the day when you should know the
truth.

" You need not be surprised at this joyful martyrdom,
Armand, the love which you had had for me had opened
my heart to noble enthusiasms.

" However, I was not able to secure sufficient strength
all at once.

"Between the execution of the sacrifice which I had made for you and your return, a sufficiently long time had elapsed during which I had been obliged to have recourse to physical means so as not to go crazy and to stupefy myself for the life into which I threw myself. Prudence has told you, has she not? that I was present at all the fêtes, at all the balls, at all the orgies.

"I had something like the hope of killing myself quickly, through excesses, and I think this hope will not be very long in being realized. My health gave way more and more, and the day on which I sent Madame Duvernoy to you to ask for mercy, I was exhausted in body and mind.

"I will not recall to you, Armand, in what manner you recompensed the last proof of love which I gave you, and by what outrage you drove from Paris the woman who, dying, had not been able to resist your voice when you asked of her a night of love, and who, like a senseless thing, thought for a moment that she could solder again the past and the present. You had the right to do as you did, Armand;—my nights have not always been paid so highly!

"I left everything then! Olympe replaced me with M. de N——, and took upon herself, I have been told, to inform him as to the reason of my departure. The Comte de G—— was in London. He is one of those men who, giving to the loves of women like myself just enough of importance to render them an

agreeable pastime, remain the friends of the women they
have had and entertain no hatreds, having never been
jealous; he is, in short, one of those grand seigneurs
who open to us only one side of their heart, but who
open to us both sides of their purse. It was of him that
I thought immediately. I went to rejoin him. He
received me exceedingly well, but he was at that time
the lover of a fashionable woman of the world, and he
feared to compromise himself by his connection with
me. He presented me to his friends, who gave me a
supper, after which one of them carried me away.

"What would you have me do, my friend?

"Kill myself? that would have been to have burdened
your life, which should have been happy, with a useless
remorse; moreover, what would be the use of suicide
when you were so near death anyhow?

"I passed into the state of a body without a soul, of a
thing without a mind; I lived for some time this auto-
matic life, then I returned to Paris and inquired after you;
I learned then that you had departed on a long voyage.
Nothing sustained me longer. My existence became
such as it had been two years before I knew you. I
endeavored to win back the duke, but I had too deeply
wounded that man, and the old men are not patient,
doubtless because they perceive that they are not eternal.
My illness grew upon me daily, I was pale, I was sorrowful, I was still thinner. Men who purchase love examine
the commodity before taking it. There were in Paris

healthier women than I, fatter than I; I was beginning to be forgotten. This is the history of the past up to yesterday.

"At present I am seriously ill. I have written to the duke to ask him for some money, for I have none, and the creditors have returned, bringing me their bills with a pitiless insistency. Will the duke answer me? Would that you were in Paris, Armand! You would come to see me, and your visits would console me!"

"December 20th.

"The weather is horrible, it is snowing, I am alone in my room. For the last three days I have had such a fever that I could not write you a word. There is nothing new, my friend; each day I hope vaguely for a letter from you, but it does not arrive, and doubtless never will arrive. The men alone have sufficient strength never to forgive. The duke has not replied to me.

"Prudence has begun again her journeys to the Mont-du-Piété.

"I do not cease to spit blood. Oh! I would indeed give you pain if you should see me. You are indeed happy to be under a sunny sky, and not to have, as I have, a whole winter of ice which weighs upon your chest. To-day, I sat up a little, and behind the curtains of my window I looked out on that life of Paris with which I thought I had indeed completely broken. Some faces that I knew passed in the street, quickly, joyfully, carelessly. Not one of them lifted their eyes to my windows. However, a few young people came to leave their names. Once before I was sick, and you, who were not acquainted with me, who had obtained nothing of me but an impertinence the day on which I saw you for the first time, you came to inquire after me every morning. Now I am sick again. We have passed six months together. I have had for you as much love as the heart of a woman can contain and can give, and you are far away, and you curse me, and there does not come to me one word of consolation from you. But it is chance alone which causes this abandonment, I am sure of it, for, if you were in Paris, you would not leave my bedside and my chamber."

"*December 25th.*

"My physician forbids me to write every day. In fact, my souvenirs have the effect only of augmenting my fever; but yesterday, I received a letter which did me good, more by the sentiments which it expressed than by the material succor which it brought me. I can therefore write to you to-day. This letter was from your father, and these are its contents:

"'MADAME: I have just learned that you are ill. If I were in Paris, I would go myself to inquire concerning you; if my son were with me, I would send him for news, but I cannot leave G——, and Armand is six or seven hundred leagues from here; permit me, then, madame, simply to write to you how grieved I am to hear of this illness, and believe in the sincere vows which I make for your prompt restoration to health.

"'One of my good friends, M. H——, will call upon you, will you have the kindness to receive him. He bears a commission from me of which I impatiently await the result.

"'Will you accept, madame, the assurance of my distinguished consideration.'

"Such was the letter which I received. Your father has a noble heart, love him well, my friend; for there are but few men in the world as worthy of being loved. This paper, signed with his name, did me more good than all the prescriptions of our great physician.

"This morning, M. H—— came. He seemed to be very much embarrassed with the delicate mission with which M. Duval had charged him. He came quite honestly to bring me a thousand écus from your father. At first, I wished to refuse, but M. H—— said to me that this refusal would offend M. Duval, who had authorized him to give me this sum at first, and to remit to me in addition all that I had need of. I accepted this service which, coming from your father, could be only a charity. If I am dead when you return, show to your father what I have just written for him, and say to him that, in tracing these lines, the

poor girl to whom he had deigned to write this consol-
ing letter shed tears of gratitude and prayed God for
him.'

"January 4th.

"I have just passed through a number of very painful days. I did not know that the body could suffer so
much. Oh! my past life! I am paying for it twice
over to-day.

"They watched with me every night. I could no
longer get my breath. The delirium and the cough
divided the remnant of my poor existence between
them.

"My dining-room is full of bonbons, of gifts of all
kinds which my friends have brought me. There are
doubtless among these persons some who hope that I
may be their mistress later. If they could see what the
disease has made of me, they would flee in affright.

"Prudence is making New Year's presents with what
I have received.

"The weather is frosty, and the doctor tells me that
I can go out in a few days if the fine weather continues."

"January 8th.

"I went out yesterday in my carriage. The weather
was magnificent. The Champs-Élysées was full of
people. You would have thought it was the first smile
of spring. Everything had a festival air around me. I
had never suspected that there might be in the sunshine

all that I found in it yesterday of joy, of sweetness, and of consolation.

"I met almost all the people whom I know, always gay, always occupied with their pleasures. How many happy people are there who do not know that they are happy! Olympe passed me in an elegant carriage which had been given her by M. de N——. She endeavored to insult me by her looks. She does not know how far away I am from all those vanities. An honest young fellow whom I have known for a long time asked me if I would come and take supper with him and one of his friends who greatly desired, he said, to make my acquaintance.

" I smiled upon him sadly and I offered him my hand burning with fever.

" Never have I seen a more astonished countenance.

" I returned home at four o'clock, I dined with a sufficiently good appetite.

" This going out did me good.

" If I should be cured !

" How much the sight of the life and of the happiness of others makes those desire to live who, the evening before, in the solitude of their soul and in the gloom of their sick chamber, had wished to die quickly !"

"*January 10th.*

" This hope of health was only a vain dream. Here I am again in my bed, my body covered with plasters which burn me. Go now and offer this body which was formerly paid for so dearly and see what they would give you for it to-day !

" It must be that we committed a great deal of evil before being born, or that we shall enjoy a very great happiness after our death, that God should permit that this life should have all the tortures of the expiation and all the pains of the trial."

"*January 12th.*

" I am still suffering.

" The Comte de N—— sent me some money yesterday, I did not accept it. I wish nothing from that man. He is the cause that you are not near me.

" Oh ! our beautiful days of Bougival ! where are you?

" If I ever leave this chamber alive, it will be to make a pilgrimage to the house in which we lived together, but I shall only leave here when dead.

" Who knows if I shall write to you to-morrow ?"

"*January 25th.*

" There are now eleven nights in which I have not slept, in which I suffocate, and in which I think each moment that I am going to die. The doctor has left directions that I must not touch a pen. Julie Duprat, who is watching with me, however, permits me to write to you these few lines. Will you not come back, then, before I die ! Is it, then, eternally ended between us ? It seems to me that, if you should come, I should get well. Of what use would it be to get well ?"

"*January 28th.*

"This morning I was awakened by a great noise. Julie, who was sleeping in my chamber, rushed into the dining-room. I heard men's voices, against which her own contended in vain. She re-entered weeping.

"They had come to seize my furniture. I said to her to let them execute what they call justice. The sheriff's officer entered my chamber, his hat on his head. He opened the drawers, made an inventory of everything that he saw, and did not appear to perceive that there was a dying woman in the bed which, fortunately, the charity of the law leaves me.

"He condescended to say to me on leaving that I could oppose the seizure before nine days, but he left a watchman! What is going to become of me, Mon Dieu! This scene made me still more ill. Prudence wished to ask for some money from your father's friend, but I opposed it."

"I received your letter this morning. I had need of it. Will my reply reach you in time? Will you see me again? This was a happy day, which made me forget all those that I have passed for the last six weeks. It seems to me that I am better, notwithstanding the feeling of melancholy under the impression of which I replied to you.

"After all, one should not be always unhappy.

"When I think that it may happen that I shall not die, that you will return, that I shall see the spring again, that you would love me still, and that we might begin again our life of last year!

"Foolish that I am! it is with difficulty that I can hold the pen with which I write to you this senseless dream of my heart.

"Whatever may happen, I loved you well, Armand, and I should have been dead long ago if I had not had to support me the remembrance of that love, and something like a vague hope of seeing you again at my side."

"*February 4th.*

"The Comte de G—— has returned. His mistress deceived him. He is very sorrowful, he loved her greatly. He came to tell me all this. The poor fellow is also troubled in his business affairs, which did not prevent him from paying the sheriff's officer and sending away the watchman.

"I spoke to him of you, and he has promised me to speak to you of me. How completely I forgot in those moments that I had been his mistress and how he endeavored also to make me forget it! He has an honest heart.

"The duke sent to inquire after me yesterday, and he came this morning. I do not know what it is that keeps this old man still alive. He remained with me three hours, and he did not say to me twenty words. Two great tears fell from his eyes when he saw me so pale. It was the remembrance of the death of his daughter,

324 THE LADY OF THE CAMELLIAS

doubtless, that made him weep. He will have seen her
die twice. His back is bent, his head drooped toward
the earth, his lip hanging, his glance extinguished. Age
and sorrow weigh with their double burden upon his
exhausted body. He did not reproach me in any way.
It might even have been thought that he derived a
secret satisfaction from the ravages which the disease
had made in me. He seemed to be proud to be still
upright, while I, still young, I was crushed by illness.

"The bad weather has returned. No one comes to
see me. Julie watches as much as she can with me.
Prudence, to whom I cannot give as much money as
formerly, is beginning to make pretences of business to
absent herself.

"Now that I am near death, notwithstanding what is
told me by the doctors,—for I have several of them,
which proves that the disease is increasing,—I almost
regret having listened to your father; if I had known
that I would take only a year of your future, I would
not have resisted the desire to pass that year with you,
and at least I would die holding the hand of a friend.
It is true that if we had lived together this year, I should
not have died so soon.

"May God's will be done!"

"*February 5th.*

"Oh! come, come, Armand, I am suffering horribly,
I am going to die, My God! I was so melancholy yesterday that I wished to pass somewhere else than in my

own house the evening which promised to be as long as that of the day before. The duke had come in the morning. It seemed to me that the sight of this old man forgotten by death would make me die more quickly.

"Notwithstanding the raging fever that consumed me, I caused myself to be dressed and taken to the Vaudeville. Julie had rouged me, otherwise I should have had the appearance of a corpse. I went to that box in which I gave you our first rendezvous; all the time I kept my eyes fixed on the seat which you occupied that evening, and which was occupied yesterday evening by a sort of boorish fellow who laughed noisily at all the stupid things which the actors retailed. They brought me home half dead. I coughed and spat blood all night. To-day I can no longer speak, I can scarcely move my arms. Mon Dieu! Mon Dieu! I am dying. I expected it, but I cannot conceive the idea of suffering more than I do suffer, and if . . ."

From these words, the few characters which Marguerite had endeavored to trace were illegible, and it was Julie Duprat who had continued.

"February 18th.

"MONSIEUR ARMAND: From the evening on which Marguerite wished to go to the theatre, she has been much more ill. She has lost her voice completely, then the use of her limbs.   It is impossible to describe what our poor friend suffers.   I am not used to these kinds of emotions, and I have continual frights.

"How I wish that you were with us!   She is nearly always in delirium ; but, whether delirious or in her right mind, it is always your name that she utters when she is able to pronounce a word.

"The doctor tells me that she cannot last much longer.   Since she has been so ill the old duke has not returned.

"He said to the doctor that this spectacle affected him too greatly.

"Madame Duvernoy is not behaving well.   This woman, who thought she could draw more money from Marguerite, at whose expense she lived almost entirely, has assumed engagements which she cannot fulfill, and, seeing that her neighbor can no longer serve her, she does not even come to see her.   Everybody abandons her, M. de G——, harassed by his debts, has been obliged to go back to London.   On leaving, he sent us some money ; he has done all that he can, but they have seized the goods again, and the creditors are only waiting for the death to sell everything.

"I wished to employ my last resources to prevent these seizures, but the sheriff's officer told me that it was useless and that he had still other judgments to execute. Since she is going to die, it is better to abandon everything than to save for her family, whom she did not wish to see, and which never loved her. You cannot imagine in the midst of what gilded poverty the poor girl is dying. Yesterday, we had no money at all. Dishes, jewels, cashmeres, everything is in pawn, the rest is all either sold or seized. Marguerite is still conscious of what is passing around her, and she suffers in body, in mind, and in heart. The great tears roll down her cheeks, so thin and so pale that you would no longer recognize the countenance of her whom you so much loved, if you could see her. She made me promise to write to you when she no longer could, and I am writing before her. She turns her eyes toward me, but she does not see me, her look is already veiled by approaching death ; nevertheless she smiles, and all her thoughts, all her soul, are directed toward you, I am sure of it.

"Every time that the door opens, her eyes light up, and she always thinks that you are coming in ; then, when she sees that it is not you, her countenance assumes again its sorrowful expression, becomes moist with a cold sweat, and the cheeks turn purple."

"*February 19th, midnight.*

"What a sad day has this been, my poor Monsieur Armand ! This morning Marguerite was suffocating, the doctor bled her, and her voice returned to her a little. The doctor advised her to see a priest. She said that she would consent, and he went himself to get an abbé at Saint-Roch.

" Meanwhile Marguerite called me to her bedside, asked me to open her wardrobe; then she showed me a cap, a long chemise, both covered with lace, and said to me in a feeble voice :

" ' I am going to die after confessing, then you will dress me in these,—it is the coquetry of a dying woman.'

" Then she embraced me weeping, and she added :

" ' I can speak, but I suffocate too much when I speak; I am suffocating ! some air ! '

" I broke into tears, I opened the window, and, a few minutes later, the priest entered.

" I went to meet him.

" When he knew in whose house he was, he seemed to fear that he would be badly received.

" ' Come in boldly, father,' I said to him.

" He remained a little time in the sick-chamber, and as he came out he said to me :

" ' She has lived like a sinner, but she will die like a Christian.'

" A few minutes later he came back, accompanied by a choir boy carrying a crucifix, and by a sacristan who walked before them ringing a bell, to announce that God was entering the house of the dying woman.

" They all three of them entered that bed-chamber, which had formerly re-echoed to so many strange words, and which was at this hour only a holy tabernacle.

" I fell on my knees. I do not know how long the impression produced upon me by this spectacle will remain ; but I do not think that, until I come to the same moment myself, any human thing can impress me so deeply.

"The priest anointed with the sacred oil the feet, the hands, and the forehead of the dying woman, recited a short prayer, and Marguerite was ready to depart for heaven, to which she will doubtless go, if God has seen the trials of her life and the sanctity of her death.

"Since that moment, she has not said a word and has not made a movement. Twenty times I would have thought her dead, if I had not heard her labored breathing."

"*February 20th, 5 o'clock in the evening.*

"Everything is over.

"Marguerite's death agony came on that night, about two o'clock. Never did martyr suffer such tortures, if we might judge by the cries that she uttered. Two or three times she rose upright in her bed, as if she wished to seize again her life which was ascending to God.

"Two or three times also she uttered your name, then everything was silent; she fell back exhausted on her bed. Silent tears flowed from her eyes, and she was dead.

"Then, I approached her, I called her, and, as she did not reply, I closed her eyes and I kissed her on the forehead.

" Poor, dear Marguerite, I could have wished that I
were a holy woman, so that this kiss would recommend
you to God.

"Afterwards I dressed her, as she had requested me
to do, I went to get a priest at Saint-Roch, I burned
two candles for her, and I prayed for an hour in the
church.

" I have given to the poor the money she had left.

"I do not know much about religion, but I think
that the good God will recognize that my tears were
real ones, my prayer fervent, my alms-giving sincere,
and that he will have pity on her who, dying young and
beautiful, had no one but me to close her eyes and to
bury her."

" *February 22d.*

"To-day the funeral took place. Many of Marguerite's female friends came to the church. Some of
them wept sincerely. When the funeral train took the
road to Montmartre, two men only followed it, the
Comte de G——, who had returned purposely from
London, and the duke, who walked supported by two
footmen.

"It is from her rooms that I write you all these
details, in the midst of my tears and before the lamp
which burns mournfully near the dinner which I cannot
touch, as you may well imagine, but which Nanine has
prepared for me, for I have not eaten for more than
twenty-four hours.

" My life may not long preserve these sorrowful impressions, for my life no more belongs to me than Marguerite's did to her ; this is why I give you all these details in the very localities in which they have taken place, in the fear, if a length of time should elapse between them and your return, that I might not be able to give them to you in all their mournful exactitude."

XXVII

" You have read it ? " said Armand to me, when I had terminated the perusal of this manuscript.

" I comprehend what you must have suffered, my friend, if all that I have read is true ! "

" My father has confirmed it in a letter to me. "

We conversed a little while longer on the melancholy destiny which had been fulfilled, and I returned to my own rooms to take a little repose.

Armand, still sad, but soothed somewhat by the recital of this story, soon recovered his strength, and we went together to visit Prudence and Julie Duprat.

Prudence had failed in business. She said to us that Marguerite was the cause of it ; that, during her illness, she had lent her a good deal of money, to obtain which she had given notes that she had not been able to meet, Marguerite having died without repaying her and without having given her any receipts by means of which she could prove her claims as creditor.

By the aid of this fable, which Madame Duvernoy related everywhere to excuse the bad state of her affairs, she drew a note of a thousand francs from Armand, who did not believe it, but who wished to appear to believe it, so much respect had he for everything that had had to do with his mistress.

Then we went to see Julie Duprat, who related to us the sad events of which she had been witness, shedding sincere tears over the memory of her friend.

Finally we went to Marguerite's tomb, over which the first rays of the April sun were causing the first leaves to expand.

There remained to Armand a last duty to accomplish, that was to go and rejoin his father. He desired me still to accompany him.

We arrived at G——, where I saw M. Duval, much as I had imagined him from the portrait which his son had drawn for me,—tall, honorable, benevolent.

He welcomed Armand with tears of happiness, and grasped my hand affectionately. I readily perceived that the paternal sentiment was that one which dominated all the others with the receiver-general.

His daughter, whose name was Blanche, had that transparency of the eyes and of the look, that serenity of the mouth, which prove that the mind conceives only holy thoughts and that the lips utter only pious words. She smiled at her brother's return, ignorant, the chaste young girl, that far from her a courtesan had sacrificed her happiness at the mere invocation of her name.

I remained for some time with this happy family, all occupied as they were with him who brought to them the convalescence of his heart.

I returned to Paris, where I wrote out this story just as it had been related to me. It has only one merit, which may perhaps be contested, that of being true.

I do not draw from this recital the conclusion that all women like Marguerite are capable of doing what she did ; far from it, but I have been made acquainted with the fact that one of them had experienced in her life a serious love, that she had suffered because of it, and that she had died of it. I have related to the reader what I have learned. It was a duty.

I am not the apostle of vice, but I will make myself the echo of noble misfortune wherever I hear it appeal.

The story of Marguerite is an exception, I repeat it ; but if it were the usual thing, it would not be worth writing.

www.ingramcontent.com/pod-product-compliance
Lightning Source LLC
Chambersburg PA
CBHW021531110726
47902CB00004B/827